Rob Phayre

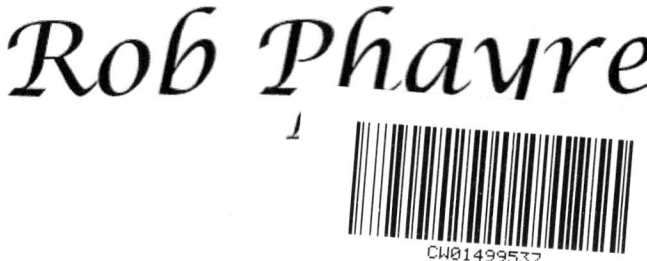

CW01499537

Copyright © 2021 Rob Phayre Ltd

Cover design by: Rob Phayre Ltd based on the concept developed by Kira Phayre

Cover image base layer: Shutterstock (Valeriy Eydlin)

Other images used under Creative Commons License

About the Author

'When a crisis hits, and all around you are losing their heads, you can't help anyone if you have already lost yours.'

Rob started his career as a British military helicopter pilot. After that, he moved to Africa and worked as a security and crisis manager. In his time there he responded to problems including terrorism attacks, kidnap for ransom, murder, massive fraud, and anti-counterfeiting. He specialised in resolving Somali piracy incidents.

Rob has led security projects all around the world. From the ice and snow above the arctic circle to the deserts in the Sahara. From the jungles in Africa to the rippling waves of the Indian Oceans.

Rob's experience in so many places, with so many fascinating characters doing such daring deeds, makes him the ideal author for the works of fiction that are The Response Files.

Rob's debut novel The Ransom Drop was published as an award-winning audiobook.

To find out more and see Rob's other book releases visit: www.robphayre.com

To leave feedback or ask questions about this title, visit Rob's author page on: Goodreads.com

Jungle Heist

Book 2 of The Response Files

Rob Phayre

To the Vaut clan.

Rob

1

To Ursie, India, Juliet, and Kira.
Thank you for your love and support.

The Kayoro Mine

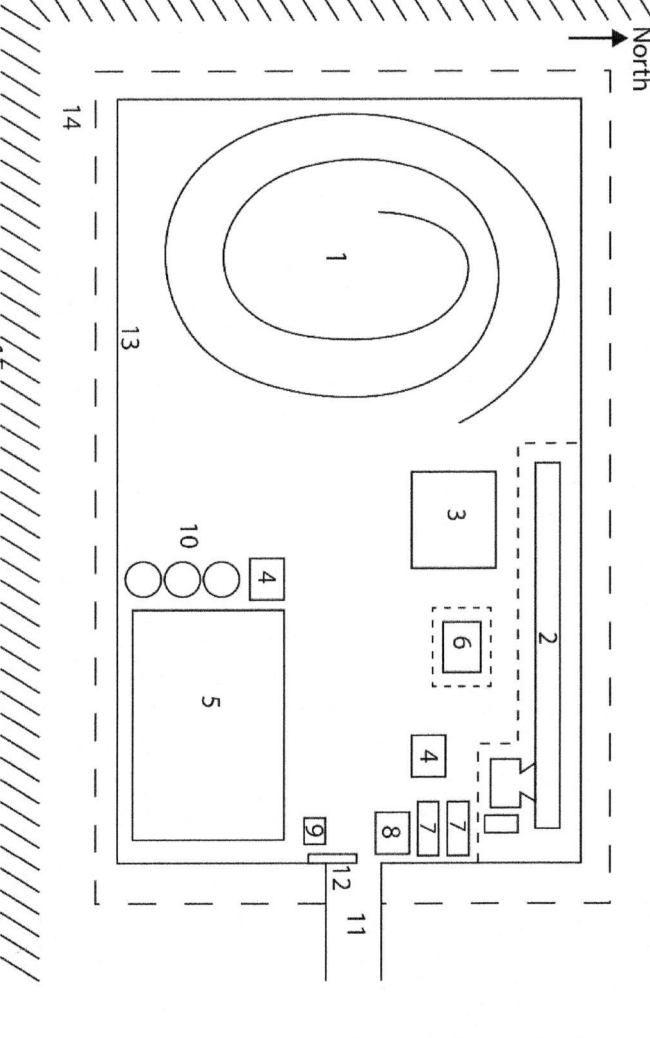

1. The Excavation Pit
2. The Runway
3. Maintenance Yard
4. Lockdown Shelter
5. Ore Processing Plant
6. The Vault
7. Accommodation Blocks
8. Office Block
9. Guard House
10. Water Tanks
11. Main Road
12. Main Gate
13. Perimeter Berm and fence
14. Barbed wire fence
15. Jungle edge

Chapter 1

September 17th, The Kayoro Mine. Ghana.

Gold. Jimmy was surrounded by gold. That dulled yellow colour of money that had an immense weight of wealth. There was no smell to it. In fact, the only smell in this brightly lit vault was Jimmy's own body odour. The vault was half full, but in this humidity and heat, Jimmy tangibly filled the rest with his personal sour stench.

Jimmy could only be described as sleazy. He had thinning hair, and instead of respecting himself and going bald, he grew it long on the left and slicked it over the top with hair oil. His habit was to run his right hand over his left ear, and then over the top to slap his hair back down over his psoriasis-scabbed dome. His jowls were deep, his belly bulged. Too much good food and beer. Jimmy had a talent though, that his looks and personal habits hid well. He was one of the best expat mine managers in Africa. If you wanted to scrape every last ounce of production out of a mine, then Jimmy was the man you got to do it for you. Whatever you paid him, he was worth it. American by birth, he hadn't been back in years. He resented every single dollar that the IRS taxed him while he was abroad. He saw no value in it. He had been married once but had decided he preferred twenty-five-year-old local girls that were half his age. He resented his ex-wife and his cash-hungry son for the money he had to give them too.

The Kayoro mine in Northern Ghana was one of the largest in the world and could produce about eight tons of gold bars per month. The vault that Jimmy was currently in was designed to hold much more than that though. Getting secure transport in and out of this remote part of Africa was logistically difficult, and expensive. It was a simple business decision that leveraged government security, which was freely given, to both guard the production and escort the convoys that took it to Accra. Gold was one of the main sources of foreign exchange in the country and the government wanted to protect it.

Jimmy reached out and touched one of the gold bars. His brain naturally did the calculations. Each bar was 24-karat pure gold and weighed twelve and a half kilograms. Eighty of them made one ton. Each ton was stacked on a steel pallet on the floor. Each brick was ten centimetres wide, twenty-seven centimetres long and five centimetres deep. Twelve bags of sugar in weight compressed into something the size of a simple house brick. In the mine they took raw rock, processed it, and ultimately churned out these gold bricks, stamped and polished, at a rate of about twenty per day.

Jimmy was doing his monthly management check. It had been a good month and there was a touch over eight tons of gold in the vault. At fifty million USD a ton or thereabouts, that was a lot of bricks. In a week or so the government planes would come, land at the mine's airstrip and the soldiers would load it all onto the planes to fly it the seven hundred kilometres to Accra. Once there it would be moved into armoured vehicles and driven to the central bank.

Jimmy took the clipboard and signed the inspection sheet. Before placing it back on the rack, he photographed the sheet with his phone camera and sent it to head office by email. He walked out of the vault, past the quartermaster who started the process of closing the vault up, and then past the pair of armed guards who protected this part of the building. He walked along the plain concrete walled corridor, through another security door, which was monitored remotely by video. It closed automatically behind him as he walked on through the more public space and out of the front door into the sunshine.

He pulled his aviator sunglasses out of his breast pocket and put them on, protection against the glare. A small gust of wind caught his hair and it flopped ridiculously on to his shoulder. He quickly flapped it back onto the top of his head and looked around vainly to see if anyone had noticed.

This part of the site was large, lots of buildings, machinery, trucks, and people. About two kilometres away was a berm of mud and soil, grassed over, but which kept prying eyes out. This manufactured three-metre-high perimeter stretched around the entire site for about twenty kilometres and included the runway. On top of the mound of the berm was a very sophisticated three-metre-tall fence. Every fifty metres were mounted day night cameras combined with the latest technology in sensors. Through artificial intelligence they could cue the security staff in 'the bunker' as it was known, directly to the source of any disturbance. Computer power assessed what the threat was. It would then categorise the level of threat and it could even automatically inform head office in Paris. Every half kilometre watch towers, with two armed guards each, dominated the land. A physical presence to back up the new technology. Beyond the berm, for three hundred metres out, the jungle had been cleared back to ground level. It created an effective fire zone for the towers and for the rapid response team that would arrive by 4x4 pickup if there was any sort of drama. About one hundred metres into that cleared zone, another formidable obstacle lay. Coils and coils of barbed wire. Expertly laid to form a pyramid shape. The coils were well tied to metal stakes that had been set firmly into the ground using concrete. Jimmy's eyes passed over all of this and settled on the dense green jungle beyond. The mine was in a large valley, and the jungle blanketed the hills all around for a hundred kilometres in every direction. No one lived in the jungle nearby except for some local tribespeople who scratched out a frugal living.

The jungle was a dangerous place, he thought. It wasn't the animals, it was the remoteness. Bugs and disease loved the jungle, the cloying, sweaty, humid heat. The lack of penetrating winds to clear it resulted in air so thick it was sometimes hard to breath. The humidity drenched your clothes in seconds, and they stayed wet until you changed them. If you went into a cool temperature-controlled building you were then wet, and cold. Travelling through the jungle was dangerous, cutting a path with a machete, following someone else's path if you knew where it went. No mobile phone comms for ninety five percent of it and no easy way to get to a hospital if you were wounded. Jimmy didn't like the jungle, but he had huge respect for it.

As he walked back to his office building, he unclipped the satellite phone that he always carried. Not the company issue one, but one he had recently bought for himself. He had so far only ever used it to call one number, and he dialled it whilst he checked that there was no one within earshot. After a couple of rings, he said, 'Sir, it's me.' He listened briefly before replying, 'Yes I think we're ready. What? Yes, yes, sorry. I *know* we're ready for Wednesday next week. We're nearly full, and the government collection will be on Thursday. There'll be just over eight tons available.'

Another pause, 'Yes, I understand.' Jimmy looked at his phone as the call ended. He paused thinking, it's all moving now, and I can't stop it. He automatically checked that his hair was in place as he continued walking towards his office. Damp, dark stains under his armpits spread nervously.

Chapter 2

September 18th, 30,000 feet above the UAE.

The Associate was sitting behind the antique desk in his modified Gulf Stream G5 personal jet. The plush pale cream carpeting, the varnished cherry wood trim, the pale suede walls matching the cream executive chairs and sofa. A widescreen TV on the bulkhead to the front was turned off so that The Associate could concentrate on his conversation with the man sitting in front of him.

The Ghanaian Minister for the Interior was relaxing a little too much in The Associate's opinion. It looked like power had made him too confident. The Associate thought he should remind him of how he got there before he made the offer that would be on the table.

The Associate was short, and he was thin. He looked as if one of his parents was African, the other from the Far East. He spoke with an accent that appeared uneducated, a mix of Nigerian and Japanese. However, you misjudged The Associate at your peril. He spoke six languages fluently and ran one of the largest organised crime groups in the world. He had his fingers in many different pies, did not shy away from killing, but he did not distribute drugs and he abhorred human trafficking. He was wealthy beyond measure, and he had long since stopped trying to just make money. These days, he did it for the game, for power, and sometimes just to see if he could. He destroyed his enemies, he nurtured loyalty and he was known in all the wrong circles for who he was, but no one knew his name.

As he sat there in his tailored blue pinstripe three-piece suit, he looked over his half spectacles at The Minister sitting before him.

'Minister,' said with surprising contempt. 'It's time to move our relationship forward.'

The Minister was dressed like a British politician, with a garish bright green silk tie over a cream hand-tailored shirt, and a dark lightweight suit. He looked languidly at The Associate. His ebony face, flat nose, and slightly rheumy bloodshot eyes. 'This sounds interesting.'

'It's time to repay my investment in you. With my support, you have risen near to the top of the pile, and with my help you will now become President.'

'This sounds really interesting. What do you propose?'

'From your side, it's quite simple. Next week, my men will steal a large quantity of gold from your country. Your job will be to make sure that the military and police are not able to stop them and that my people can escape without too much difficulty.'

'But the Central Bank is too well protected. It's in the middle of our capital city, it will look too suspicious if I order a reduction in protection before a major raid happens. Also, I can't control the immediate police response and...'

The Associate, bored of the whining cut him off. 'Did I say it was the Central Bank?'

'No. But you said...'

'Just listen and do what you're told.' Chastised, the Minister went quiet. 'Next week, my team will steal a month's supply from the Kayoro mine. Your job will be to delay any major decision making on the response. You don't need to make any adjustments to the site security in advance, but I don't want the police responding too quickly. We must have enough time to load the escape aircraft. Then I need enough time to get my team out of the country. I don't want the Air Force shooting them down during the escape.'

'That's easy enough, I can order an immediate readiness demonstration in another part of the country. It will just look like bad timing and then I...'

'I don't need the details. You'll manage, I'm sure.'

'But how will this help me with the Presidency?'

'Firstly, a concerted media campaign will rapidly begin against the current President, next you and your lead investigator will recover a proportion of the gold for the Central Bank, making you shine. Finally, you will be given fifty million US dollars to fund your campaign in next year's election. How you spend it will be up to you.'

The Minister was thinking rapidly. The plan was simple. There was little risk to him personally, he only needed to make some phone calls, delay things a little. Then next year, he would have a vast budget to bribe whom he needed to, create the campaign materials he desired, and plaster himself all over the TV and news sheets. Of course, even better was that a large chunk of that money would stick to his hands and end up in his personal account in the Virgin Islands. 'This sounds possible, but many people will die.'

'Again, I don't need the details.'

'I hope you have a team that is well led?'

The Associate was losing his patience a little, 'This time, *Minister*, you don't need the details.'

As the conversation continued, the plane flew through the clear blue sky, its pristine white hull with bright red sash livery glinting in the sun.

Chapter 3

September 18th, Dibulo. Ghana.

Abdi had been in Dibulo for nearly a week now. Somali by birth but educated in London, he had recently proven himself to The Associate as being highly competent. He had made his name and fortune by creating a new business model off the coast of Somalia, pirating ships, and charging huge sums in ransom to release them. For this project, his task was quite different. As the eldest son of a Somali warlord, he was used to automatic respect from those who served him. That wasn't the case here. The Associate had briefed him and flown him to this remote place in the jungle just over a week ago. Since then, a massive logistics operation had happened around him. More than forty fighters had arrived, one by one. Some brought battered old Toyota pickup trucks with them, some carried weapons, all came with a story or two and a nefarious past.

    To help Abdi there was a Nigerian man named Cheko. About half of the newly-arrived fighters personally knew Cheko, and they followed his word as gospel. He was quiet, thoughtful and he listened. He rarely made rash decisions, but when Cheko had to, he could fight. He was middle aged, short curly black hair above a rounded face. His beard, which was only occasionally trimmed, was patched with grey. If Abdi was the General, then Cheko was the Sergeant Major who made things happen. Abdi and Cheko had only met briefly on the phone, after an introduction by The Associate. Coming from different parts of Africa, with different criminal pasts, there was very little trust between them. They both knew The Associate though and that had to be good enough for now.

    Cheko and many of his men made their living in the illegal logging trade. They were at home in the jungles of West Africa. They could sniff out rare hardwoods, mahogany, ebony and teak. Find the groves where they were concentrated. Then they cut them down, dragged them through the jungle, cutting further paths where needed, selling them to the highest bidder. Cheko didn't care that the trees were rare, or about global warming. He cared only about feeding his family.

At the moment, only Abdi knew the final target. A gold mine about fifty kilometres away. The men who were arriving in this remote part of Africa knew that they were there to attack and to kill. They just didn't know what or who yet. They did know that they were being paid a fortune to do it. Enough to set themselves up for life.

Abdi wasn't enjoying the jungle. This camp, beneath the speckled green canopy of trees was too humid. Abdi was used to humid and hot from his hometown on the Somali coast, but he didn't like the bugs, this lack of breeze. Sweat beaded on his forehead and stayed there until he wiped it off with his sleeve. He felt claustrophobic, surrounded by the giant tree trunks reached into the sky. Their branches spread, their leaves filled every possible gap. The canopy was swaying up there, he noticed, driven by some high wind. Down at ground level though, amongst the musty, smelly, rotted leaves that crawled with insects, there wasn't a breath of air. Around Abdi it was dim and dusky, yet above the tree tops, out of sight, the sun arced as a distant halo across the sky.

Abdi was sitting outside his canvas tent in a cheap white plastic chair. Next to him, Cheko was taking a sip from a coffee mug. They were watching the men unloading large crates from the back of a truck.

'So, when will you tell me what the target is?' Cheko asked in his strong Nigerian accent.

'The day after tomorrow. I'll have everything confirmed by then.' Abdi was lying a little. He already knew the attack would be in five days' time, but he had to strike a balance between preparation and secrecy. 'I'll tell you, so that we can plan in detail, but you'll not be able to tell the men the exact target until we're on the road.'

'They won't like that.'

'They'll like someone betraying us and getting killed even less. Besides, I'm paying them to obey and to fight. The risk is simple. If one of them says one word on a phone to their mistress, we could lose the whole project. You and I could lose our lives. If that happens, we'll both be dead, and I'll be really pissed off.'

There was a lot of shouting all of a sudden from the back of the truck. As they watched, a large crate fell from it and onto the floor. The wooden crate smashed revealing printed boxes with pictures of remote-control drones on them.

Abdi stood up and shouted. 'The next man that drops one of those crates will have one dropped on his head! That equipment is vital to our success!' Having vented, he sat down again fuming slightly.

'What are we going to do with sixty drones?'

Abdi looked at him. 'Well firstly we're going to use them to knock out some guard towers, and then we're going to use them to kill anyone who tries to stop us.'

'How is a plastic drone going to do that?'

'Tomorrow our explosives expert gets here. She can turn each one of those into a bomb that can be flown from a distance outside the range of small arms.'

'Seriously, we can kill without risk to us?'

'There's always risk. I don't know yet if there are any armoured vehicles on the site, or any defensive bunkers or mortars.'

'What the hell are we attacking?'

'You find out in two days' time. For now, get those men working as a team and practise their drills. Tomorrow the drone pilots arrive. I need them to prepare their kit, practise flying, changing drones rapidly, flying with weights on. That kind of thing.'

'Do they know what they're doing yet?'

'No. They think they're here for survey work, but once the three of them arrive, they won't leave until the job is done.'

Chapter 4

September 20th, Accra. Ghana.

The Minister was at his home on a hill in Cantonments, the wealthy suburb on the Southern side of the city of Accra. In his living room, he was standing with a cut crystal glass of whiskey in his hand, looking out of the expansive window at the beach less than a kilometre away. It was late evening, and the gaudy lights from the beach bars blinked, almost synchronised with the lamps from the squid boats out in the bay. Tourists and locals alike were partying as normal on a Saturday night in the humid sea air. The monsoon rains were only a few weeks away; everyone looking forward to when they would wash away the layers of dust and filth that clogged the streets.

All those people, they don't know what's going to happen yet, the Minister thought to himself. All of them, blissfully ignorant in their tiny little lives. Worker ants, for me to take advantage of and do with as I please.

His maid, wearing a red uniform servant's dress with a white apron, entered the room quietly behind him and announced, 'Sir, your guests are here.'

He stirred from his toxic revelry. 'Thankyou, Anne, please show them in.' He was always polite and courteous to his staff. He needed loyalty and discretion from them. He paid them well and treated them with respect. These men who were coming to see him now, he would treat them the same way, he would stroke their feathers. Make them feel important. He needed them, for a little while, and he would entice them into his confidence. The Minister adjusted his tan slacks and sat on one of his soft chairs, looking composed, creating an effect. Four men were brought into the room. As they entered, The Minister stood, a beam of a smile on his face, all warmth. These were his men, not the President's. Over years he had nurtured these relationships, grown them from small corrupt seeds. Mentored them, fed them on opportunity, kept them close. Today he would give them an offer, that he wouldn't admit even in the darkest recesses of his mind, that he needed them to accept.

As they sat and were given drinks by the maid, there was a little small talk. Children being sent away to international schools, a new Mercedes, a new apartment for a new girlfriend. As far as the Minister was aware, these men had never all been in the same room together. He looked at them one by one as they chatted. There was the Deputy Inspector General of police, who was the second in command of the country's police force. The Chief of The Airstaff, the most senior man in the Air Force. The Minister of Transport, an up-and-coming member of the elite with the backing of a powerful family, and finally his Deputy Minister of the Interior.

The Minister waited patiently for an opportune moment, a lull in the conversation before he started. There was a little bit of Oxford in his diction. 'Gentlemen, thank you so much for coming. I'll start by stating that I trust you all absolutely and I would like for you all to trust each other.' Wary nods around the room. 'You're the first to hear it, but next year I'll be announcing that I'll be running for President.'

There were the usual platitudes, congratulations and such given by the men in the room. They were uncertain as to why they were all there, being invited into this inner circle.

'If I'm successful, I see excellent opportunities for advancement for all of you.' The Minister looked around the room slowly, gauging the men. In his mind, the police officer, the ex-pilot and the deputy minister were already in the bag. The Minister of Transport wasn't though, and he spoke first.

'Minister, that is exciting news of course, but we're but a small group of men. What is your plan, how will you finance your campaign?'

With hunters' eyes, glowing, the Minister replied, 'I'm glad you asked. The funding is secured, but there is one area that I need your help. Next week, something remarkable will happen. I can't tell you what it is, but when it happens you will know.'

The Minister for Transport queried again. 'So how do we help if we don't know what "it" is?'

'You will know, I assure you, when it happens. And as far as help is concerned, you'll all be able to play a part, subtly without any risk to yourselves. What I need from you is time. Inefficiency, a delay in your decision making, hold your subordinates back. Respond, with the minimum that you can get away with.'

'This sounds illegal?'

'Undoubtably. It is. But if I succeed, I guarantee two things; One, you will all be considerably richer than you are now and two, you will all be given positions of power that you never dreamed of.'

'And if you fail?'

'Then no one will know that we had anything to do with it. And then, we will try again.' The Minister was beginning to wonder if he had made a mistake bringing in the Minister of Transport. He made a note to keep a very close eye on him.

Chapter 5

September 20th, The Kayoro Mine. Ghana.

Jimmy was out doing one of his daily checks. The Kayoro mine was a hard rock mine, Kilometres across, a vast open pit which when looked at with a bird's eye from above, spiralled down hundreds of metres from the surface. The spirals were wide roads, along which a constant procession of Caterpillar 747 dumper trucks trundled.

Those huge, bright yellow, well-used dumper trucks could carry four hundred tons of gold ore per load. The mine had thirty of them, and that was a hundred-million-dollar investment just there. The dusty black wheels were enormous. Each wheel was wider than a saloon car, taller than two fully grown men. The boxy looking snub-nosed trucks packed two V12 engines and delivered 3400 horsepower. Even with that power, as they crawled their way up the road, they came slowly. The noise was constant, much of it shielded by the depth of the mine. But when they finally, like a rhino released, broke free on to the flat ground above, the vibration and hum increased hugely. There was a reason why Jimmy was wearing a hard hat with ear defenders on it.

Down at the base of the mine, where the live quarrying was happening, vast cranes worked in unison, hauling ore, fifty tons at a time and dropping it into the hoppers on the back of the trucks. Blasting had been completed yesterday. Large boulders were still being fractured by huge pneumatic machines, breaking them down into smaller chunks, the cranes and the dumpers worked constantly.

The latest truck to escape the pit trundled past Jimmy on its way to deposit its load on the pile awaiting processing. There, huge bulldozers were already at work moving other ore into the processing plant. Jimmy cast his eye around. Today wasn't a normal manager's check. Today he was trying to remember all of the security measures that were in place around the site. He had a phone call to make on Monday. It was with the leader of the team that was coming to steal the gold. Jimmy was a cautious man and didn't want to write anything down, even on paper. As Jimmy cast his eye over the vast site, he made some mental notes. In addition to the forty guard towers, the site had a lot of security infrastructure. There were hundreds of CCTV cameras, or Video Monitoring Systems as the last memo from the security team had started calling them. There was an impressive gate structure that could be locked up tight. There were external fences, internal fences, trenches, and barriers to stop vehicles from ramming. There was a contingent of armed police on the site, but Jimmy couldn't remember for the life of him how many people that was. There was even a large police station about twenty kilometres away down the main road whose job it was to respond if there was a major problem.

The thing about this site, Jimmy mused, was that it was closed up tighter than his ex-wife before he divorced her. No one came in without an appointment, in triplicate, in advance, if they were lucky.

There was also government vetting, a security check on the way in, and one on the way out. Even the airplanes when they landed on the runway inside the perimeter of the camp were thoroughly searched. The airfield part of the camp was sealed off from the rest, of course. Jimmy wished he had paid more attention to the site's security manager. That guy was good at his job and that worried Jimmy a lot now that he thought about it. What was he missing? How would that guy respond to an attack? Jimmy would have to work something out there. Another thing that Jimmy worried about was the safety of the crew working the mine. There were several safe havens built around the camp. One in the ore processing area, one near the accommodation and a portable one in the base of the mine. These safe havens, bulletproof, self-contained spaces, were designed as places for the workers to shelter in the event of a major problem. The practical drill a couple of weeks ago showed that once people were inside the safe havens, they were indeed safe. But would they all get in there when the attack began?

Jimmy's radio beeped. The digital Motorola's allowed individual calling instead of everyone on the net having to hear a conversation. He unclipped it and spoke to his production manager. 'Go ahead, Salim.'

'Jimmy, I thought you might want to know. We're going to crush our production targets this month. The last couple of thousand tons that we processed had nearly triple the gold concentrate in it than forecast.'

'Thanks Salim, that's good news, especially when bonus day is coming up.'

Clipping his radio back onto his belt, he did the math. An average ton of ore would have between five and eight grams of gold in it. By a process of crushing, milling, chemical treatments, heating, more chemical treatments and purification, you could take basic ore and turn it into one of the most desirable metals in the world. Jimmy thought that the current grade must have perhaps eighteen grams of ore per ton. An exceptional quality, but it never lasted long. Still, the bump in production meant there would be a little bit of extra gold to be had on Wednesday.

Chapter 6

September 20th, Dibulo, Ghana

Abdi was sitting, as had become his habit, on his plastic chair outside his tent. The green canopy of the trees above him swayed gently. Inside his tent was his hammock, the only way to sleep in the jungle. It kept you off the floor and then you could hang a mosquito net above to keep the worst of the bugs out. His chair gave him a sweaty arse, but it also gave him a good view of the camp. It was a place where his men knew they could find him. If they had a question, they would approach, and like some lord of old, he would nod so they could come closer and ask their questions.

Cheko approached with a petite Indian-looking woman in tow. He didn't pause as he walked straight up to Abdi and introduced Azrah.

Abdi stared at this woman, a mistress of death. She was so small, so innocuous, harmless looking. Her black hair was tied back and hidden with a dark grey shawl. She wasn't pretty, some childhood disease had left her with a pock marked face, but intelligent eyes behind battered scratched glasses stared at Abdi without fear.

They did the usual introductions and pleasantries before getting to the meat of the meet.

'Has Cheko told you what I need you to do?'

Azrah replied in a Pakistani accent shaking her head as she did so. 'Yes, yes, yes. It sounds highly interesting. I have never attached such large bombs to drones before. Can they carry the weight?'

'I am told so. My question though is, are they safe?'

'What, my bombs?'

'Yes, with the vibration of the drones. Might they go off accidently?'

'No, no, no. My bombs very safe. Until of course you don't want them to be.'

'Will that size of bomb be able to destroy a guard tower?'

'What is the tower made of?'

'Wood, steel, tin metal roofs.'

'There is your answer. The metal roofs will turn into fragmentation and shrapnel when the bombs go off. It will shred anything underneath that isn't hit by the immediate blast.'

Abdi, who was not even remotely experienced in explosives, having studied finance and economics for a degree, nodded. He had assumed that the bombs would blow up the towers like some Hollywood stunt film, but he didn't want to show his ignorance. 'Good. Now, my next problem is the bunker with all the gold in it. How do we crack that one?'

What followed was a technical discussion between the three of them. Options were discussed that verged much more on civil engineering than fighting a contact battle. In the end, Abdi had to accept that this expert really did know what she was talking about. It sounded as though she could do everything that was needed and would have a busy couple of days putting all of her devices together.

'Abdi, my question to you is, have you got all of the materials that I need to do this work for you?'

'That's a fair question. I think so, but let's take a walk and I'll show you.'

Chapter 7

September 22nd, Accra. Ghana.

All of the members of the cabinet of the government of Ghana were sitting in the State House briefing room. Well, all but one of them, and the President. The room had a large oval mahogany table, that seemed to float above the rich, thick cream carpet. Adorning the walls were portraits of the previous presidents. Stern-looking photos, not paintings which would have had more gravitas. Arched over each window spaced all the way along the length of the room, a wide, silk sash, horizontally striped in the red, yellow, and green of the country's flag.

Everyone in the room knew why they had been called in at the last minute today. Told by the whips that no excuse would be tolerated. They knew, but no one was talking about it. Despite the power that they all held, they sat in that room, waiting anxiously for the President to arrive. School boys and girls awaiting the principal.

The door opened, and they all stood. The President, scowl on his face, chins wobbling, bags under his eyes. An immaculate Savile Row suit, pastel yellow shirt from Pinks of London, and green tie hand woven from silk in Paris. He paused, peered over the rims of his spectacles, and said in a quiet voice, full of disappointment, 'Sit.'

With a shuffling of chairs, and the odd furtive glance amongst the cabinet, they sat. A couple of murmurs of 'Good afternoon, Mr President,' were ignored by the man in charge.

He sat and undid his jacket button. He slowly took a sip of water from the glass on the table in front of his seat. Deciding that he had everyone's attention he began. 'I have just come from a meeting with the Attorney General, and the Minister of Energy. Ah, excuse me, the former Minister of Energy.' This was news, so he let it sink in for a moment. 'The news that broke around the world last night, about his financial relationship with the Chinese conglomerate, Palm Gold, appears to be true. He told me that the allegation of more than two hundred million USD being paid to him over the past seven years, is not correct. However, he agreed that it was in the best interest of the country that he resign. To be clear though, he didn't resign. I sacked him. I have also given him one month to return that money to the Central Bank of Ghana. In addition. I spoke to the U.S. Attorney General who informed me that they will be requesting his presence in America for trial. It appears that he not only broke our laws, but also a host of international money-laundering laws as well. The Americans want blood.'

Stony faces around the table didn't give much away. Politicians always knew how to mask what they were thinking. Behind lidded eyes though, there was a riot of questions. Without exception, everyone around that table had a finger in a couple of meaty pies. Some were more obviously corrupt than others. None of them thought they were stupid enough to get caught though.

The President continued. 'What disappoints me most, is that this man who I vouched for, who I nurtured, was stupid enough to get caught on the international stage. To bring down the reputation of the country in such a public fashion. I know that all of you have some side businesses, and whilst I don't condone it, I know that it will take more time before corruption is ruled out of this country completely. What is unforgivable is the size, scale and arrogance displayed in this case.' His voice began to rise in tone and volume. 'I have told the Americans that they can have him. I have told the former minister that too. The only way to save his skin is for him to repay the whole goddamned lot! If he does that, then maybe the Americans won't have him, but he will never be able to leave Ghana again.'

More than one or two people in that room thought that was a little unfair. Some of them though, liked the fact that a wealthy rival had just been removed from the chessboard of power. The Minister of the Interior caught the eye of The Minister of Transport. Last week's meeting had ended well. They held eye contact for a mere moment, with no change of facial expression, but it was a look that communicated at a visceral level.

Was the President really saying that he would hand over one of the inner circle to the Americans? That would not be popular. Even the recovery of all that money, if it happened, would only gain a couple of sound bites on the TV, a few column inches. Perhaps he was eyeing up a leading role at the UN, or the IMF. Trying to make it onto the world stage. Either way, thought the Minister of the Interior as he looked at the competition around the room, next year's Presidential battle had just gotten a little easier. He lost himself in self-congratulation and images of success, as the soon to be a 'has-been' droned on and on about corruption.

Chapter 8

September 22nd, Dibulo, Ghana

Cheko was playing hard man. Or at least that's what one of the newly-arrived drone pilots had thought. If only he had known that Cheko wasn't bluffing, he might have saved himself a lot of embarrassment and pain. Actually, on reflection, it was the pain that he had been most uncomfortable with at that particular moment. Three drone pilots had arrived about two hours ago. Sitting in the back of a battered old pick-up truck for a three-hour journey through Northern Ghana had given them numb buttocks and senses. Arrival in the camp shattered any final illusions about this being a simple survey gig. It was the weapons on show that reinforced that. They had been invited cordially to sit and get a briefing from Cheko. They sat on crudely cut logs which served as chairs. Cheko had been courteous at first, passing them water, all smiles. Then he had started to talk about what their role was going to be. As he saw the stunned faces, above the expensive bush clothes, bought especially for this little adventure of a contract, he knew he would have to take a tougher line.

When the first guy had stood up and said that he wanted no part of such a thing, Cheko had smiled a crocodile smile. He had of course prepared for this. Two of his men stepped forward and pinned the drone pilot by the arms, pulling them back so that his chest puffed out. Cheko went to a table behind him on which was a small box. He opened the box and pulled out the largest scorpion the pilot had ever seen. Twenty centimetres in length, it was all pulsating black body and furry legs. It had massive front claws and of course a tail, arched like the tautest of bows. At the tip, a single stinger waved angrily. Cheko was holding the scorpion by the middle of its tail, taking great care. It waived its claws menacingly, straining its whole body as it tried to snip or sting the fingers that held it like a vice. Cheko advanced towards the pilot with this furious monster at arm's reach in front of him.

'This is a giant forest scorpion. If you didn't know, in the jungles of the world there are twenty-five scorpions whose venom is fatal to humans.'

The pilot looked at it petrified. Cheko knew that actually, a good rule of thumb was that the larger the claws and the bigger the scorpion, the less deadly their venom was. Evolution had made it so that if you had big claws, they were designed to scare an attacker and the venom wasn't so bad. Generally, it was the tiny little scorpions with small claws that could kill you with their sting. Of course, Cheko wasn't going to tell the pilot that. Not until he had shit himself first. 'The three of you are going to do what we say. You'll fly like your lives depend on it. In fact, your lives do depend on it and so does mine. If you don't do your job, I might die. If that happens, I'll come back like the jungle spirit I'll be and I'll pursue you to the ends of the earth!'

'But, but... I don't want to kill anyone!' the pilot blurted.

'OK, then you die here and now.' In a swift movement Cheko put a finger to the man's throat, pulled at the neck of his shirt and dropped the scorpion down his front. The man screamed, a high effeminate pitch and he started dancing and jiving as he tried to keep the scorpion away from this skin. He beat with the flat of his hand against the bulge and then screamed as the scorpion stung him. He ripped the tucked-in shirt out and the scorpion dropped to the ground. It had a damaged front claw and it stood there, tail arching threateningly, whilst the pilot whimpered in fear examining the growing red spot on his stomach.

Cheko addressed the other two pilots who had gone pale. 'Do either of you have any objections?' When it was apparent that they didn't, he continued. 'You'll check your equipment, check the drones and the controllers. Work out how you're going to do this. The bomb maker has already prepared the devices and you'll help her secure them to the drones. Then I want you to fly them with the weight. Later, you'll tell me how you'll operate so many drones at once and how you'll get them to their targets.' He paused and addressed the pilot who was actually crying now. 'You!' he shouted. 'Stop whimpering. You're not going to die from that sting. Whilst painful, that one wasn't deadly.' He kicked it away and into a nearby bush. 'You do what we say and when we say. Not only might you live through this, but you will be paid handsomely.' The pilot actually looked grateful now that he knew he wasn't going to die, at least not today.

Cheko left the group under the care of some of his men as he walked to Abdi's tent. As he arrived, Abdi smiled at him. 'That was nicely done. I don't think I've heard a man scream like that in a long time. Do you think they'll give any more trouble?'

'No, but we'll need someone to watch them and threaten them if needed when the battle starts. I don't like having to rely on coerced men for such an important part of the plan.'

'It can't be helped. You're right of course, it's vital. If they can't destroy all those towers quickly then we'll lose the element of surprise and be fighting a much larger force. If we have any drones left over, then I want them up above us and able to come down and destroy any police that are being problematic.'

'If it works, it'll set the way that people attack places like that for years to come.'

'Perhaps. Keep a personal eye on them, will you? For now, I have to prepare for a call with the mine manager. He's going to give me a final briefing on all of the security measures. I'll let you know if we need to adjust any of our plans.'

'Can we trust him?'

'That man just wants money. He'll do what is needed as long as he thinks he'll get paid.'

Chapter 9

September 22nd, The Kayoro Mine. Ghana.

The white pickup truck was perched on top of a hill inside the perimeter of the mine. Its engine plinking metallically as it cooled down. Already on the dust under the car, a puddle of moist sand was forming. The air conditioning unit worked frantically, trying to remove water from the sodden jungle air inside the cab. Jimmy was standing, leaning up against the hood of the truck, his beer belly protruding over a belt that was two notches too tight. A large dark stain of sweat sat in the middle of the back of his cream shirt. That stain was centred in the middle of rings of salt where other sweat patches had long since formed and dried. He had his satellite phone in his left hand and was mustering his thoughts. His right hand reached over his left ear patting his hair in place over the top of his balding pate. He briefly looked at the residue of hair oil on his palm before wiping it on his trouser leg. There was one other number stored in his phone, aside from The Associates, He scrolled through to a contact called Mr A.

Jimmy hadn't slept well last night. All of a sudden, this thing, this project, was getting very real. He was about to betray the trust of all those with whom he worked. It wasn't that over which he lost sleep though. He was more anxious about his own skin. He knew if he disappeared either before or after the attack, then all the fingers of blame would fall on him, and he would never be able to set foot in the Western world again. So, he was going to hide along with the rest of the crew. Sit it out in one of the safe havens. It would be pure coincidence when the first shots were fired that he would be near one of the places to lock down securely. He might even be able to become a hero he thought, react quickly, keep people safe. The investigation after the attack wouldn't be pleasant, but there shouldn't be any evidence that he was involved. He just needed to dispose of this phone at the right time. Then in a year or two, he would retire early, access the vault where his share of the gold was stored. His lecherous bitch of an ex-wife wouldn't see a penny of it.

He extended the phone's antenna and gave it a few moments to acquire a satellite. When he saw the bars light up on the display, he pressed call on the keyboard.

'Yes?' an oddly London, English sounding voice, answered with a twang of an overtone that Jimmy couldn't quite place.

'Is that Mr A?'

'Yes. I assume this is Mr B?'

'Yes, it is. I have some information that I think you're expecting.'

The voice that was clear on the other end because of the digital technology said, 'Go ahead.'

Jimmy started. Detailing everything that he could remember of the physical security measures: the infrastructure, the guards, the police, the response teams. This download of information took about twenty minutes and then Jimmy finished, confident that he had remembered everything. Then started a question-and-answer session.

'You haven't told me where the main vault is.'

'Haven't I? Well, it's a concrete block of a building, in between the processing plant and the offices. It looks extremely low to the ground, because a lot of it's underground. I assume you are going to blow into it.'

'Yes'

'Well, don't plan on blowing the main vault door off. It's designed to need so much explosive that the corridor leading up to it will collapse, and that makes getting the gold out very time consuming. I suggest that you get your explosives man to approach it from the outside. It's still hard, but I have something that will help.'

'It's a woman.'

'Umm, what?'

'It's not an explosives man, it's a woman.'

'And why is that important?'

'Because, if this fails, and you haven't told me everything, I will get her to blow your balls off with some detonation cord and force what's left of them down your throat!'

Jimmy paused for a moment, visualising that. He continued uncertainly, 'I've, um, organised for a spot inspection on the jack hammer rig, so it will be up in the maintenance yard tomorrow, not down at the bottom of the pit.'

'What is a jack hammer rig?'

'Well, you know the machines that make a goddamned lot of noise when breaking up roads and fixing potholes? It's a massive one of those. I thought you might like it to help break into the vault? It's designed to shatter huge rocks and pull them apart. It should have the ability, after some explosives have done the main work, to cut through that concrete vault and its steel reinforcement like a drug dealer through a packed dancefloor.'

Abdi, on the other end of the phone grunted approvingly, 'Fine, that's a good idea. Maybe you arrange for a forklift truck and a bulldozer to be nearby as well. It will all cut down on the time needed to get the gold out.'

'I will do, now let me tell you about the air defences. At the moment it's a weak spot. The air defence system is old and has never been used. My security manager is always going on about how worried he is that it doesn't work.'

'Does it work?'

'I have never seen it do anything. The men that are supposed to work it are lazy, sleeping all day. I don't think that it'll be able to do anything.'

'Think or know?'

'Well, nothing is certain, but I am confident.'

'Will it work against drones?'

'What? No. It's designed to protect the runway. We have never even thought about drones. What could drones do against us?'

'Don't worry about it. So, it's some good news and some bad news.'

There was a slight lull in the conversation and Jimmy was a little uncertain, but he needed to ask. He took a deep breath before asking, 'What happens to all my employees?'

'If they don't fight against us, and stay in the buildings, then we won't kill them on purpose.'

'On purpose?'

'Yes, there will be a lot of explosives, a lot of shooting, anyone that is an obvious target will be killed. Some may get killed accidentally. If they stay inside those little protective bunkers you told me about then we won't kill them. As long as we're able to get into the vault.'

Jimmy didn't like that, but he was committed now. He couldn't back out and tell anyone without revealing what he knew. 'Do you have to kill all of the security guards?'

'Anyone who resists will be killed. It's that simple. If they're not a threat, they may live. You're sounding like the bride before her wedding night. All nerves and afraid of what it will be like. All you have to do now is shut your mouth and hide in your bunker. Then you'll be a rich man.'

The conversation continued for another ten minutes before Abdi had finished with his questions. When Jimmy eventually hung up, he spent a while leaning against his truck, looking around the site, sweating and worrying.

Chapter 10

September 23rd, Dibulo. Ghana.

The day before the attack. Abdi, his men, and one woman were all standing around in a circle beneath the trees. There were forty or so of them, and they were a rag-tag crew. There was no uniform, no standard dress. Some wore shorts, flip flops and a football shirt. Some had camouflage trousers, boots and dark t-shirts. There were beards, dreadlocks, and shaved heads. Some had blingy watches of fake gold and some had teeth of real. On the floor in the middle, was a model, a representation of the mine site.

Abdi was standing in the middle of the circle with a long stick in his hand. Everyone had had their phones taken off them that morning and it was time to finally tell then what the target was. Abdi wasn't one for pleasantries and inspiring speeches. At the age of twenty-six he was probably younger than most of the men there. His frame was skinny, his Somali face sallow. He was properly dressed in dark green long trousers and a long cotton shirt. He wore boots that allowed his feet to breath properly, but they were still quite new and chafed his toes a little. He was getting sweat rashes under his armpits and swore that something was eating him alive each night.

He had already started the briefing, making sure everyone knew who was working with whom for the attack tomorrow. It was time to describe the plan and he stood in the middle of his model, aware that everyone was watching him with interest. The model had taken Abdi most of the morning to make, done from an arial photograph taken on a discreet flyover months before. The model was a couple of metres wide and several metres long. The buildings had been made of rocks or big pieces of wood. The runway from long green leaves, the fence lines by scuffing his boot along the soil. He used his stick to point as he spoke.

'This is the Kayoro gold mine.' It was the first time he had named the site and there was a lot of excited chatter. 'Quieten down and listen.' He waited. 'The site is six kilometres long and four kilometres wide. The whole site has a mound of earth around it three metres high and it's topped with a fence. The jungle is cleared for three hundred metres out to the treeline to give the defenders a firing zone. There's an extra fence about half-way around and there is a road that goes all the way around the perimeter. Every five-hundred metres there are guard towers, each with two guards in. There's lighting, security cameras and sensors of all kinds. It's a hard place to get into.'

A voice popped up from the crowd, 'So how do we get into it?'

Abdi looked in that direction and continued, 'There's a runway in the top right-hand corner, which is the Northeast. There's one gate only, on the Eastern side. There's a huge processing plant on the Southeast corner. On the Western edge of the site there's a river, too wide for us to cross. The whole of the Western side is a huge open pit mine kilometres long and wide. But we don't need to go to that part of the site. Offices, accommodation and the guard room are all here by the gate on the East side. And this little building here, next to the maintenance yard, is the vault.'

Eyes stared at that innocuous looking piece of wood that represented the target and wealth beyond measure. 'The battle starts tomorrow morning at dawn. We'll move from here tonight and lay up near enough to the site but hidden in the trees until we need to show ourselves. We'll attack through the front gate and from the Northeast corner over the airstrip at the same time.'

That same questioning voice piped up again, 'But how are we going to defeat all of those defences? There are so many of them and so few of us.'

This time Abdi answered him directly. 'We're going to use a drone swarm.' He saw the questioning looks. 'A drone swarm. You've seen all those shiny little airplanes. Well, each one of them now has a bomb attached. Think of it like a grenade which we can direct exactly to where we want it. At the beginning of the battle, we launch them all up into the air, where they will hover until directed by our fine brave pilots.' Abdi indicated the three drone pilots who looked anything but. 'One of those drones will destroy a whole guard tower, a vehicle, a group of soldiers in a trench, whatever. We'll direct them to destroy the guard towers first, and then we'll use them as we need to. Death will rain from the sky and there's not a single defence on that mine that can stop them. The soldiers will run in fear when they realise that. Once the towers at the main gate are destroyed, we'll approach with RPGs and the vehicles which have the .50 Cals on the back. It shouldn't be too difficult.'

'So, what happens next?' another voice this time, and there was a bit more respect in the general tone now.

'Next we break into the vault. We use special shaped charges to blow a hole into the side. Someone goes in and then presses the emergency exit button on the inside of the vault. It automatically opens the vault doors. Then we drive the gold out on pallets using forklift trucks. Whilst all that is happening, the airplane arrives. We load the gold onto the plane, we all get on and we fly out to Liberia where you all get paid.'

'What about police response?' It was Cheko this time.

'One of the first drones will destroy the radio masts on the guard house. But as a backup we will also lay an ambush on the road outside the camp to hit any police that respond. It will look like a war zone by the time they arrive, and we don't know how many police or military might respond. Basically, once it starts, we need to move quickly.'

'How do we control all the workers inside the camp?'

'Their procedure when an emergency happens is to go to their safe havens. They're like concrete bunkers which we won't try to get into. We don't need to interfere with the civilians, unless they try to stop us, in which case you kill them. I expect them to stay hidden in their safe little houses until we leave. Soldiers on the other hand might try to counterattack us. And that's where our drones come in again. We can hit them when they're still a long way away.' Abdi paused for a moment for any other questions. 'That's the overall plan. Now let's break you into your attack groups and go through what each of you needs to do, if we're going to make this plan work.'

It was by no means a military operation, and as a result the briefing took a long time. Abdi needed to make sure that each man and woman knew exactly what they needed to do tomorrow. They were fighting together for the first time and communications might be very difficult. It wasn't the first time that Abdi thought to himself that this was a really complicated problem. He would be heavily reliant on Cheko to make it work. He was going to have to trust him implicitly after all. But, he thought, Cheko had to trust Abdi too.

Chapter 11

September 23rd, The Kayoro Mine. Ghana.

The convoy of pickups and the truck carrying all the drones crept along the road, sneaking surreptitiously under the stars. All headlights had been turned off and brake light bulbs removed about ten minutes ago, during a brief pit stop. This lack of light had made driving very difficult and there had been more than one rear end collision. The worst had happened when the lead pickup simply drove off the road and into a ditch. The crunch of the accident, the shouted expletives of the fighters sitting in the back, sounded ridiculously loud to Abdi's stressed-out ears in the quiet night. Luckily, the pickup had quickly been pushed back up onto the track by muscles and the power of Abdi's muttered swearing.

The forty or so fighters had been split into two groups of twenty and allocated their vehicles for the insertion. Cheko was in command of one group and Abdi had the other. Abdi also had Azrah, the bomb maker with him and the three drone pilots who were under close guard. Where Azrah looked completely composed, and in control, the drone pilots looked scared shitless. The massive armoury of weapons and bombs made them think that next time, before they accepted a freelance contract, they should do a little more due diligence. It didn't matter what the day rate was if you were never going to get home to collect it.

One of the things that had really brought it home to the pilots was when the 'technicals' turned up. These technicals were fitted out for jungle fighting. Toyota Hilux single cab pickup trucks, with a tripod mounting for a fifty calibre M2 Browning heavy machine gun fixed to the flatbed of each vehicle. The baseplate was crudely welded to the floor, and then a sturdy steel pole brought the weapon mount up high so that it could fire clear of the cab in front. The mount allowed the weapon to swing through an arc of 360 degrees and the gunner could stand holding the weapon for support whilst it drove along. Pinioned to the top of the mount was a shelf for the ammunition crate and for the weapon itself. The gun barrel extended well out in front and ended in a flash suppressor. The bulky rectangular breach finished at the gunner's end with two small handles and the trigger mechanism. The weapon was already loaded with dully glinting brass .50 calibre rounds on an ammunition belt that fed from the box on the weapon's left.

Bench seats in the back of each pickup concealed storage bins for more ammunition crates, as well as food and water for the driver, gunner and loader. Three of these vehicles, all painted in a jungle camouflage of greens and browns, had menaced their way into the camp yesterday. The final things to arrive.

Tonight, one technical was leading the convoy and one was bringing up the rear. The third was Abdi's command vehicle and it was driving just in front of the truck that was carrying all of the drones, prepared with their explosive loads. If Abdi thought about that too hard, truth be told, he got a little nervous. Interspersed throughout the rest of the convoy were a further five pickup trucks. They were battered old vehicles; none had the same paintwork, some had brightly coloured decals, but they were all scratched and dented to hell. All were loaded front and back with fighters. Had there been anyone to see them as they crept down the road through the jungle, the silhouettes in the starlight would have looked strange. Ghostly vehicles, men sitting uncomfortably on the flatbeds in the back, some wearing hats, all carrying a weapon. The occasional long tube of an RPG was visible as was the sporadic dull glow of a cigarette. From the fighters came a low rumble of chatter, though not any louder than the droning of the vehicle's engines. Occasionally there was a burst of laughter. That laughter when it happened, sounded strained and forced. Pretty normal for warriors about to go into battle.

Five kilometres or so short of the main gate to the mine, and at about midnight, well ahead of schedule, the whole convoy pulled off the road. The drivers gently steered the vehicles through a gap in the foliage to an area just beyond, where widely-spaced trees allowed them to lay up. Even the truck was able to come off the road and park discreetly. Its higher profile bashed some branches on the way through. The spot had been identified a couple of days ago and was the perfect place to hide until it was the right time to attack.

Cheko and his men were leaving the rest of the group at this point. Their task now was manoeuvre to the Northern side of the mine, pass through the jungle and create a second point of attack. They were leaving their vehicles and had to cover the final few kilometres on foot, in the dark. It was not going to be easy, but Cheko had his seasoned veterans with him. He was confident he could get to his attack point before dawn. As his men unloaded their kit from the back of the pickup trucks that had brought them this far, Cheko walked up to Abdi who was leaning against his vehicle in the dark. He whispered, 'We made good time.'

'Yep. Have you got everything you need?'

'Yeah, the men are nearly ready. Now we just need to find our way. We'll track along beside the road for a little while and then cut across the bush to the North.'

'And you're certain you can make it in time?'

'Of course. We all know that if we don't, then you're going to have a hell of a fight on your hands. We have to distract enough of the guards and soldiers to make your job a little easier.'

'Well, if we fail, then the area will be crawling with soldiers before mid-day. We'll all get caught.'

'Then we must pray to our gods that we don't fail.'

'To success then, Cheko. March well, fight better, and tomorrow we'll be rich.'

Cheko nodded and walked back down the line of vehicles to where his men were all now ready. Most of the experienced fighters were going with him and had put mud on parts of their faces and hands. With their dark clothing, they blended right in to the jungle. Those less experienced in combat and who were staying with Abdi, were wearing a mix of football shirts, shorts and bright t-shirts. Looking at the men that passed them, they made a conscious note that they wouldn't look like novices again, if they were lucky enough to get through this.

As Cheko and his men started to walk out, they left with an arrogant gait. They were not going to show fear as they left and sauntered past their comrades. They carried with them water, their weapons, bullets, and some had first aid kits. A couple of men shared the weight of some pipe bombs, put together by Azrah. Abdi had heard of this idea from an old British Army pamphlet he had bought back home in Somalia. These three-metre-long 'Bangalore Torpedo's' would find a use later in destroying some of the barbed wire fences. Other men carried RPG's as well as their rifles. The weight on rotting green straps was crippling, and they would be chafed and sore by the time they reached their target. However, it was better to have one and not need it than the other way around. At least, if you wanted to win the fight. The men moved out and across the road as they started to head North. When they passed into the jungle on the other side, they quickly faded into the murky gloom.

Abdi walked along the line of vehicles as his men readjusted their equipment, spreading it out now that they had more space. They left the technicals with just their operators and split out amongst the other pickups. Their immediate job when that was done was to rest, to sleep if they could. Nerves were likely to keep them awake, fretful, tossing and turning uncomfortably. The mosquitos, sensing a feast, descended to do their part in keeping the men awake.

Chapter 12

September 24th, The Kayoro Mine. Ghana.

Just before five in the morning, Abdi's convoy moved out. The plan was for two of the technicals to lead the truck, and then for the rest of the pickups to follow after. Bringing up the rear was the last technical. Azrah was a passenger in that one, with a couple of her boxes of magic tricks. Cheko and his men had had just over four hours to cover the five kilometres through the jungle. Abdi thought that even with slow going they would be in position by now. He knew that walking at night through the jungle was very dangerous, and should be avoided where possible, but in this case the risk had to be taken.

As the convoy made its way out of the jungle and back onto the tarmac road, all was quiet and tense. Men who until so recently had been in the doze of semi-sleep were getting their first hits of adrenaline as they realised what was coming with the dawn. Some had smoked cigarettes, some had drunk water from a canteen, and some had drunk a little cane spirit from hidden bottles. There had been no laughter or grinning, each man was absorbed in their own thoughts. It was getting serious.

Abdi was in the second technical from the front, with the truck just behind him. They crept along the road, careful not to over rev their engines. Again, no lights, no chatter. About a kilometre short of the main entrance to the mine was a bend in the road. The convoy came to a gentle stop. Abdi got out of his technical and the two front vehicles pushed forward ever so slightly to provide cover and to give the drone pilots a secure space to work in. The technicals remained hidden in the dark, but the eyes of the gunners were wide awake. Around the bend, the glow of the mine lights was clear above the trees. It reflected off the ever-present halo of dust above the plant polluting the starlight. Even the smell here was different to the damp of the jungle. There was a dusty, musty odour with a tang of unknown chemicals too. The fighters could hear a constant rumble of noise from the operating mine, those huge trucks hauling ore, the processing plant grinding rock into gravel and dust. It was literally a twenty-four hour a day, noisy, money-making machine. Abdi heard that din. He was pleased to think that there was no way that the guards on the main gate only a kilometre away, could have heard his men approach.

The tail gate of the truck was gently lowered, screeching a little in protest. Several men jumped into the back and formed a human chain, passing the packaged drones out carefully. Azrah came forward and, sly as a cat, stood to one side, ready to pounce on any idiot who didn't understand how dangerous their cargo was.

The drone pilots were behaving now, unpacking the drones, and lining them up on the road, giving them plenty of space between each one. One of the pilots erected a five-metre antenna that had a slim white box on the top. It was tied to the rear of the truck and would go with it when it moved forward. With forty of the drones unloaded, he jumped up into the back of the truck, unpacked a laptop and booted it up. The other two pilots were carefully switching on the drones whilst Azrah followed them removing the final safety device for her bombs. Once the devices were turned on and ready, both of the pilots and one of the fighters climbed into the back of the truck. Behind them were twenty more drones still in their boxes but otherwise ready to go. Two pilots picked up large and bulky drone controllers, strapping a harness around their neck and waist. These portable computers had joysticks, and a couple of tv screens. The first screen was for the real-time video camera on the drone. The second was flight information, height, speed, direction of flight, battery remaining, and location. There were a number of buttons as well. Autopilot hover, auto return to start location and an all-important covered red switch that had been repurposed as a trigger for the bombs.

These state-of-the-art setups would allow the pilots to control each drone one at a time. The master pilot with the laptop was going to control the swarm. At the right time he would send a command and all forty drones would take off moving automatically to a high hover about two hundred metres above the mine. This swarm commander would then pass individual drones to the pilots to control using their drone controllers on their final attacks. This way, the pilots could rapidly and effectively deploy the drones with their lethal payloads.

Abdi's fighter, in the truck with the drone pilots, was an experienced and battle-hardened old man. Whilst he was there to guard the pilots, he was also there to direct them if necessary and make sure that they did their job.

There was one other critical part of the drone plan, and this was under the control of the swarm pilot. Two drones were going to be on auto pilot high in an overwatch position. One above the gate house with its camera pointed back down the main road. The other would hover over the top of the camp and use its camera to identify any problems within the boundary. Abdi felt that keeping two drones for this purpose would give him an edge in the battle. He just hoped that the batteries would last.

Chapter 13

September 24th, The Kayoro Mine. Ghana.

Once Azrah had enabled the bombs on the drones, she walked back to her technical, which was the last vehicle in the convoy. As she walked past the five pickups loaded with fighters steeling themselves for battle, she looked at them coolly. They hadn't regarded her as very important during the past few days. Some had even been disrespectful until Cheko had sorted them out. She was an enigma to some of the fighters. A foreign woman, in the jungle fighting beside men. They didn't trust her and couldn't understand why she was there. She knew though. Once the battle started, the biggest impact would come from those "wet" drone pilots and her. Between them they would kill or maim more of the enemy than all the fighters put together. She had grown up in a culture in Pakistan where women were expected to know their place. She had a better idea though. She would make her place in the world instead on her own terms. It just so happened that she had made a life by bringing pain and death. She was very good at what she did.

Preparing for the death of others was what Azrah was doing now. She walked to the back of the technical and collected her bag. Then, as she walked off to the side of the road, the gunner and the loader watched her warily. Using the light of the stars, Azrah jumped across the drainage ditch and selected a large tree. She placed her bag at its base. Azrah pulled out three boxes, each about the size of a small juice carton. Using duck-tape she secured them to the tree. Two of the boxes were opposite each other around the trunk at just above ground level. They were the cutters. The pusher was the third box, and she taped that high on the opposite side of the tree to the direction she wanted to force the tree to fall. It was hard to get her arms around the girth of such a large tree and she had some awkward moments, face up against the rough bark, trying to keep the bombs in place whilst she secured them. Azrah then picked up a similar set of devices from her bag and walked across the road to another large tree on the opposite side. She repeated the procedure and once the bombs were fixed, she looked at the switches on the tops. She double checked the configuration and then double checked the first bombs. Fishing around inside her bag, she picked up a box the size of a cigarette packet. It had a number of switches on it, and she started by turning on the unit's power supply. In the centre of the box were three rocker switches, each shielded by a hard cover that needed to be moved before she could press them. Underneath each, in her handwritten text were the words, test, arm, fire. For now, she activated the test button. The bomb trigger units indicated a small green LED light on the top. Satisfied, she revisited each bomb and twisted a small safety switch which made them fully live. Despite knowing that she had made the devices well, she couldn't help an almost pleasurable, involuntary breath hold as she did so.

Now that she had prepared the explosive block on the road, she started preparing the killing field. As briefed in advance, the loader in the back of the technical helped her carry a large heavy wooden box. He staggered about fifty metres down the road, in a direction away from the mine, to the other side of the already prepared trees. The man was sweating as he carried the box, and it wasn't just the humidity of the jungle. He grunted with effort as he put the box down on the floor where Azrah indicated and then she dismissed him. He walked back to the technical, maintaining personal control not to run, breathing easier with each step taken. As Azrah watched him go, she smiled grimly. He might think he was safe now, but then he didn't know the killing distance of the devices that she now laid out on the ground.

There were two large anti vehicle mines, ex-military stock and shaped like giant ice hockey pucks. They were painted green and weighed about fifteen kilograms. Then there were two claymore mines, slightly concave, dark green, plastic containers, that were filled with explosives and ball bearings. Azrah proceeded to place the devices in order. Mine, claymore, mine, claymore in a line along one side of the road so that they spanned about seventy metres. The mines were right up against the edge of the road, but the claymores were set back by about five metres. That way her devices would have the best possible effect. If she had had the time, she would have preferred to bury the mines under the road surface, but there wasn't, so she settled for covering them with a few hastily cut branches. Finally, she connected their firing cables to her creation of a remote trigger mechanism and planted a small antenna off to the side of the road. Her radio signal, when she sent it, would definitely get through.

With the devices all armed she walked back to the convoy of vehicles. Her first task was done, and now it was vital that she stayed alive so she could crack the vault. She wasn't going to participate in the firefight, and she was going to stay well away from the attack against the main gate. She had already decided though, that she would find somewhere to enjoy the view.

Chapter 14

September 24th, The Kayoro Mine. Ghana.

Abdi was feeling very exposed and vulnerable. All of his fighters were lined up on the road, ready to go, charging headlong around the bend in the road to their front. He knew his back was covered by the technical at the rear and by Azrah's' welcoming gift. In reality though, there was nothing stopping a military convoy from coming from that direction, or even a guard patrol coming out of the front gate of the mine. He had agreed with Cheko that they would start the attack at precisely ten minutes to six o'clock, but that was still a few minutes away. Abdi cursed himself for bringing his team out too early. He paced anxiously walking up and down the length of vehicles. He was no military-trained commander. He didn't give any inspiration to his men, no small words of reassurance to boost their confidence. He kept his head down, looking at his boots as they scuffed along the road. The sun was beginning to rise away in the East, a glow of light well over the horizon. Unseen birds were waking and squawking the dawn chorus. The night insects wisely shut down some of their chatter. An instinctive reaction to avoid becoming breakfast.

Abdi finished his stroll next to the drone pilots who were still sitting in the back of the truck. He surveyed the multitude of drones laid out on the road. They were large, white, quadcopters. Cruciform shaped with ten-centimetre-long propeller blades on the top side of each corner. The pilots had disabled the red and green lights on their undercarriage that helped a pilot visually understand which direction they were flying in. It was a safety measure to try and stop them being shot down, but it meant piloting them would be a little harder. Costing about three thousand dollars each, the drones were state of the art. Inbuilt live 4K video feed, a top speed of seventy kilometres per hour, the ability to carry well over a kilogram in weight and with a three-hour battery life. Abdi had been staggered at how easily he had been able to buy a shipping container full of these devices from China. He was just as stunned with how little paperwork was needed to import them into Ghana. Perhaps, he mused, that might change if he was successful today.

Abdi looked at his watch, focusing in on the second hand as it ticked through the bottom of the clock. Dawn was well on the way now, light spreading across the canopy around him. He took a deep breath, looked at the pilots and quietly said one word, 'Begin.'

The swarm pilot nodded, looked down at his keyboard and using the mouse clicked the word "execute." Fully autonomously all forty drones spooled up their rotors, and then in a simple pattern to avoid crashes on take-off, launched themselves into the air. There was no being silent now. Abdi and all his men tilted their heads back to watch, as sounding like a huge swarm of angry bees, the drones climbed rapidly. Abdi looked at a screen that was hanging from the wall in the back of the truck. On it was the direct feed from one of the drones, its camera slaved and locked onto the gate. The 4K resolution zoom was moving to focus on the guards idling there. They were rubbing bleary eyes, tired from a night on duty. The guards didn't show any indications that they had heard the noise of the drones over the plant and machinery. It was a bit of a gamble, but Abdi had asked if the drones could go high enough that they wouldn't be heard, before they passed over the top of the camp. It seemed to be working.

On the swarm pilots' screen was an overlay of Google Maps in terrain mode. On top of that, forty red dots were moving fast. Each red dot had a number next to it from one to forty. That was going to be important in a moment for the pilots' combat awareness. The drones were up at nearly one thousand metres in altitude now and were flying rapidly towards their holding point above the site. The swarm pilot was frantically sending orders to the drones now that he could see the site more clearly. One by one, he clicked on a red dot, and then using his mouse sent it to a new holding location. He had a target list, and he sent his drones to them now. First up, were the perimeter guard towers. With one tower every five hundred metres and a twenty-kilometre perimeter, there were a lot of towers. A drone was sent to hover above each one in this near half of the camp. Six drones were sent to hover high above the main gate. One of them would be the overwatch drone that monitored the approach road. The other five would be used to help the fighters breach the site. Finally, a number of drones were left centrally as a reserve. It only took a few minutes for the drones to reach their positions. The swarm pilot typed a few strokes on his keyboard. Then he informed the drone pilots which number drone their individual controllers were now connected to.

Using their personal screens, the pilots could look down using the camera for that drone and view their target. The swarm pilot nodded at Abdi.

Abdi looked past the truck, towards the two technicals that were in the front. He made sure they were ready and waved a hand at them. Then he turned to the line of pickups immediately behind him and waved them forward. He instructed the two drone pilots to start the attack.

Time moved rapidly as the vehicles started moving. The first drone attacks started at the main gate. Either side of the gate were two guard posts. Within a second of each other, piloted individually, drones ploughed into the top of each tower. On the screen as Abdi watched, one moment he was flying down at the tower from a great height, the next the screen went blank. There had been a surreal moment of the camera zooming right up to the tin roof of the guard post. And then visually, nothing. Abdi heard it though. Two large bangs as the drones exploded. The swarm pilot was alert and already telling the drone operators the numbers of the next drones in their control. They looked at the central screen, to see where they were, and then started piloting again. Their nerves seemed to have evaporated as they became engrossed in their jobs. Bringing death was much like the computer games they played in their time off. Over the next minutes, the radio antenna at the guard room was destroyed. Then, guard tower after tower were blown to kingdom come. Groups of people in the open, carrying weapons, were fair targets. A group of men in combat clothing, hiding behind a concrete barrier, were wondering what the fuck was going on. Explosions all around them but no enemy to be seen. The camera showed them looking frantically around, not understanding, but they never looked up, and didn't worry for long. The drones were stinging like hornets, and the drone pilots, now merciless behind their "video game" killed, again, and again.

Chapter 15

September 24th, The Kayoro Mine. Ghana.

With the drones doing their job, explosions were happening almost every minute. Smoke and flame erupted with no notice, death reaching out and clasping its grip around increasingly terror-filled guards. The pilots started directing their efforts to the perimeter towers, working their way methodically around the camp. The swarm pilot kept handing them drones and monitored activity by the main gate. Some of the buildings there were scorched and blackened, a couple of small fires had started, adding to the carnage and confusion. The bombs on the drones were not hugely powerful, but they were having the desired impact. The guard towers, with their tin roofs, turned into death traps for those cowering in them. The force of the explosions caused massive rents in the metal work, they fragmented, penetrating flesh. One of the towers by the main gate had been structurally damaged on one leg and it started to lean precariously.

Outside the main gate, two of the technicals which had driven closer, started to open fire. The heavier thump of the .50 calibre rounds, hitting concrete, and penetrating the thin walls of the guard house to the left of the main gate. The five pickup trucks filled with fighters surged forward under their cover before stopping and disgorging men. Somewhere inside the mine, an alarm button had been pressed, a high-pitched wail began undulating throughout the camp.

Abdi looked up from the drone screens to see Azrah waving at him from about a hundred metres away. He was pleased to see that she was staying out of trouble. She held up her detonator and gave him a questioning shrug. There was too much noise to try and shout, even over that short distance. Abdi looked back down the road to where the explosives had been attached to the trees and gave an exaggerated nod.

Azrah looked at the small, innocuous box in her hand. For her, detonations released feelings of pure pleasure and absolute control. It gave her a freedom of expression, an unbundling of the repression of her youth as a girl in Pakistan. She looked at the switches, test, arm, fire. Quickly, as though needing release, she lifted the cover on the arm button and flicked the switch. Three hundred metres down the road, the devices came alive, straining, listening for the final signal. Bringing herself under a little more control, her finger caressed the cover guard of the fire button. She savoured the moment, pleasuring herself. Her finger, with its clipped and grubby nail, searched under the cover, flicking it upwards, revealing the short stubby button underneath. She teased it for a moment, then, looking down the road, she applied a gentle pressure. The button sank, a frisson of current flowed through the box and milliseconds later, the two devices strapped to the trees detonated.

The explosions scythed through wood, vaporising the cellulose structures across the base of the trees. Further up, through the instant mist, giant white splinters were forced out in a cone of debris. For a fraction of a moment the trees stood there, as they had done for many years, before toppling ever so slowly towards the road. The top-heavy branches fell gracefully, arcing through the air as the heavy trunks followed. The two trees collided slightly as they fell across the road, and then with a final rustling crash they lay, dead as they now were, branches quivering with shock.

Azrah, ecstatic with the release, rotated to face a mining camp that was turning to ruin. Smoke drifted like a blackened haze, but it barely shifted in the fuggy air. The mistress of death surveyed her work.

Chapter 16

September 24th, The Kayoro Mine. Ghana.

Jimmy had set his alarm early that morning. He had been to the 24-hour canteen in the camp, thinking that he would down a big breakfast. Once he had got there though, he had found that he wasn't very hungry after all. The acidic bile in his stomach was turning and churning, he had tried to chew on some toast, but it was hard to swallow. He managed a cup of coffee, but that didn't help the acid. He had gone back to his room and picked up his day sack. Last night he had packed a couple of essential items, two bottles of water, some snack bars, his iPad, a satellite phone, and a battery buddy. In his trouser pockets he put his wallet and his passport. He hadn't wanted to leave much of value in his room in case it got looted.

As dawn approached, he took his bag and started to walk around the accommodation blocks. He looked like the manager that he was, just doing a management check. To keep up the façade, every now and again, if someone walked past him, he would pull out his phone, take a photo and make notes about some non-existent problem. The closer it got to dawn, the closer he meandered to the safe haven. The mine site had three of them. One near the accommodation block, one near the processing plant, and one near the mine pit. They had been designed with a number of potential incidents in mind. Firstly, tropical weather. Monsoon floods were occasionally so awful that there was risk to life. It hadn't happened whilst Jimmy had been the manager, but someone somewhere had done a risk assessment that said it was possible. The security manager had a more realistic risk in mind. The potential for a large-scale robbery. This was a gold mine after all. Jimmy rolled his eyes. The guy would be insufferable after today's incident.

The safe houses were built to withstand armed attack. Solid concrete, huge pneumatic doors, air purification systems, food, water, standby power, and even chemical toilets. The concrete buildings were huge. Each one designed to hold seventy five percent of the mines' occupants. Assuming of course that all the workers were able to get to them in the event of a drama.

Jimmy looked at his watch. The sun was definitely rising now. Where the hell were the attackers? They should have been…

A pair of blasts came out of nowhere. Despite his advanced knowledge, Jimmy nearly shat himself. It was so loud! It boomed above the continuous grinding of the processing plant. The sound was closely followed by a slight pressure wave. Not enough to cause concern, but enough to be felt deep within the ears. Jimmy turned towards the front gate where the noises had come from. He saw workers wearing coveralls and hard hats in the open areas stunned, confused, mouths open in shock. Two columns of dust and debris were growing rapidly near the gate. It all looked so real. Then came the next blast, this one much closer. It was this side of the fence line and looked like it hit the antennae on the guard house. Then another blast as a guard tower was hit. Enough was enough. Jimmy, keeping up the ruse, shouted to those few workers he could see, 'Don't just stand there! Get to the safe havens!'

Men and women came running. Those curious few, coming out of the canteen, or the accommodation block were looking around wondering what the hell was going on. They quickly realised as more blasts rattled windows. Someone was screaming now too. 'Come on! Run!' Jimmy didn't need to pretend to panic. His voice was climbing a few octaves, screeching the words out. He was standing near the entrance to the strong room now. He grabbed a woman that was running past him. 'Push the panic button! Sound the alarm! But listen. Keep the door open until the last possible moment. We need to get as many people inside as possible!'

With eyes wide with fear, the woman nodded and rushed inside. Soon after, the camps alarm system started screeching its warbling tone. Buildings were emptying now, rapidly. People flooded towards the safe haven. Some almost completely naked, obviously fresh from bed. There were cleaners, cooks, miners, drivers, office workers and even the security manager. Still Jimmy couldn't work out where the blasts were coming from. He wondered if they were mortars. RPG's? Even artillery. He had no idea about the deadly woman, less than a kilometre away, and her flying toys.

The security manager, with black hair covered in foamy shampoo, and a towel around his waist, ran up breathless. 'Jimmy! We're under attack!'

Jimmy ignoring the obvious statement decided to play along. 'Yes, I know. You take over here at the entrance. I'll go in and see if I can get on the phone to the police!'

'Roger that. I'll stay here until the last safe moment!'

Jimmy, grateful for the excuse to go inside the shelter and avoid any more bombs, nodded before turning and walking in through a concrete tunnel to the large room. Inside was pandemonium. Panicked voices, obvious shock, and fear, such fear. You could smell it as it tanged the air. 'Everyone quiet down!' Jimmy commanded. It took a moment, a repeat or two, and some nudges, but there was a little more calm. People continued to pour in through the door behind him as he addressed the room. 'Is anyone hurt?' no reply. 'Have we got any first aiders here yet?' A couple of hands raised, and Jimmy directed them to one side of the room. 'Any line managers?' Those with hands up went to a different part of the room. Jimmy was really getting into his stride now. He thought he was doing really well, looking like he was in control, not panicking. He started to dish out tasks to individuals. Things that sounded good and for which people would remember him afterwards. Of course, he conveniently forgot to make that phone call to the police.

Chapter 17

September 24th, The Kayoro Mine. Ghana.

Outside the camp, at the front gate, there was more resistance than expected. The two guard towers had gone, and some guards had been killed that were hiding behind a concrete barrier. But there were still some men firing from a couple of holes in the guard room wall to the left of the gate. The drone pilots had ineffectively tried two more drones whilst trying to silence them before Abdi had stopped them from trying again.

The .50 calibre heavy machine guns on the back of the technicals had also fired hundreds of rounds at them. Whilst they were creating holes in the concrete and a lot of rubble, somehow, they weren't reaching out and touching the pink bodies inside. Abdi told them to reduce their rate of fire, conserve ammunition and keep the men under cover. He ran up to a group of Nigerian men lying down on the ground and threw himself down beside a young man wearing an Arsenal football shirt.

'Arsenal!'

The young man looked quizzical until he realised that Abdi hadn't just turned up to talk about a football game. 'Umm, yes?'

'Have you ever fired an RPG before?'

'No.'

'So why are you carrying one?'

'Because my boss told me to!'

As bullets continued to fire over their heads, Abdi tried to keep his calm. Of course, this boys' idle boss hadn't wanted to carry the heavy weapon himself. Inside Abdi's guts were squirming with terror, but he tried hard to keep his voice calm and sound under control.

'Arsenal. I will make you a deal. I want you to take that RPG and fire it at those camel fuckers in that building. If you kill them, I will give you a thousand dollars before this day is out.'

Arsenal looked at the building and weighed up the risks of having to kneel up, work the unfamiliar weapon and hit the target, all without getting shot himself. Understanding the thoughts behind the boys' eyes Abdi said, 'I will tell everyone to fire, to give you cover. Then you get up and kill them.'

Arsenal nodded. Abdi shouted to everyone near him. 'In a minute, when I say, everyone is to start firing at that building!' The seconds passed slowly, Arsenal shifted his body, still lying on the ground. He pulled out the RPG, removed the covers and plugs, mentally rehearsed what he would do. He was hyperventilating. Bullets continued to crack overhead, passing close. 'Ready?' Abdi asked. When Arsenal nodded, Abdi shouted 'Fire!'

The rattle of gunfire increased considerably. Arsenal knelt up, raised the long tube to his right shoulder. His right hand was on the trigger guard, his left holding the balance of the weight of the barrel. He leant in with his head, to put his eye to the aiming sight, and then he died.

The bullet that killed him blew clean through his skull. A single shot that sprayed blood and bone behind him. Abdi stared, whilst the boys' body, now sightless, toppled back and collapsed in a crumpled heap.

Abdi was horrified, he froze for just a moment, but he had been in combat before. He had had to find his courage then, and he dipped into that place now. He grabbed the RPG, pulling it free from the boys' body. All his senses were hyper alert. For him, time slowed as he put the weapon to his shoulder, knelt up and fired. With a crack and a swoosh, the rocket propelled grenade with its bulbous head and thin tubular tail, flew like the bastard firework that it was, towards the building a couple of hundred metres away. It hit the brickwork square on. The shaped charge forced the weight of the explosion through the smallest of holes, punching through the concrete to expand out into the volume of the room beyond. The shooting stopped. The enemy were dead. With whoops and calls, the fighters ran forwards to take the gate with their vehicles following shortly after them.

Abdi took a breath. He was still kneeling with the tube on his shoulder. His hands were sticky with sweat. He looked down at the body of the boy with a cold look in his eyes. He dropped the tube onto the ground and wiped something from his face. He was disgusted to see clumps of curly black hair and brain matter sticking to his hand as he brought it down. He had to flick his wrist a couple of times to jettison the disgusting goo. In a slight trance, but buoyed by success, he acknowledged that they must have been stuck to the weapon. There was blood on his cheek too. Lots of it.

Abdi looked around, taking stock. There was another dead body lying on the ground, one of his. Another name that he didn't know. There was also a man with a gunshot wound in his leg. He looked fearful as he wrapped a bandage around it, grimacing slightly with the pain as he tied it tight. The jungle was not a place to be injured like that thought Abdi as he walked towards the main gate. His men were well in control of it now and not many of them were firing, which told Abdi that there wasn't much to fire at. As he got there, he could see well inside the camp. Over to the right, one of the safe havens sat low and squat to the ground. Even as he watched he saw its large metal doors closing. 'Well done!' He was able to say, out of breath, to the men nearby. 'Now move to your agreed places.' Men and vehicles moved forwards and started to spread out into groups inside the camp. Some headed to the processing plant, some to the airstrip, and some through to the mine. Drones continued to destroy perimeter towers at regular intervals. The noise of an explosion reminded Abdi of something. He stepped to the side and looked behind. He could see Azrah standing next to the drone truck several hundred metres away and gave her a wave. She acknowledged, climbed into the back of the truck and it made its way forward to the main gate.

Abdi looked around as the truck drove up and parked next to him. When it stopped, he saw Azrah's face as she recoiled in surprise. 'Abdi! Are you hurt?'

'What? No, No! It's not my blood.' He unconsciously touched his face smearing the blood more.

'Good. Err, would you like some water?' Azrah handed him a large bottle of water from the back of the truck. He took the blue cap off the top and poured the first half of the bottle over his head. Pink fluid ran down his face as he rubbed. It poured onto his clothes and then it dripped onto the yellow dusty floor where it sank into a darkened stain. 'You should do that again.' She said as she handed him another bottle. He began washing his face and hands a little more thoroughly.

The drone pilots who had been busy flying, and who had never seen so much real blood, looked at Abdi. Disgust evident on all of their faces. Abdi looked at one of them straight in the eye as he brought the bottle down and proceeded to take a long drink with pink froth dripping off his chin. 'Keep doing your jobs. You're doing well.'

Abdi threw the bottle down on to the floor and walked away to lead the fight.

Chapter 18

September 24th, The Kayoro Mine. Ghana.

Cheko and his men were exhausted. Their night-time move through the jungle had been a colossal mistake. It was one of the cardinal rules. Never move at night in the jungle. The gloom of darkness, no light penetrating the canopy, the risk of tripping, or falling. That all increased the risk of injury and needing to be left behind to fend for yourself. Movement was incredibly slow. They had come across a vast patch of 'wait-a-while' vine. The plant was the curse of all those who knew the jungle. It was a cross between the type of vine that Tarzan swung on, a cactus, a bramble and a sea urchin all wrapped into one. It grew in great tendrils across the forest floor. It climbed up on itself, intertwining tentacles reached up until it created a dense impenetrable bush. It was Satan's Velcro. If you ever got ensnared in it, you had to wait-a-while. The thorns hooked into your clothing, your legs, your arms, your face. Anything exposed and soft enough for it to get a grip on. Then, as you gingerly tried to extricate yourself, another tendril of the vine would grip another part of your anatomy. Eventually, you could hack your way out using a machete and take stock of your bloody hands. Hook-like thorns, which easily detached from the vine, would be latched into any exposed soft places. Many penetrated clothing and stayed in your skin. Hooks that you couldn't remove would irritate, fester, and go septic. The triffid-like wait-a-while was a bastard of a plant.

The fighters had come across a patch that stretched for hundreds of metres. After a time- wasting search in both directions, Cheko decided the only way through was to hack and cut. It had been slow going. Painfully slow. The lead person would get five minutes at the front, a hundred percent energy, machete flying in the dark, then they would swap out with the next man. Luckily, no one was seriously injured, but at one point they had had to risk using torches. It was tactically ridiculous and a massive risk, but Cheko knew how important it was for them to make their attack on time.

As the dawn light came and started to illuminate the canopy above, Cheko started swearing at the men, urging them on. They were still five hundred metres away from the edge where the jungle had been cleared from the camp when the first bombs went off. All ideas of being in place and having had a rest before the attack had long gone out of the window. Cheko's men were knackered, they had been carrying all their ammunition, the pipe bombs, and their weapons throughout the night. Even experienced, calloused hands were sore from using their machetes, clothes were drenched in the humidity.

Hearing the battle begin without them, the men dug into whatever energy reserves they had, and trudged faster towards the camp. Cheko didn't know it, but the delay saved many of his men's lives. The guard towers on the perimeter, where the fighters breached the treeline, had already been destroyed. Twisted metal, dead defenders. Cheko breathed a sigh of relief knowing he wouldn't have to lead a frontal assault. As they entered the cleared area, the fighters blinked in the dim light of the dawn, but they knew better than to stop.

Cheko urged one of the pairs of men sharing the weight of a pipe bomb to go forward. In the second world war they were called 'Bangalore Torpedoes', but that name had gone out of fashion. The device was effectively a metal pole, similar to a construction scaffolding pole with the hollow interior packed with explosives. At one end, a push button electrical timer was connected to the detonator, which was plugged into the explosive. That was then taped up to secure it. The two men ran forward to the forbidding-looking razor wire fence in the centre of the cleared area. It consisted of six coils, a pyramid shape, three on the base, then two coils in the middle which were topped by the last. They were tied to metal stakes hammered into the ground at ten-metre intervals. To the unprepared, and to wild animals, it was a formidable obstacle.

As the fighters took cover behind large trees, Cheko stood on the edge of the cleared area looking at the camp. He saw the towers of smoke, he heard the siren alarm and even as he watched, the next guard tower, about a kilometre away to his right, was hit by a drone. There were no guards visible at all, but that didn't mean that they were not there. Cheko could see clearly beyond the well cleared ground and the razor wire obstacle to the mounded soil and chain link fence that was the perimeter of the camp. Aside from the roofs of some buildings, he couldn't see what was behind the berm.

The pipe bombers, now a hundred metres ahead, reached the razor wire obstacle. They lay on the ground and fed the five-metre-long pipe through the base of the barbed wire coils. The pipe was heavy, and it bowed the wire slightly and rested on the ground. One of the bombers turned and started running back to the tree line. The other removed a plastic safety cover and then pushed the button of the electrical timer switch. He knew he had thirty seconds. He quickly stood up, turned, and ran back to Cheko.

It was an odd moment of calm reflection for the fighters as they waited for the detonation. It wasn't peaceful, because the ongoing firefight was not so far away. But it was a moment for them to collect their breath, pray to their god, grab a drink of water.

The pipe bomb exploded with a large crack of noise. The rounded shape of the pipe focused the forces. This caused the pressure wave to brutally eject its way up into the air above, and down into the ground below. Soil, sand and stone were blown out in a V shape, creating a shallow trench along the ground. The combination of blast and pipe shrapnel upwards melted the wire above so rapidly it appeared vapourised. As the tensioned coils separated, the blast cleared a path like Moses parting the sea.

Cheko and his men surged forward, charging out of a wide expanse of the jungle, but converging as they ran, focusing on their crossing point in front. There was no breath for shouting, just more slog as they ran the hundred metres to the broken razor wire. There was confusion as many reached it at the same time, the razor wire reminding them of their struggle last night with the wait-a-while. The headlong dash paused, embarrassed in its exuberance, as the men had to wait for each individual to pass in single file. Once through though, the men spread out again, lying down on the ground whilst the last pipe bomb went forward to the berm and the perimeter fence. Cheko went with them this time and it was a two-hundred-metre dash. The thick grass underfoot wasn't high or treacherous, it was obviously regularly trimmed by some machine to keep the field of view clear from the camp. As they approached the berm of soil that was piled up around the whole perimeter, it seemed to tower above them as they got closer.

This three-metre-high obstacle kept prying eyes and vehicles out of the camp. A further three-metre-high chain link fence was well bedded into the top of it and created a visual deterrent too. The steep slope of the berm was grassed to keep dust down, and as the men approached, the front pipe bomber slipped on the morning dew as he tried to run up it. He crashed to the floor, dropping his end of the pipe as he fell. For a moment, the three of them were stumped. They realised that the sides were too steep and slippery to climb, surely not something that was built in. But, then Cheko had an idea. 'You man! Put the front of the pipe under your arm and hold on tight.'

'What yo' on about?' said the bomber, confusion on his face.

'We'll run you up the ramp!'

The man did as he was told. He turned to face up the steep ramp, put the pipe under his right armpit and clamped his elbow to his midriff. Using his left hand, he clasped the end of the pole. Behind him Cheko and the other bomber took a firm grip of the opposite end. Like jousters of old, forcing the lance forward they charged. It went well. The man in front, legs pumping, ran as he reached the steep incline. He just kept his balance, with his legs moving while he maintained a vice like grip on the pole. Behind him, Cheko and the other bomber gripped the pole, ran and pushed. The bomber in front was catapulted forward and up the slope. His shout of victory was rudely interrupted as his body slammed into the fence line. He was just beginning to turn when suddenly he convulsed. There was a spark and a snap. The fence line was fully electrified. Both Cheko and the other pipe bomber felt the sting of the current too, as it travelled down the metal pipe and into their hands. Its impact had been mostly absorbed by the man at the top but they both swore and were able to drop the pipe. The other man appeared stuck to the fence, and he continued to vibrate and convulse oddly. Finally, gravity found that it did rule the universe after all, and the man crumpled down onto the ground. He started to slide slowly back down the slope. The pipe was wedged through the fence and stuck there, one end high about a metre above the ground and the other low and on the floor at Cheko's feet.

'Fuck, boss, that hurt!' said the pipe bomber that was still standing.

'I didn't see that coming.' admitted Cheko.

'Neither did I. I thought it was a good idea.'

'It would have been perfect if that fucking fence hadn't been electrified.'

'Wait!' said the bomber. 'Could the electric shock have started the timer?'

There was a moment of dawning comprehension before both men turned suddenly and ran. Cheko as he ran, tried hard to guess how long he might have remaining. Five seconds? Six? His shoulders were hunched, and his head tucked down as he pumped his arms and legs. He had no idea if he would make it.

The bomber who had been electrocuted saw his fellow men running. He stood up shakily, swaying on his feet, his blitzed brain forced him to run.

When the bomb exploded, that same v shaped charge went upwards. One moment there was a man running, the next there was pink mist hovering over a pair of legs. They flopped to the ground an obscene half-mannequin wearing trousers and boots. Cheko and the other bomber were out of range of the blast, but the pressure wave hurt their ears and punched them in the back. Thankful he was alive, Cheko turned to look at the fence. Given the pipe bomb had not been set properly, they had been lucky. The fence had been cut sufficiently enough for them to get through and the blast had churned up the slope of the berm making it climbable. Once again, the dash started as the men made for the gap.

As Cheko waited by the fence line, he looked down briefly at the mangled half corpse on the floor. The squishy, bloody entrails, partially burned by the blast, made his men retch as they passed. When Cheko looked up, it was to see a video camera, attached to the post of the fence line, moving on its electric motors to stare directly at him. Someone somewhere, he thought, was watching. He gave them his best leer.

Chapter 19

September 24th, The Kayoro Mine. Ghana.

About a kilometre away from the main gate, inside the camp, was the vault. The low, squat concrete square sat between the safe haven and the maintenance yard. Beyond the vault to the North, Abdi could see the bright orange runway windsock hanging listless against its pole. That was the direction that Cheko should be coming from, mused Abdi. In fact, now that he thought about it, where the hell were they? Surely they should be inside the perimeter by now? There should be a lot more noise from over there.

Abdi watched as the fighters who had come through the front gate with him started to spread out to their objectives. One of the technicals was staying near the drone truck at the gate, to cover the main road. The other two technicals were accelerating away to the West. One to take up position by the vault, and one to move to the maintenance yard where it would cover the main mine area and make sure there were no nasty surprises. Abdi guessed that perhaps twenty or so of the drones had been used so far, and to great effect. Even as he watched, more towers were hit. The guards in them were not stupid, he could see a long way down the camp perimeter that those towers that hadn't been hit were being evacuated. That caused him some concern. If they weren't killed quickly, they could all get together and launch a counterattack.

Abdi's fighters that were on foot were spreading out now. Some went to the office building and the accommodation blocks to the North of the main gate. A group headed towards the processing plant to the South. Now that they were all inside, the site looked huge to them. So much space, so many places for people to hide.

A new noise hit Abdi's ears. A different type of gunfire and it sounded heavy. It was a rhythmic sound, about two shots a second, fired in short bursts. Thud, thud, thud, thud, barked this new weapon. Abdi focused, alert, trying to find the new threat. The technical that was travelling fast towards the maintenance yard started to swerve. It veered sharply to the left, the gunner in the back, holding onto the .50 cal. It looked to Abdi that it was firing towards the bunker. The vehicle was about a kilometre away so Abdi couldn't see the detail, but he did see the result. With a sustained burst from the hidden weapon, the pickup truck took the full force. The driver tried to turn, but the vehicle flipped, rolling at speed. The gunner and loader in the back were thrown clear. They flew awkwardly through the air before landing in crumpled heaps on the ground. The vehicle continued to roll for a moment more, windows shattered, the engine screaming itself to death.

From behind the bunker trundled a nightmare. A military armoured personnel carrier, painted in dapples of greens and browns. It had a wedge-shaped pointed nose and boxy square sides that stretched to the rear. The front led up to a long slanting top side that culminated in a rounded turret. In that turret, somewhere behind the armoured glass, sat a gunner. The whole crew was protected by armour and even though the vehicle was ancient, rusty, battered; they were the kings of this battlefield.

A drone hammered its way down onto the top of the vehicle, there were puffs of grey smoke and a few surface scratches appeared as fragmentation glanced off. The vehicle trundled on, driving on six massive black rubber wheels. Nothing was stopping it. Another drone thumped into it. It was similarly useless, like throwing darts against a concrete wall.

Abdi's fighters who had been in the open were scattering rapidly, several of them falling to the cannon fire. The APC continued trundling, driving towards where Abdi stood next to the truck with the drone pilots in. The truck driver had seen the danger and was already reversing, trying to get back out of the main gate before they were in range of the merciless gun. Abdi stood there helplessly trying to work out what to do. His men were ineffective. His technicals had run for cover, useless against the armour. Why the fuck didn't I know about that killing machine thought Abdi. Had that son-of-a-goat mine manager betrayed them?

The APC was getting closer, heading straight for the main gate. Thud, thud, thud, went the gun as it slewed left and right. Men fell, brutally assaulted by the carnivorous shells. Its cannon slaved towards Abdi, and he was looking right down its throat.

Chapter 20

September 24th, The Kayoro Mine. Ghana.

Cheko had climbed over the perimeter berm a few moments previously. They were crossing the runway and still they hadn't had to fire a single shot, but they had heard the calamitous sound of the unseen heavy weapon. Their entry to the camp had so far been completely unopposed. As expected, they could see the vault a couple of hundred metres away to their right. The gate, offices and accommodation were off to their left as they approached.

The heavy cannon continued firing, Cheko also heard the blasts of drones. As they continued running towards the vault, in a belching cough of black diesel smoke the APC appeared, its focus on targets by the gate. Cheko looked around him. Years of minor skirmishes had removed some of the edginess of combat. He had never had military training, but he was able to make reasonable judgments under pressure. He didn't like commanding others to take extraordinary risks, and whilst his followers respected and even loved him for that, it meant he carried those higher risks on his own shoulders. The situation required RPGs and thankfully his team had some with them. He ran to the nearest one and almost tore the weapon from the man's hands.

'Quickly. Quickly! Give me that!' he barked.

The other man, a little slower on the uptake, had to duck his head as Cheko pulled at the weapon. Even so, the canvas strap tore at his ear as Cheko violently pulled. Cheko pivoted and knelt down on the ground to create a solid platform. One knee flat on the dust, the other raised to waist height. He removed the safety covers from the long cylindrical weapon and lined the sight up just in front of the moving vehicle. It was oblivious to the threat and about two hundred metres to his front. He had to track with it to give himself the best chance of success. Somewhere in a deep recess of his brain, he remembered the gnarly old man who had taught him how to shoot one of these. He shouted, 'Clear behind! Firing!' The man whom he had taken the weapon from, jumped out of the way as the weapon fired. Debris and smoke engulfed Cheko as the rocket leapt forward. His men, observing, watched the shot fly true. The bulb shaped head of the rocket hit the flat side plate of the armoured vehicle and squashed on impact. A millionth of a second later it detonated. The now shaped charge of high explosive ripped into the armour in a condensed jet of energy. Plate steel melted instantly. The force of the explosion through the tiny hole caused a massive over pressure inside the cabin. Molten metal was forced inside, fragmentation sheared from the inside of the metal plate and ricocheted around the interior. It sliced through men and passed into the ammunition storage area kicking off a chain reaction. Inside was a maelstrom of hellfire and the occupants died in a burning rictus of pain.

Abdi, who thought the end was near, had started praying to Allah. Then he had seen the flight of the rocket, the puffs of smoke, and the licking flames escaping from the gaps between the turret and the chassis. As the vehicle ground to a halt, he looked around him. Very few remained of his group of soldiers, perhaps four from what he could see, plus the pickup truck drivers and the two crews on the technicals.

There were no more enemy to be seen, but that only meant that they had fled for now. Abdi turned towards Azrah who was standing at the gate about a hundred metres away. 'Azrah!' he shouted. 'Keep the truck with you and get the drone guys to prepare all of the rest of the drones. Then, prepare your additional surprises at the gate. After that get over to the vault as quickly as you can. I will meet you there.'

Azrah waved in acknowledgement, and Abdi started walking towards the vault, where even now Cheko and his men were grouping. The burning hulk of the APC was emitting a lot of heat as it cooked off, so Abdi gave it a wide berth.

'Abdi m' man. I'm sorry. It took us too long to get through the jungle last night.'

Abdi looked at him, weighing up his thoughts. Had Cheko tried his best? Did they stop for a rest? Did the fact that they were late mean that he had lost many more men than he was expecting? What he said was, 'Did you try your hardest?'

'Yeah, I swear, man.'

'The timing was unfortunate, but you just made an incredible shot. Anyone would think you'd been firing those rockets since you were on your mother's teat.' Cheko looked Abdi in the eye, realised that he was truly forgiven and nodded. Abdi continued talking. 'Have you lost any men?'

'I lost one guy, the freakin' fence was electrified. We didn't know that.'

'Yeah, and that whore of a mine manager didn't tell me about that piece of armour either!' Abdi was furious now and continued venting. 'I bet that goat fucker is locked up inside that bunker as well. If I ever see him again, I'll rip his forked tongue out.'

'D'ya think he betrayed us?'

'I don't know, perhaps he hedged his bets. I'll tell The Associate when we get out of here and ask his opinion on how he wants to deal with the situation.'

'If he betrayed us, I'll throw him into a spear pit in the jungle and let him rot.'

Abdi reflected for a moment. Which was the worst way to die from that? Would it be thirst, hunger, would you bleed out, or would infection from the excrement-covered spears do the job? 'If he betrayed us, I'd help you do it. I have only a small handful of men left, so we need to adjust the plan a little.' For a couple of minutes, they discussed what needed doing, and then Abdi sent Cheko off to get it all organised. Abdi meanwhile sent one of his men to go to the maintenance yard to collect one of the giant pneumatic rock-shattering vehicles. It was part of the plan to get into the vault. He was just walking around the perimeter of the building when Azrah appeared by his side. They spoke as they walked, examining the structure for any cracks or tell-tales of poor construction.

'Are you all done at the gate?'

As per her custom, Azrah shook her head. 'Yes, yes, yes. I have laid a couple more mines. Seeing as they have APC's, I thought I had better dig them in properly. We were lucky with that RPG shot. It hit the side of the vehicle square on. If it had been a front shot, the RPG would probably have deflected right up the glacis plate and done no damage at all. Abdi didn't want to think too much about that, or the fortuitous arrival of Cheko just in time. Azrah continued speaking in her rapid-fire way. 'Anyway, the mines will blow under the vehicles and should hit the weakest parts'

Even though Abdi had been educated at university in London, and had socialised in a hugely multicultural environment, he had to work hard to understand Azrah's rapid speech and her Pakistani accent. 'Um, great. I don't see any weak points on this bloody vault though. Do you?'

Azrah nodded this time. 'No, no, no. I think we will have to just start our work a few metres in from the Southwest corner.'

'OK, this is your expertise so let's do it your way.'

'The concrete is too thick to do it in one blast, so I am going to use progressively increasing sizes of shaped charges. That way, I will blow the hole larger each time and maximise the effect of the explosives. When we need to start using the mechanical tools, I will let you know.

Abdi agreed, leaving this petite, incredibly skilful, and really quite scary woman to get on with her work.

Chapter 21

September 24th, The Kayoro Mine. Ghana.

Five kilometres away, over towards the edge of the huge oval pit that was the mine, a group of the guards were gathering. Confusion and fear were in charge. The bombs that had come out of nowhere had killed a large number of their colleagues before they realised the guard towers were death traps. There was a leadership vacuum, and panicked people had been making poor decisions. That had finally changed now though, and they were being organised by Daniel, a slightly chunky Ghanaian man with a greying goatee. He had been with the mine as a junior guard supervisor for nearly ten years, and until today it had been one of the best jobs he had ever had. Clean accommodation, as much food as you could eat, regular hours, and great pay. As long as you were honest, it was a job for life, and he was able to send nearly all of his salary home to his wife and kids. He was building a small house on his farmstead, it was going to have three rooms, running water and electricity. A palace compared to the tin shack he had grown up in.

All of that was just a dream at the moment though. To get to retirement he had to get through this day, and that was proving tough. He had started to bring a semblance of control to this panicked gang. Although junior in rank, he was experienced and grandfatherly to many. He had been gathering the men running in from the exploding guard towers. They had soon learned that any cluster of men attracted the bombs in their direction. The bombs had stopped for now and the twenty or so armed guards were spread out all the way along the lip of the mine. They had identified now that the bombs were mounted onboard drones. They had seen some of them falling, even following groups of men as they ran. Lying down on the floor they were using the rock and stone as cover from ground fire, ducking down if a technical aimed in their direction. Those lucky enough to find a large rock with an overhang, crawled into those darker spaces too, with cover from above. There was a catch-22 in play. The technical either didn't want to, or couldn't, advance to solve the problem that was brewing. The men couldn't advance across the open ground because the .50 Cal had much longer range than their rifles. Daniel was trying to work out what was best. The attackers obviously wanted the gold, and that was in the vault. Where the guards were now would keep them safe, and they were protecting the safe haven at the pit end of the site. But if they stayed there, then the robbers would get away with the gold.

Daniel thought it best to wait it out for now, see what developed. He kept peeking around the rock he was hiding behind, trying to monitor what the thieves were doing. He saw a small group go into the maintenance yard. What the hell were they going to do there?

Chapter 22

September 24th, The Kayoro Mine. Ghana.

Cheko and three of his men advanced into the maintenance yard. They were informal in the way they were sauntering around camp now. Not professional soldiers, they carried their AK-47's loosely in their hands. They hadn't seen any more mine workers for a while and assumed that they were either in the safe havens, had fled, or were hiding around the vast mine site. However, Cheko was still recovering from the armoured vehicle incident, and he wasn't going to take any risks. There were so many guards on this site that he didn't want to be surprised by some guy who had watched too many Arnold Schwarzenegger movies.

As they walked into the maintenance yard, Cheko was awed by the size of the machinery. It was like the designers of this equipment had taken your average piece of road building kit and then said, let's build it ten times bigger, just for a laugh. There was a huge dump truck, up on a concrete ramp, something being done to its undercarriage. The ramp was large enough to drive a modified flatbed pickup under it. There was a bulldozer, the width of two tanks, with huge tracks and a massive front blade. The blade was easily ten metres wide and nearly a foot thick, of plate steel. It must have weighed a hundred tons. It was built for one purpose, to move massive amounts of earth and rock. Cheko looked at it, thought for a moment, and then spoke to one of his men.

'Sammy, see if you can get that beast started. Then drive it to the front gate of the camp and use it to block the entrance.'

'Cool mon, nah problem.' Sammy, with thick dreadlocks and a bit of a Bob Marley fetish, was grinning from ear to ear as he turned towards the massive toy.

'Sammy don't piss about, I know you! Just drive it to the gate, park it and then come back here and find me.'

Sammy grinned. 'Sure boss. I gotta work out how to lift the blade. I've neva played with one of these before.'

'Sammy! Playing with it's what I'm afraid of!' Cheko said good naturedly.

As Sammy walked towards the bulldozer, Cheko turned to look at the other bits of machinery. The bulldozer was an unexpected gift, but what they had really come for was waiting at the far side of the workshop. Parked there was a huge, mechanised hammer drill. Its purpose was to use the vast pneumatic chisel on the end of its manoeuvrable arm to crack vast boulders. Any advert might have said it was 'well used'. To Cheko it looked knackered. It was bright orange, though he couldn't tell if that was the old paintwork, or the rust. One or the other looked to be the only thing holding it together. The tiny glass square cabin on the front of it was about ten metres above the ground. It was accessed by a long ladder with one of those wrap-around oval cages on it. The vehicle was tracked and caked in dust. Cheko was deeply concerned that part of their plan to crack into the vault, rested on this rusty dinosaur's shoulders.

As they walked towards it Cheko heard the coughing belch of the bulldozer starting up. He turned to see it moving forward in a plume of black diesel smoke. There was a crunch as whether by accident or design, Sammy drove forward and smashed a pickup truck out of the way using the blade.

Rolling his eyes, Cheko turned back. 'Omar, this one's yours'

Omar, the only one in the group who had worked as a road builder before and had some experience of driving pneumatics, looked at Cheko.

'You t'ink 'dis is gonna start? It don't look like it's moved nowhere for years!'

They were close to it now. The wheels on the base of the tracks that towered above them looked dented and battered. The rubber hoses of the pneumatics system had perished and cracked, to the point where they looked like they would fracture if someone coughed near them.

'Well, Omar, you'd better get it to start. This piece of crap is what we need to get into that vault. Let's see what we can do.'

Nervously, Omar climbed the ladder and got to work.

Chapter 23

September 24th, The Kayoro Mine. Ghana.

Azrah was thinking. She was standing on the Southwest corner of the huge, squat vault building. The sun had still hardly risen over in the East, and she would have been in the shade except for the bright orange light of the site's sodium flood lights. The drone truck had come forward to where she was. With help she had disgorged several of her boxes of tricks and an acetylene blow torch, before telling the truck to move away again. She heard the constant chatter of the drone pilots in the back, still coordinating strikes as they went.

Over the past few days, she had prepared several shaped charges, designed to the best of her ability to force their way in through reinforced concrete. The physics was incredibly complicated and still wasn't fully understood in science. She wasn't a physicist though. She had spent years researching, practising, and generally just blowing stuff up. She had created devices that were tubes about twenty centimetres in diameter and thirty centimetres deep. Inside one end she had formed a hollow cone, almost the entire depth of the tube. She had then lined the cone with a thick copper sheet. The whole device had been placed in a slightly larger box, so that she could place them more easily against the concrete.

Azrah had already lined up the first device. It was placed on the floor and the hollow, concave shape of the cone was up against the smooth grey concrete of the wall. That wall towered above her now about three metres. She knew that the room beyond was dug into the ground and so by placing the charge on the floor outside, it should be about halfway up the wall on the inside. What she didn't know though was exactly how thick the wall was. She also didn't know how well it was reinforced.

She had used a couple of steel tent pegs to make sure the box didn't move, hammering them into the ground using a rubber mallet. Having looked around to make sure that the area was well clear, Azrah went around the corner to where all of her boxes were. From one, she pulled out a detonator, and some electrical cable. Clipping the amount of cable she needed using pliers, she went back to the device. There she attached the wires to the detonator and then the detonator was inserted through a hole in the casing at ninety degrees to the wall and directly into the high explosive. She had a last look around, walked back around the corner, connected the cabling to the trigger and pressed the switch. There was a lot of noise, some dust, and an obvious vibration through the concrete wall. As Azrah walked back around the corner of the vault, she peered through that dust to see what the effect of her first device had been. The answer pleased her. As the environment cleared a little, she saw first the slight cratering of the ground where the charge had been placed. She saw that the charge had penetrated into the wall by about half a metre. Large cracks, like a spider web, flowed outwards from the epicentre. Concrete rubble lay on the floor, white lumpy blotches like mushrooms growing out of the scorched earth. Inside the crater in the wall, two-inch-thick iron bars lay in a contorted lattice that was so wide, it surprised her. Hmm, she thought, either they never really thought that someone would try to enter this way, or the building contractor screwed over the owners by saving on the cost of the iron.

Azrah was tempted to try to pull large lumps of concrete out of the hole but didn't think it would do much good. She opted instead to do the next charge. She propped this one up against the same hole and used a couple of wooden posts to keep it in place.

A minute later, after that detonation she saw that it was time already to use some mechanical help. Relieved, she looked over her shoulder to see the vehicle, with the huge pneumatic chisel, lumbering across the dusty ground. She waved it towards her and then took a moment to have a break, cracking open a bottle of water. There wasn't much firing going on now. Just the occasional blast from a drone, the odd thump of the .50 Cal.

As Omar approached, Azrah, using hand signals, told him she wanted him to start working on the hole. From above her, in his Perspex cabin, Omar gave her a thumbs up. It took him a moment to get the controls right, and he slammed the head of the chisel into the wall a couple of times, scraping grooves into the smooth concrete. He eventually got the head lined up in the hole and started the hammer action.

The noise staggered Azrah, it was teeth jarring, she shoved her hands up to her ears and quickly walked back around the corner of the vault. Omar sitting high, couldn't see everything that he was doing

74

down below him and so he reversed slightly, away from the wall. He stretched the long arm of the machine out, octopus like, almost flat. That was better he thought, as concrete and steel started sheering off in chunks.

Ten minutes later, Abdi was standing with Azrah around the far side of the vault when the pounding stopped. They cautiously poked their heads around the corner and saw Omar give them a thumbs up. As they walked up to the hole, Abdi was delighted. They were already through. An obvious two-metre-long tunnel had been carved. It wasn't possible yet for a man to get through, because the steel rebar inside made the hole look like a twisted game of Kerplunk, but it wouldn't be long now.

Ten minutes later and using malleable plastic explosive, Azrah had clipped those two inch steel bars to the point where now a man could get through the tunnel. As soon as she was clear, Omar, who had abandoned his vehicle, went in through the tunnel headfirst. Some of the bars were hot to the touch and scorched him slightly as he went. Some were sharp, and they cut through his trousers and his shirt. With a torch in his hand, he crawled forward. As he reached the far end of the short tunnel, his torch beam penetrated into the gloomy room. There was dust and debris, and he couldn't see very well. Then he realised he had a problem. He started backing out of the tunnel quickly.

Abdi, on the other side, hadn't expected to see Omar coming back. 'What's wrong? Was there no gold?'

Out of breath and gagging on the dust, Omar replied, 'I don't know, I couldn't see! The only thing I could see was the drop. I couldn't turn around in the tunnel, I have to go feet first this time, or else I will land on my head when I drop!'

There was a moment of incomprehension and then Abdi laughed. 'Ha, of all the complicated things I planned for, that wasn't one of them! Well done, Omar, in you go. Call out when you can tell me what you see.'

A few minutes later, Omar, really scratched and bruised now, landed on the floor of the vault. Torch in hand he turned. The vault had no lights on. There was a green emergency exit sign, dimly lit on the far side of the room. It gave an eery glow. Dust was settling now, and Omar, heart thumping, paused at what he saw. His jaw dropped.

Abdi was agitated on the outside. So much so that he started to climb into the hole. 'Omar, what do you see? Omar!'

'Gold, Abdi, I see gold! Pallets of it. Great big, beautiful bricks of it. More than I can count, Abdi!'

Abdi's head popped out of the hole, and he looked into the murky space, following the line of Omar's torch.

'Allahu Akbar! That is the sweetest thing I've ever seen!' They both spent another moment staring before Abdi recovered first. 'Omar, go and see if you can find the emergency exit button. It should be over there by the vault door. Have your weapon ready, just in case.'

Omar picked his way across the floor, careful not to twist an ankle on a piece of debris. He walked past the steel pallets on the floor, each with two layers of gold bricks, forty bricks to a layer. Laid together like pieces of jigsaw puzzle, though he didn't know it, each pallet held exactly one ton of gold.

Reaching the far side of the small room quite quickly, he hit two switches. The first was the light switch, the second was a green push-button that said 'Emergency Exit'. As he hit that one, in the flickering of the lights as they came on, the vast steel vault door started to open outwards. Abdi, staring into the room saw the pallets in all their glory now. Despite the fact that the golden sheen was covered in dust, he could see six of them. He closed his eyes for a moment. In that cocoon of a tunnel he gave himself a moment to think. On the whole, things were going well. He had lost more men than he wanted, but he had the gold. Now all he needed were two things. The first was the airplane and the second was for someone to turn off that bloody alarm.

Chapter 24

September 24th, The Kayoro Mine. Ghana.

Daniel and the other guards had watched all the work going on at the vault with a keen interest. Even though it was some five kilometres away, they saw the smoke and heard the boom of the charges as they went off. Daniel was mentally torn. His loyalties to the company were high: it had paid him well and looked after him for the past ten years. They were nothing compared to his loyalty to his own skin though, so he had stayed where he was, hiding on the lip of the vast mine site. Gradually, however, something had gnawed at him. How many times had he fantasised about such a situation when he was a younger man? Here was such a situation, unfolding in front of his eyes. No one more senior had turned up yet and so the decision really did fall to him. The twenty or so men spread out around him were mostly young and scared, though some looked like they might be up for a fight.

Daniel tried to think. They were heavily out-gunned by the robbers. Those drones and the technicals gave them an edge that was unbeatable. But, he thought, where would they be going next? Are they going to drive back out of the main gate, down the one road that leads all the way to the police barracks twenty kilometres away? Surely not. Perhaps their plan would be to leave and escape through the jungle. It was certainly not impossible but with several tons of gold it would be very difficult. Really, that left only one option: fly the gold out. If that was the case, then there would be a point where all of those men and weapons would be on board the airplane. Would that give him an opportunity to strike? Making up his mind, he spent a few moments trying to plan.

'Hey you!' Daniel shouted to the man about thirty metres to the right. 'Pass this up the line. We're all going to move to the North end of the mine near the airstrip. I think they'll try to get the gold out by plane. Make sure that everyone stays spread out and use the side of the pit for cover all the way. For God's sake, don't bunch up or those cursed drones will have us.'

The man shouted an acknowledgement before turning to his right and passing the message along. Daniel turned to his left now and was about to repeat the message when the guard there shouted, 'I heard! Let's do this!'

'Yes, but carefully! Let's move but keep low and try not to get killed!'

Chapter 25

September 24th, The Kayoro Mine. Ghana.

Everything seemed to have settled down a little now for Abdi. He was standing next to the Drone truck, which had become his informal headquarters. It was parked outside the entrance to the vault. By being here, Abdi could listen to the drone pilots and see what targets they were seeing. The best resource by far was the eye in the sky drones. One was still hovering above the main gate, watching the approach road, the other was above the mine pit. It was monitoring the guards that had suddenly started moving towards the Northern end of the pit. The pilots were watching them closely, waiting to see if they bunched up and were worth striking from above.   There were only about ten drones left now with that strike ability, so they didn't want to waste them. There were two others that were being used for camera work, and they only had about half an hour of battery life left.

The morning was moving on rapidly, thought Abdi with some concern. The sun was well into the sky now, and the orange light of dawn well past. As Abdi looked around the site, there were several fires burning. The largest and nearest was the armoured vehicle. Its burning tyres were melting in the fiery heat. They were sending out an acrid, foul grey smoke that sat over the camp, refusing to disperse. There wasn't much wind to blow it clear and it drifted thinly towards the vault and the drone truck, making people cough.

As he watched, a forklift truck, with a pallet of gold bars on it, came out of the vault, and made its way towards the airstrip. In terms of moving the gold, they were nearly halfway there already, this part of the plan was going quickly. He looked up above his head to see an outdoor speaker mounted on the outside of the vault building. It was still warbling the emergency alarm and was ridiculously loud. He pulled his weapon off his shoulder and aimed at it. He let off a couple of short bursts prompting some of the fighters to turn rapidly and stare. Then they just grinned and got on with their jobs. The white plastic cone shattered off the wall leaving wires exposed. Some of the bullets ricochet off the concrete. When the firing stopped, Abdi heard the done pilots' continued exclamations of surprise. One of them poked a

79

frightened head out of the rear of the truck, saw what Abdi had done and then ducked back inside. Whilst the alarm was still sounding around much of the rest of the camp, here at least it was a little quieter.

Abdi fiddled with the satellite phone in his pocket, pulled it out, and extended the antenna. He dialled and pressed send, waiting a moment whilst it rang. A Czech voice answered in English but with a heavy guttural slant. 'Ano! Hello!'

'Petr, it's Abdi.'

'Abdi! Abdi, my friend, how are you.' Petr's voice was hard to hear over the background sound of turboprop engines.

Abdi wasn't in the mood for idle chitchat. 'Petr, where are you?'

'As you asked, we are circling about fifteen miles North of you at low level. I see a lot of smoke where you are. Is it going well?'

'Yes. I need you to come and land immediately.'

'OK. Is it safe?'

Abdi thought for a moment. If he said no, he was fucked. This pilot could just say goodbye in the confidence that Abdi would likely not survive the day. So instead, he lied a little. 'Yes, there are still some small problems but it's manageable. We've broken into the vault, and you'll be on the ground for less than thirty minutes.'

'OK, we will come in to land shortly. Let us keep it brief, comrade.'

Having hung up, Abdi reflected on the call. Something flagged in his brain. The pilot had, to be honest, sounded a little drunk. He hoped not, but he had heard about these old mercenary pilots. Veterans of so many conflicts, paid by whichever wannabe dictator had the money. Some of them, who fought in the cold war, made their money any way that they could. No task was too dirty. Abdi knew for a fact that Petr had escaped across some Soviet border in his youth, stealing the aircraft as he left. He now had a reputation and a profitable business with a freight plane that he hired out on a day rate. The higher the risk, the higher the day rate. The Antonov AN-12 was a heavy-lift aircraft, designed for work in remote areas and on difficult airstrips. It could carry about twenty tons or a hundred people, which was far more than Abdi needed. Truth be told, the aircraft was Abdi's largest concern. This one had been built in the 1970s and so had been flying for fifty years. Petr had stolen it in the 80s and since then had been living in Chad, using it to service a number of African states, whenever needed. Abdi hadn't wanted to use an ancient plane, with an ancient alcoholic pilot, but he had figured that there were not many British Airways captains that would want to do this type of job.

Coming back to the present, Abdi thought about the next steps. He needed to bring his men in closer now, protect the vault and the airstrip. He also wanted to keep the main gate under tight control. Given he had less than twenty men left, that was going to leave him quite stretched.

Azrah was sitting in the shade of the drone truck. She had little to do at present and she knew it was best to just stay out of the way for now. 'Azrah, I'm going to start to bring in the men. Stay here and make sure these pilots keep doing their job.'

'No problem,' she said, sitting comfortably cross legged in the dust.

Abdi saw that Cheko was still managing the looting of the vault and the move to the airstrip. Abdi looked up suddenly and waved his arm to catch the attention of a passing pickup truck. He had made his decision and wanted it to take him around camp, so that he could start to implement the withdrawal.

Chapter 26

September 24th, The Kayoro Mine. Ghana.

It was too good to be true thought Azrah, as one of the drone pilots leant out of the back of the truck and called her name. She picked herself up off the floor from under the shade of the old canvas-sided, battered wagon, and walked to its rear. The pilots were chittering and chattering like nervous birds. They were obviously panicked. The first hour of the battle had gone well with them, and they had done exactly what was needed. Azrah suspected that now that the adrenaline of the computer game was wearing off, they were realising exactly what they had done, and were coming to terms with taking life. Azrah had gone through that barrier many years ago and had defeated her demons.

Still, she looked at the screen when they pointed, and felt even her cold heartbeat flutter a little. The drone that was monitoring the road towards the camp had picked up a police or military convoy. There were perhaps fifty armed men, lots of pick-up trucks, but worst of all, at the front, another armoured vehicle. Immediately focused, Azrah spoke to the man who had been guarding the pilots. 'You! Go find Abdi and tell him we will soon have company at the gate. Tell him about that,' she said, pointing. The man nodded, jumped down from the truck and ran.

Azrah told the pilots to take the drone overhead. She watched the screen, as the armoured vehicle approached her delaying tactic, the two trees that had been dropped across the road earlier that morning. She watched with an analytical, calculating eye, trying to assess where exactly she had placed the mines and the claymores. She welcomed the feeling of being turned on, anticipating what was about to happen. She had never had such a clear view of her work before: a bird's eye view of the death and mutilation that was to come. What she really wanted now was for the enemy force to show how poorly they were trained. With luck, they would bunch up and offer her a better target. In her hand she had the remote detonator. As she caressed the small black box, she visualised the two anti-vehicle mines and the two claymores, spread over a space of about seventy metres.

The armoured vehicle at the front, and one of the pickups, paused at the trees. An obvious commander got out, walked around the obstacle, and then gestured at the driver of the armoured vehicle. From above, Azrah could see the weakness that she thought the commander had observed. In the middle of the road, the two trees overlapped. They were hefty pieces of timber, thick trunks, and bushy green tops. At their stump ends though, and off the road, they were only one tree thick. She saw the armoured vehicle reverse slightly and reposition on the side of the road. Irritatingly, it was the side furthest away from her mines. The armoured vehicle, which was similar to the one the Cheko had destroyed earlier, nudged forwards on its six rubber tyres. It pushed its pointed glacis plate up against the trunk, and with a belch of diesel pushed forwards, testing. It was too easy. Azrah thought for a moment that the commander would get brushed aside by the top of the tree as the base was levered forwards, but no such luck. He leapt backwards and seeing that his plan was working, moved back to his vehicle. That was where his luck ran out. Azrah, deciding that the best time was now, pushed the button. She shivered with her own release as the claymore nearest the obstacle caught the commander and his tin can of a vehicle in its full force. Ball bearings shredded forward under the force of the explosion, tearing up metal and flesh. The two anti-vehicle mines, designed to penetrate armour upwards had little effect. It looked like some fragmentation went out sideways, but not enough to really matter. The last claymore had more impact, catching all the men in the back of one pick up and tearing up the bonnet and driver of another. Like an ants' nest poked with a stick, there was a flurry of activity, men running, vehicles reversing, lots of visible screaming and shouting, but none of that was heard by the team watching the drone images in the truck. The only sound they heard was the dull thump of the detonations up the road. Proof that the speed of light really was far faster than the speed of sound. Azrah looked at the drone pilots, who had turned white seeing such carnage. 'They are coming.'

Chapter 27

September 24th, The Kayoro Mine. Ghana.

As Abdi's land cruiser pick-up truck skidded to a stop by the main gate, he opened the door and jumped out. He heard the blasts from outside the gate and realizing how little time he had, looked to see what resources he had available. Not many, was the answer. This part of the camp entrance was walled, and the gates themselves had been destroyed during this morning's attack. Parts were still standing, but large sections had been turned to rubble. The gates themselves hung at obscene angles, contorted off their hinges. At the moment, the giant bulldozer was plugging the gap in the gate area with its chunky metal blade. There was still a large enough space though, for a man to step between the curve of the blade and the edge of the gate posts. Abdi peeked through it. The road was currently clear, all the way to the bend in the trees about a kilometre away and so far, the police had not recovered from Azrah's mines. Behind him, inside the camp, one of the technicals was about a hundred metres back from the entrance. Its .50 Cal. was aimed lazily towards the main gate, and the gunner and loader were sitting in the back, smoking but alert.

To Abdi's left and right were only a handful of men. They were perched on the rubble of the wall peering over the top. One of the men to the side had an RPG, but otherwise they were all armed with only light weapons. Abdi looked at the pitiful force that he had. Not enough to counter a large contingent of armed men, especially if they had an armoured vehicle. He decided that he needed to take a risk and started barking out instructions.

'Hey, bulldozer driver! Reverse the vehicle and get it out of the way. I want them to think that the gate is open.' Seeing the questioning eyes of the driver he shouted, 'Do it now, goat fucker!'

Then, to the driver of the pickup that had just brought him here, 'You! Bring that vehicle and park it on the left-hand side here. I want you to block only half the gate. Watch it though. There is a mine on the right-hand side and unless you want us all to meet Allah sooner than we should, drive carefully!'

'You, with the RPG! Move further up that wall. When the armoured vehicle comes, if it doesn't trigger the mine, you'll hit it on the side. If it does, then you hit the next vehicle that tries to come through.' Abdi continued. 'Everyone, listen carefully! I want them to think that there's no one left here. Do not show yourselves, do not fire until the armoured vehicle comes through this gate.'

The men around him started to realise that Abdi had a plan, and that it was a good plan. Some of their nervousness left them. Those armed only with AK-47's spent a moment looking about for a better firing position. Abdi stepped back from the gate and walked towards the technical. He would stay with that for now and position it out of sight until it was needed. As he walked towards it, he thought briefly about the airplane that was incoming. In fact, as he looked, he could see it at the far end of the runway approaching to land. It was too late now he thought, to tell that drunken pilot to stay away for a little longer. All Abdi's pieces were on the board now, committed. He just needed his opponents to make an opening move.

Chapter 28

September 24th, The Kayoro Mine. Ghana.

The Antonov AN-12 was a solid brute of an aircraft. This one had been around so long that it was a miracle it still flew. It was noisy, stank of fumes and vibrated like a petrol-powered sex toy. On the outside, it was white hulled on top and a mottled grey underneath, as though it had been dipped in a vast tub of paint. It was high winged, with four turboprop propeller engines, the best configuration for landing on remote airstrips. It had a standard cockpit window spread, but having had so many potential roles when designed, it also sported a glass nosecone. From there, in times of old, a gunner or bomber might have plied their trade. Inside the cockpit, it was pre-historic: huge toggle switches, faded markings in Cyrillic, giant dials, and gauges. No hint of a modern "glass cockpit" here. In fact, the only glass in sight was Petr's vodka bottle.

Petr took a large gulp from that now. He belched slightly as he called out the pre-landing checks to his co-pilot. As the speed kept bleeding off and the flaps lowered, the nose dipped, giving the pilots a clear view of the landing strip and gold mine below them. Towers of smoke, burning vehicles and something new. A convoy of vehicles coming out of the jungle in the far distance, heading towards the main gate. Petr paused. Abdi hadn't told him about that. 'Svoloch!' he thought. 'Bastard!'

There was no such thing as an easy job in Petr's life. He always had to weigh up the risks. As he had gotten older though, he realised that he didn't do it for the money any more. There was only so much premium vodka a man could drink and only so many nubile young women he could pay to fuck. No, aside from being addicted to vodka, he was addicted to the adrenaline of the work. He had few qualms now. He wouldn't touch people-smuggling, but he didn't have many other principles. Making up his mind, he stayed on the approach. 'Fuck it!' With one hand still on the controls, he took another swig from the bottle, wiped the top of it in his armpit, and handed it to his co-pilot, who also took a long pull.

Chapter 29

September 24th, The Kayoro Mine. Ghana.

Daniel and those guards that were willing to go with him had reached the far Northern camp boundary now. For some reason that he didn't understand, the technical that had been keeping them in place had left and headed back towards the main gate of the camp. That had meant that the fifteen or so the guards had been able to leave the safety of the mine ridge behind and move to the nearest end of the airstrip. Two kilometres away, down the length of the pale grey surface Daniel saw plenty of activity. The robbers were obviously moving all the gold to the dispersal area. Even as he watched, a forklift truck deposited another pallet of gold. Daniel's problem now was that between him and them, there was a huge open space. There was no cover for them to be able to approach unseen. Daniel was worried that if they popped their heads up, then the 'technical' would come racing back. With its superior range it would kill them in moments. He was trying to work out how they could get through the electric perimeter fence. If they could do that, then they would be able to get up over the fence line berm, use it as cover and get close enough to attack. He was in the middle of pondering that when he heard the roar of engines behind him. As he turned, he saw a huge plane, less than a kilometre away, and about to pass directly over their heads, as it came in to land.

Throwing all caution to the wind, he shouted to his fellow guards. 'See that plane! That's how they're getting out! Shoot it down!' Lying flat with their backs on the ground the guards all brought up their weapons. 'Go for the engines, go for the cockpit! Just make sure you hit it with everything!'

The noise was immense now, the power tangible. The whirling propeller blades were less than a hundred metres above them. So close, he could stretch an arm out and be worried about losing his fingers. It felt like the exposed undercarriage would leave tread marks on his face. His weapon in his shoulder, a fully automatic AK-47 with a thirty-round magazine. The monstrous airframe passed overhead. The harsh multi-crack of all the weapons firing, time expanded, spent brass dropping down to the ground beside him, the smell of cordite. Small black holes appearing on the fuselage, dot, dot, dot. He saw a hundred rounds firing up at the cockpit. The crazy glass nose shattered, spiderwebs forming. His magazine emptied. He ejected and inserted a new one, then rolled onto his stomach. He tracked the plane as it passed and touched the ground, wheels puffing in the smoke. He kept firing. He watched in frustration as the plane raced away from them, down the runway. 'How the hell did we not bring it down?' he shouted. He looked around him at the other guards. They too were in disbelief. Daniel had a realisation. 'Oh man, they'll know we're here. Quick, everyone! Back to the mine!'

The guards turned and ran for the edge of the mine again. They didn't see the plane, as it continued along the runway. Ever so slowly, it started to veer to the left. Petr's and the co-pilot's lifeless hands were beyond the ability to steer it, or even to slow it down. With no brakes applied, the aircraft came off the tarmac, little by little rattling over the hard ground. It hit the perimeter berm at a hundred miles an hour, leaped briefly into the air, for a final short flight, bits breaking off it as it did so. Then, the knackered old bird came to rest in the cleared no-man's land on the edge of the jungle. The trees, which were older than the airplane was, looked on silently.

Chapter 30

September 24th, The Kayoro Mine. Ghana.

Abdi and his technical had moved to the office building near the gate on the Northern side. The bulldozer had backed well away, leaving a trail of diesel smoke that Abdi hoped would just blend in with the other fires around the camp. What he really wanted now was for the police to be suckered straight into the camp and into an ambush. He had sent the drone pilot guard back to the pilots, to tell them not to detonate any more drones, until he had taken care of the armoured vehicle. Then they should throw everything they had at the remaining police.

Abdi found it hard to keep his focus. He couldn't see past the buildings, or through the berm that surrounded the entire camp. He couldn't see the enemy approaching, so he had to trust his men nearer the gate to keep him informed.

He was convinced that the armoured vehicle would come in first, and whilst it probably could climb over the berm, he was trusting to the fact that a poorly-trained crew would take the easiest option. Right through the main gate.

It was during the wait for the attack that the plane crash happened. One moment things were going well, pretty much to plan bar a couple of snags. The next, the whole world went wrong. Abdi's attention was grabbed by the crescendo of small arms fire, somewhere within the camp behind him. He turned to see the plane coming into land, then he watched helplessly as it smashed into the berm and launched into the air, for its final time.

That was when Abdi started to panic. He felt absolute fear and his was heart racing. It was difficult to breath, a tightening chest and he felt like he was being smothered. He realized he had lost control of the situation. His escape route had just disintegrated and now he was afraid.

He didn't know for how long he was like that, almost catatonic. He was rudely interrupted by another detonation. He found himself crouching on the floor, head between his knees. He looked up to see the armoured vehicle at the main gate. It had made it, most of the way through, when the mine went off. On shaky legs, Abdi stepped forward to get a better look. To his horror, the cannon on the turret rotated towards him and started firing. He dived for cover behind the nearest building, landing in the dust as the cannon rounds continued to blow chunks out of the walls. Abdi had to pick himself up and run further to safety.

Behind him, and on the far side of the gate, the RPG man took advantage. The armoured vehicle had been immobilized by the mine, but not destroyed. At less than a hundred metres range, the RPG fired into the square side of the vehicle. The result was brutal. White hot metal, at 10,000 degrees, spewed into the armoured vehicle and it brewed up, as drones started to drop on the police vehicles which were all lined up behind. With eight men still sitting in each one, three were shredded before they even worked out what was happening. In blind panic, vehicles started turning, reversing, men were jumping clear and onto the ground, some were run over. Other men tried to jump back in, as vehicles accelerated away spewing gravel and dust. More drones struck, adding to the carnage. Of the fifty or so police officers who had come charging to the rescue, less than ten made it away. They ran back to the cover of the trees. Seeking sanctuary from the death and the slaughter.

Abdi picked himself up off the floor. He reached out and touched the top of his head to find a nasty cut. He couldn't remember where he had got it from, but it bled a river that coursed down his face. The loader from the technical bounced over with a field dressing. Relief all over his face he shouted, 'We won, Abdi, we won!'

Abdi, still groggy, looked at the young man as he tied the dressing on to the top of his head. He wrapped the bandage part under his chin and tied a knot. 'We haven't won yet, boy. We just lost our plane ticket out of here. Get me some water and let me think.'

As Abdi stood there, trying to contain his panic, he realised that at a cognitive level he wasn't thinking clearly. Waves of fear were gushing through him. It wasn't the same as being in battle, where the fear was of getting hurt. At least you could do something then, even if it was hide. Now, he felt completely hopeless. Out of control, and no plan left. Allah be merciful, how would he get out of this mess? Things weren't helped when the swarm pilot ran up to him.

'Abdi, Abdi! We've used up all the drones. There are none left. We don't even have any power left for the 'eyes in the sky'! What do we do now?'

Chapter 31

September 24th, The Kayoro Mine. Ghana.

The loss of the drones was enough to tip Abdi into a different headspace. It was almost as though things were so bad that he had accepted that he had lost. Because he had lost, in his twisted logic, he would try anything to crawl out of the pit into which he'd fallen. With a flash of inspiration, he thought of one thing that might save them. A way out of this mess, a way of kicking defeat in the balls and making a grasp for victory.

Abdi looked at the main gate and confirmed that there was no way that anything was getting in past the burning armoured vehicle, not for several hours at least. That was good enough for him. He waved to the driver of the huge bulldozer who came over at the run. Panting and out of breath, the man said, 'Yeah Abdi. Waz up?'

'I need you to do something, and it's vital for us all to get out of here. You see the berm over there to the South, halfway between the processing plant and the mine?'

The man followed where Abdi was pointing. 'Yeah.'

'Take that big old bulldozer of yours and cut through that berm. You have less than thirty minutes before we'll be there. We're going to escape from this camp using the vehicles, so the gap needs to be flat and wide enough for the pickups to get through.'

'Thirty minutes! It's gonna tek twenty just to drive this big old beast over there!'

'Well, I suspect that if you take any longer than that, then we'll never leave.'

'Right mon, nah problem.'

As the driver started to run back to his bulldozer, Abdi called after him. 'And don't forget! Push through the electric fence and clear the barbed wire in the middle too! We need a clear drive to the treeline!'

With that started, Abdi jumped up into the back of the nearby technical. 'Take me to Cheko and the gold.' he commanded, banging on the roof. As the vehicle turned sharply to head over towards the runway, Abdi had to hold on tight to the weapon mount, to avoid being thrown about. It was less than two kilometres away and only took a moment. As he jumped down off the back of the wagon, he called to the driver. 'Go collect all of the pickup trucks and bring them here immediately!' Spewing gravel, the technical drove off at speed, to round up all the vehicles it could find.

As Abdi looked around, he saw Cheko and a couple of men standing around a forklift truck. They were visibly worried. At their feet were six pallets of gold, thickly coated in dust. Six tons of precious metal, about three hundred million dollars' worth. According to the plan, instead of it all lying on the floor, it should have been loaded into the back of the airplane by now.

'Did you see what happened to the fucking plane, Abdi?' Cheko's anger was spilling over.

'I saw.'

'I'm going to take some trucks and go and kill every single one of those bastard guards.'

'You could do if you want. Or you can help me load all this gold into the vehicles and then we can get the hell out of here?'

'We won't last five minutes on the road, Abdi. We'd have to drive past the police barracks!'

'We're not going to go by road. We're going to drive through the jungle.'

'What? Are you crazy? There are no tracks in there!'

'We don't need tracks; we'll make our own. The trees are huge, there's plenty of space between them.'

'But what about boulders, rivers, streams, gullies, swamps? Abdi, think about it! Where the fuck will we go? There's nothing but jungle, for hundreds of miles. It'll take days to get anywhere!'

'Well, I for one would rather be anywhere else than here.'

'And then there's the military, they'll follow us, Abdi. We'll leave huge tracks.'

'Cheko, stop bleating like an old goat. We don't have any option other than to buy time. In time we can get some help. That there,' he said pointing at the gold, 'will buy us a lot of help.'

'If we can get it out of here!' said Cheko obstinately.

'Yes, if. Now how are you going to help here? I need you to step up.' Abdi could see the battle going on behind Cheko's eyes. It took a moment, but clarity came, and determination flooded his features,

'Well, if we're going into the jungle, we need resources. I can do that.'

'Fine, we need to leave in thirty minutes, let's get moving!'

Chapter 32

September 24th, The Kayoro Mine. Ghana.

The first pickup to arrive was there a moment later. The driver was directed by Abdi to pull up next to the pallets of gold. In short chaotic order, the forklift truck picked up a pallet, hoisted it over the tailgate of the pickup and then lowered it into the back. The leaf springs groaned as the battered wagon took the load. The pallet was too wide to fit snugly, and it lay at an angle, overhanging slightly. The steel pallet dented and scraped the metal on the side. Cheko looked at it and barked some orders. 'Get that gold off the edges and into the truck, keep it balanced out. Hurry up you dogs!' Three men jumped into the back of the vehicle and worked like demons, lifting each twelve-kilo brick, and trying to balance out the load. There was no consideration to their value, their worth. They were just bloody heavy bricks that were in the wrong place. When they were done, Cheko left Abdi to supervise the loading of the gold for the next wagons and sped up to the maintenance yard, with the laden vehicle.

As they arrived, Cheko directed the vehicle to the fuel pump and told one of the men to fill it up. He then started looking for essentials, things that they would need if they were to have any hope of making a long drive through the jungle. First and foremost were two more land cruiser pickups. With the ones lost in battle, Cheko wanted at least eight. Six for the gold, and two for supplies. One of the pickups was parked next to the fuel pump and four empty fuel drums were placed on the back deck. They were to be filled next. Cheko sent the other pickup to the main kitchen with instructions to pile in as much food as possible. Especially tinned food. He then found cables and ropes, tarpaulins, axes, saws and empty barrels. God knows what chemicals the containers had had in them, but they were going to need water and a lot of it. Frantically he threw it all into a pile so that as each vehicle came to fill up fuel, they could pick up the extra stores.

Over the next pandemonium-filled half hour, all the pickups were filled. As they became ready, they lined up outside the maintenance yard. Abdi took stock of what he had left. Eight pickups, fifteen men and one woman, and that was it. Two of the pickups were technicals. They had caused a bit of a delay, as the gold had to be loaded on to them by hand because of the heavy-weapon mounts. It had been decided that there was no way that the drone truck would be able to navigate the jungle and so the three pilots had been told to drive pickups instead. When one resisted, no force was needed. Abdi just told him he would be left behind to face the consequences and the pilot quickly changed his mind. Azrah, who still had some tricks left in a box, was put onto the back of one of the pickups. The driver was nervous because of the extra load, but she was sitting quite happily there, waiting for the next part of the adventure to begin. She noticed the driver's concern: 'It's quite OK, if anything goes wrong, we won't know anything about it. There is so much explosive in this box that we, the vehicle, and perhaps even most of the gold would be instantly vapourised.' She gave him a winning smile. 'Oh. Do me a favour though. Avoid any large bumps, won't you!'

Almost immediately, driven by a mixture of panic and the lash of Abdi's tongue, everything was ready. The convoy moved out with Cheko leading, towards the breach that had now been made in the berm wall to the South. Pausing only to collect the driver, the snake of battered old wagons, carrying fantastical wealth, crossed the berm line. They drove over the grassy no man's land, through the gap in the barbed wire obstacle, and there Cheko chose a point of entry into the jungle.

Once through the first fifty metres of thicker undergrowth, where light was in plentiful supply, the vehicles started into the primary jungle. Widely spaced tree trunks reached up and out to a dense, fully-covered canopy. It was only just past mid-day, and yet the light was gloomy. Very few ground shrubs survived here. The musty smell of the leaf mulch, a metre thick on the floor, stirred as the heavily-laden vehicles trawled through it. Bugs of all shapes and sizes were disturbed, some flew up angrily in protest. The increase in humidity was tangible, clothes were soaked in moments. Slowly but surely the convoy moved like a giant anaconda weaving through the trees across the forest floor. No real idea yet on a destination; Abdi just knew they needed to be anywhere but here!

Chapter 33

September 24th, The Kayoro Mine. Ghana.

From a safe distance away, Daniel had watched the convoy as it left the camp, disappearing through the gap in the berm and out into the jungle. From the side profile, seeing the wagons hunched down on to their back axles, he knew that they had the gold with them. As it trundled out, he realised that he had failed. His job had been to protect that gold, on behalf of his country, but he hadn't been able to that. He wasn't going to give in though. He was interested to see that there were very few men sitting in the back of the pickups. How few people there must be left in that gang of thieves. Confident that there were none of the robbers left on site, he and the rest of the guards started to move back into the main part of the camp. Daniel spoke to one of the guards and told him to go to the safe haven at the base of the mine and tell them that it was all clear. Another man was tasked to go to the production area for the same reason. As Daniel moved, he had a sudden thought. Did anyone else know what had happened here this morning? He hadn't seen anyone else more senior and was unsure. To be safe, he pulled out his mobile phone and dialled the number for the company's operations room in Accra.

'Guard Services International, operations, how can I help you?'

'Hi, um, my name's Daniel, and I'm a junior guard supervisor at the Kayoro mine. I just wanted to check to see if the incident has been reported in?'

'What incident is that, sir?'

'The robbery?'

'Not that I am aware of. Are you sure you've called the right number?'

'What? Are you telling me that no one has reported the robbery?'

'Which robbery, sir?'

'Listen you idiot. I just told you. There's been a robbery at the Kayoro mine!'

'And what did you say your name was, sir?'

'Are you fucking kidding me! Put the Ops manager on the phone. Now!'

'Please hold.'

'No! I don't want to…' some kind of light-hearted mood music started to play down the handset. Daniel was getting seriously pissed off. When someone at the other end finally picked up Daniel blurted out. 'Listen you fuckin' idiot. The Kayoro mine has just been robbed. Most of the guards are dead, and all of the gold has gone!'

There was a pause. 'Who's speaking please?'

'What! Are you…? My name's Daniel. I'm the junior guard supervisor at the Kayoro mine.'

'Great, thanks, Daniel. Can I speak to your supervisor please.'

'No! You can't! He's dead! They're all fucking dead!'

Chapter 34

September 24th, Accra. Ghana.

The Minister was having lunch at one of the beach restaurants in the Osu district of Accra. Expensive white linen tablecloth, a view of the ocean, delicious food, excellent service. He had been jumpy and nervous around his staff in his ministerial office that morning and had decided that he needed to get out of there.

As each minute passed, he expected to get a phone call, describing the national calamity that he knew was scheduled for today. The delay preyed on his mind. Had something gone wrong? What was happening? He couldn't of course precipitate any conversations on the subject. He had to let things take their course. It was painfully frustrating.

He was in the process of shelling a king prawn when his phone went. His hands were covered in garlic butter. He dipped them in the bowl of warm lemony water in front of him and used his napkin to wipe off the rest. It was his deputy. 'Yes?'

'Minister, there's been an incident at the Kayoro mine.' His deputy was very strait- laced on the phone, knew that he was playing an important part of this game. Knew that the intelligence services conducted random phone monitoring activities.

'Oh dear! How awful. Tell me more.' said the Minister playing along. Over the next few moments, and a quick report later, he hung up. He was irritated that the police response had happened so quickly. He would need to talk to the Deputy Inspector of police about that. It sounded like it had been a close call. Somewhere in the deepest remnant of his remaining humanity, he was saddened to hear of such extraordinary loss of life. So many police officers, so many guards!

Moments later, a call came in from the Chief of the Airstaff. It was a simple apology, accepted with good grace by the Minister. He smiled as he recalled how genuine it sounded. "So sorry, Minister. The police have asked for helicopter support. Some robbers escaping into the jungle. Unfortunately, we have a lot of maintenance going on at the moment. We will of course do our best, but we'll try to have something available tomorrow."

The Minister had nearly managed to finish his lunch and was just taking the last sip of an excellent chardonnay when the Minister of Transport called. 'Are you behind this?'

'Am I behind what, my friend?'

'The robbery, Kayoro! I didn't think it would be this big!'

'What an odd thing to say. Of course I'm not. I know nothing about it other than in the reports I've just received. Obviously, I've put all available resources into the hands of the police. I do hope they catch whoever did it.'

'You are either incredibly intelligent, or fatally stupid. I will reserve judgement on that and make my decision at the right time.'

'Do that.' And with clear venom in his reply, 'And when the time comes, so will I.'

Chapter 35

September 25th, Lake Naivasha. Kenya.

The hippopotamus yawned a jaw-cracking yawn and gave a long barking grunt of annoyance. Yellow incisors a foot long displayed as the mother protected its young. There was a tide line along her back and poetically, a waterlily frond hung around her neck. Moments before, they had been relaxing in shallow water and mud. The arrival of the small speed boat driven by one of the local fishermen had disrupted their wallowing and they were angrily making their way to deeper water. The boat was perhaps ten metres long, and about a metre wide. It might have once been an eggshell blue. The ancient fifteen horsepower engine was enough for the boat's purpose today, birdwatching and a picnic on the lake. Athwartships were cracked and worn varnished benches. Apart from the captain, there were only two other people on board. The man was nearly sixty and had curling blond hair, going a little grey in places. It was hidden by a pale leather, wide-brimmed bush hat. His physique told the tale that, at one point in his life, fitness had been important. His open-necked, pale pink, thick cotton, long-sleeved shirt protected him from mosquito bites. He also wore shorts and Caterpillar walking sandals, so he had liberally applied mosquito repellent that morning.

Opposite Max sat his wife. Ariana, a couple of years younger, with sleek brown hair, tied into a ponytail. She wore a light cotton print dress and a straw wide-brimmed hat with pale green ribbon.

They were both watching the hippos with great interest through binoculars. It didn't matter how many times you went on safari; you always saw something new. As the hippos submerged, the birdwatchers' attention shifted to the fish eagle sitting at the top of an acacia tree on the edge of the vast lake. It peered constantly into the water below it, waiting for a sighting of a juicy tilapia. Every now and then it honked a piercing cry to its unseen mate. However, it wasn't the mate that replied. Instead, Max's phone chirped in his pocket. He brought down his binoculars and fished it out. He looked apologetically at Ariana, whom he saw frowning over the top of her binos, trying to ignore him. He looked at the unknown number on the

100

screen. It began with +233. Africa somewhere he thought, but he couldn't quite tag where. 'Hello, this is Max.'

A clipped, educated, female voice on the other end. 'Please hold for His Excellency the President of Ghana.'

Max had only a moment to rue his slightly boozy lunch, before a deep masculine voice, ponderous but authoritative, came onto the line. 'Max, I'm grateful for your taking my call at no notice.'

'Hello Mr President. Not at all. I find that people such as yourself, sir, only call me unexpectedly when they have emergencies that need, shall we say, immediate attention.'

'Ha yes! You're quite right. I am, as you might say, a referral. I've just been given your number by a good friend of mine, the President of Angola. He says that you're dependable, resourceful, and above all discreet.'

'Oh, I wouldn't be able to comment on that, Mr President. I am delighted that I and my team have a good reputation though.'

'Yes, you do, and as you correctly guess, I have a problem. A very large problem and I need immediate, considerable help and support.'

'Go on, sir. How can we help?'

'Simply put, yesterday afternoon we had a massive theft of gold bullion from one of our mines. I don't know who did it, or why. But I do know it will have catastrophic impacts on our country's finances. The people who did it are currently on the run somewhere in our jungle to the North. I've obviously mobilised as many military and police forces as I can, but I get the sense that there are internal forces working against me. I need you to come and find the gold, get it back and then take it to safety.'

Max, his mind a whirl said. 'One moment please, sir.' He took the phone away from his ear and whilst still sitting, bent forward into the boat. With unseeing eyes, he stared at the timbers around his feet. A thousand thoughts went through his mind. People. Aircraft. Planning. Weapons. Additional consultants. Legal issues. Reputation. Future business opportunities. Current company finances, and the ability to bankroll it. It didn't take very long.

'Mr President, my gut feeling is "yes", we can help. We'll start working up a plan immediately. I have a lot to do though in the next few hours. Could you please give me someone on your team that I can speak to about this tonight?'

'Well, I'll give you my number, Max. I only want you to talk to me about this. As I say, something is off here. I suspect that political opponents may be "gathering" before the next election. I need to stop them in their tracks.'

'Very well, sir. Do please send me your number and I'll call you this evening.' As the call finished, Max turned to the boat's captain. 'Captain, please could you take us back to the car, as quickly as you can.'

Ariana muttered under her breath. 'Oh dear,' as the boat turned on a dime, and with a boost of unexpected speed, cut a bow wave across the lake.

Max was holding on to the gunwale but wasn't listening. He was already making another call. This time to Tom, his business partner and Operations Director. 'Tom, very fast ball. I need all the key players in the main briefing room in… two hours. Most of them are going to deploy shortly. Also, ask Charly to get a Hercules transport aircraft lined up for the day after tomorrow. We'll need it for a couple of days.' He listened for a moment. 'Where? Oh, Ghana. Tell the team to prepare for jungle warfare and find out which consultants we have immediately available.'

After he hung up, he went straight back into thinking mode. Ariana was staring at him, cross. Max must have felt the laser beams boring into the top of his head, and he looked up. 'Sorry, darling. Have you had a lovely time?'

Chapter 36

September 25th, Nairobi. Kenya.

Ariana had driven Max directly to the office and the trip had taken about ninety minutes. He hardly said a word in all that time, but he was furiously typing notes into his device. He barely noticed as they entered the private airfield at Orly, just to the Southwest of Nairobi. It was there that Max's company had its offices. A converted private residence on the Southern side of the airstrip. He did remember to kiss his wife and say thank you before he got out of the car, whilst also saying that he would likely be home late. Ariana, his ever-forgiving wife smiled at him. She knew that Max was enjoying life most when he was setting up a new operational project.

The office building was multi-purpose. The company administrative office was there, as were the Ops room, the briefing and planning rooms, and they were all exceptionally well equipped with the latest technologies. There was a dormitory room, always prepped to receive guests and finally, out in the garden, the garage had been extended to become a technical workshop and storage facility. The business had rapidly outgrown even that facility, so Max had leased one of the airplane hangars as well. There his team could store the larger items of equipment that they kept for projects both live and completed.

Max walked through the Ops room, desks occupied, wide screen TVs monitoring other projects in real time, a professional hubbub of noise. He walked straight into the main briefing room.

There was general chatter going on in there and as he walked in, he looked at the faces that had come in at short notice. He was relieved to see some of his most competent staff in the room. Tom, Mike, Raj, Miguel, Charly and half a dozen other team members who had just completed another project. All the chairs in the small cinema-like auditorium were filled, and at the front of the room Tom was holding court. The only display screen that was on, showed a large Google Earth image of Ghana. As Max walked in, Mike, a huge barrel-chested African American, spoke up in his deep slow bass.

'Max! I thought you had the day off. Apparently on Safari?'

Max had the grace to look sheepish, 'Yes, Ariana thought that too.'

Mike, who was good looking enough to have starred in a Gillette advert, laughed. 'Oh dear, in the doghouse again?'

Raj, who was Mike's best buddy, chimed in. 'Well, you should know, you've pulled enough dogs in your time. Ha. Woof Woof!'

For once, Mike didn't laugh. Instead, he looked embarrassed and gave Raj daggers. He tried to subtly nod and flick his head backwards, indicating that there was someone sitting behind him whom might take offence. Raj though was being slow witted. 'What's wrong, buddy, got something in your eye?'

'I think,' said Charly, the gorgeous blonde pilot sitting in the row behind, 'that Mike is trying to not so subtly indicate that he and I are in a relationship.'

Raj was suddenly flustered. 'What? Hang on Charly, I don't think you're a dog! Umm, that's not what…'

Charly smiled at him sweetly, interrupting him. 'I'm so glad to hear that, Raj. It means the world to me. Anyway, I'm a pussy cat, just watch out for my claws,' then she gave a very sexy 'miaow.'

Raj wanted to sink into his chair. His best buddy Mike had always had a problem getting a regular girlfriend, despite his looks and physique. Finally though, he had landed the awesome Charly. Mike looked at him. Quietly he said, 'Dude, sometimes you are such a dick.'

Max took that as an opportunity to cut in. 'Excellent, well, with all the pleasantries out of the way, here's the problem.' Over a ten-minute period, he briefed the team on what he knew and what his preliminary thoughts were. He didn't offer any solutions. He was a highly competent leader and knew that the best ideas often came from his team. They were experienced, from many walks of life and his job was to lead the discussion, listen and ultimately make the decisions. 'I'm going to give everyone 24 hours, before we mobilise the advance team. In that time, what can we plan for and what are the nearest crocodiles to the boat?'

As the ideas started to come in, Tom typed them into an action log, which he flicked up onto one of the other screens in the room.

Miguel, who had formerly worked as an enforcer for a large South American drug cartel, spoke up first. 'I have some experience of working in the jungle. It's not a good place to fight or get injured. We need to think about the right equipment. Helicopters, quad bikes with trailers, a lot of explosives, the right clothing and sleeping systems.'

Mike chimed in, 'Yeah, we need a really good rotary pilot for the jungle work. We'll have to carve the helicopter landing zones out of the jungle ourselves, so they'll be really tight places to get into, both day and night.'

Tom added, 'Agreed. Next up we're going to need some kind of legal authority, or get out of jail free card, signed by the President. That's if we are expecting to engage in direct combat in Ghana.'

Max nodded. 'I think we can safely assume that this is going to be a combat task. That's a good point though. I'll speak to the President about that and also tell him that we'll need to import our own weapons.'

Raj's turn and in his Indian accent he asked. 'We need to know the approximate area of operation, so that we can ask for a forward staging area. Ideally a military airbase, or disused civilian airfield. The closer we are, the better our logistics in terms of resupply and medical evacuation are going to be.'

Mike added, 'Good one, also we should probably have a good field medical service, whatever we can get our hands on at that location. It needs to have an international evacuation aircraft pre-positioned on the ground, if we have any known or forecast combat periods.'

Max came back in. 'Good, let's keep these ideas coming, track them, allocate people to lock them down and keep things moving. I'm not worried about the budget too much on this one. We'll demand a large sum in advance, so that we can finance it. Anything you need to order, buy, or rent, get onto it, especially the big-ticket or long lead-time items. I have a good contact in Ghana, who'll help with some support services on the ground. I want to send a bunch of you first, with as much kit and weapons as we can, whilst we mobilise the remaining consultants. Next up. I think we need to go back to our military days and break the problem down into phases. First, how are we going to find the baddies in amongst vast tracts of jungle? Second, how are we going to mobilise our resources, so that we can intercept them there? Third, how do we extract ourselves and potentially four or five tons of gold? It would be nice to have contingency plans, but we'll have to work on those later. The time frames are too tight. What I want now is for you to split into groups. Tom will give you phases, and I want you to work together on your phase. We'll meet in here again in two hours. If anyone else is using a planning room, kick them out. Your task takes priority. Got it? Good. See you shortly.'

Chapter 37

September 25th, Nairobi. Kenya.

After the meeting finished, Max caught up with Charly in the flight planning room. Charly regularly flew Max's team and was qualified on several aircraft types. She was in her early thirties, but had lifetimes of flying experience already, having started legally flying at the age of sixteen. Before joining Max as a consultant, she had been a stunt pilot for the Red Bull team. She was fearless in her flying, was always willing to fly to the limits and had an exceptional network of contacts. If Max ever needed a plane and a pilot, she would be involved in sourcing it and co-piloting, even if she wasn't exactly able to write it in her own logbook.

'Charly, how are you getting on with sourcing the Hercules?'

'Hi, Max' she said, knowing full well that Max didn't always remember the common courtesies. He wasn't intending to be rude, but sometimes his brain was being overly efficient. 'I have one. I'm just waiting for the email with the banking details. It's a minimum hire of a week and it's quite expensive I'm afraid. If we pay today, it'll be here tomorrow night for loading.'

'Excellent, well done. I'll pay the invoice as soon as you send it to me. Now what do we want in terms of helicopters in Ghana?'

'Well, I know what we want but the question is, can we get one.'

'How so?'

'I spoke with Mike and Raj, and we want a Chinook. But there are so few available globally and those that are in the civilian space are either firefighting, or permanently leased out. They're too expensive to have just sitting around.'

'And why does it have to be a Chinook?'

'Well, simply put, it's the single fact that we can get all of our people, kit and equipment into one airframe, in one load, along with several tons of gold. They're multi-engine, fast, powerful, and really good in the heat and humidity at sea level. The alternative is having four or five medium-sized helicopters and all of a sudden, we have a lot more maintenance crews, pilots, things that can go wrong. It won't be very subtle if we have a huge fleet.'

'OK,' said Max. 'That's all logical. See if you can get a Chinook, but just to be safe, start on alternatives as a plan B as well.'

Chapter 38

September 25th, Nairobi. Kenya.

Mike and Raj were in the hangar piling up kit and equipment. Raj was Mike's gym buddy and best mate, though they came from very different backgrounds. The Sikh had a murky past and was an expert in explosives and weaponry. As a result of the mixture of his beliefs and interests he didn't read Playboy. He read Janes Defence Weekly instead. Raj was stacked on top, on thin spindly legs as Mike would say. He ate very well, a lot of protein and vegetables and would go green just looking at a McDonald's meal.

Mike on the other hand was an ex-US Navy Seal. His uniform these days was nearly always pale cargo trousers and a black T-shirt. Tight around his frame of course. He spoke with a Southern drawl that, when combined with his physique, his looks and his deep black skin made him a lady slayer.

The two men had been friends for several years and had worked together on so many projects that they trusted each other completely. Max had long ago stopped trying to send them on separate projects and accepted the fact that these two were his best operators by a long shot.

Mike was extremely calm under pressure and would never get rattled or lose his cool. Never that is, unless Raj was trying to wind him up, which with the banter of military operators was often.

'Sorry about earlier in the ops room, man.' said Raj.

'That's OK, I am used to you being a dick by now.'

'What! I suppose I'm just finding it hard to believe that you actually have a girlfriend now, that's all.'

One of Mike's insecurities, despite his looks, was exactly that. 'Yeah, right.'

'I mean in the office sweepstake on when you two are going to get married, I obviously said never.' Raj looked at Mike slyly, whilst he was stacking cargo crates.

'What office sweepstake?'

'Well, one of the ops team has started a sweepstake. Personally, I think by the end of this year is too soon, but you know.

The way you two are always mooning around each other, holding hands when you think no one can see you...'

'We don't go around holding hands!'

'Well, I know that! Although Charly did mention to me the other day that she wished you'd hold her hand more.'

'What! Really?'

'Yeah, she said she wished you'd be more affectionate.'

'Fuck off!'

'Nah, she did mate, seriously.' Goal! Thought Raj.

Mike went silent for a moment, thinking about that. Not really knowing how to reply, he changed the subject. 'I think tomorrow we'd better take those quad bikes out and make sure they're all good to go.'

Over the next hour, Mike and Raj pulled out a pre-deployment list and ticked off a long list of kit and stores that they would want to take. As they didn't know what would be available at the other end, they would take everything they could. Fortunately, with an organisation that was used to rapid response, much of it was prepacked and in tagged storage crates. Each crate had a kit list on the lid, and were only ever put back on the shelf if they were complete.

They knew that they had a large transport aircraft for the deployment and so space for mobilisation wasn't going to be too bad. One of the things they didn't have, was enough sleeping systems and logistics support kit for the large size of the team which would ultimately be deploying. Mike made a note. The stores team would have to procure that kit pretty rapidly, but ultimately it could deploy with the main team in a couple of days' time.

While they were working, Miguel joined them. He had been in the armoury preparing the available weapons, which were not many, and drawing up a list of what would be needed. Miguel, who had a deep scar on his cheek, wore his long black hair in a ponytail which exposed the tattoos around his neck. Those who might have been able to identify them were thousands of miles away, but they would know that they were the marks of The Western Cartel. Miguel had been lucky to escape from the cartel, and coincidentally arrest, by fleeing to Africa a few years ago. He had settled in Kenya with an unknown amount of cash. It was a lot, but not enough to never have to work again and so he had bought fake ID, changed his name and built his reputation. As a civilian sniper, there were not many organisations that needed his type of services. When they were needed, it was his name near the top of the list. 'Hey guys,' he said in his thick Spanish accent, as he entered the hangar and closed the door behind him. 'I have been thinking about operating in the jungle. As you know, I spend a lotta time there and I think we are gonna need a lotta night vision and thermal devices.'

'Hey buddy,' Mike replied. 'Good job, I'm just writing the main kit list now. What do you want to have?'

'How about some thermal optic sights for da weapons, and helmet-mounted night vision goggles. Also, let's have a couple a larger handheld thermal optics for the sentry positions.'

'Sounds good.'

'Also, we are going to need a sheet load a batteries.'

Raj cut in, 'Oh yeah, a sheeeet load.' He paused and grinned as Miguel blanked him. 'Those lithium-ion batteries are a mother to get hold of. You're right though, we're going to need bucket loads. Mike, let's...'

Mike interrupted so that they both said it at the same time, 'Add it to the list!' They laughed.

Chapter 39

September 25th, Nairobi. Kenya.

Tom and Max were sitting in Tom's office. Tom, who looked like a skinny version of Desperate Dan, was behind his desk. Max was on a more comfortable couch, with a cup of coffee in his hand. They were discussing the local support that would be needed in Ghana and Max was talking about one of his contacts. 'Glenn is an old foreign office chum of mine. He's semi-retired, having set up a company that specialises in helping multi-national companies establish footprints in new countries. He's not into security risk management, but he's ex-military, lives in Accra and has a lot of business contacts. Importantly, I think we can trust him to a certain extent.'

Tom nodded, 'Quite right. When you start talking about the potential sums that we're talking about, I think trust is going to be in short supply. Do you think he can discreetly find us the kind of forward operating base that we want?'

'I hope so. I'm certainly going to try him, that's for sure. I'd rather go to the President with a full plan, and save any requests for help for things that might be really tricky. Now, what were your thoughts on the search part of the project? How do we find them in the jungle?'

Tom, who had once been a British Royal Marine commando and who had done numerous projects in various jungles around the world, knew the answer to that one. 'Our biggest problem is the size of the area we're going to have to search. There's no way to do that from under the canopy. We are going to have to use aviation resources with a serious observation suite on board.'

'What sort of thing are you after?'

'Well, I've seen externally mounted rigs that are used by some anti-narcotics and anti-poaching agencies. They have a really sensitive thermal detector on board, a lot like a thermal camera that you see in the airports these days, monitoring people's temperatures. They can cover huge areas on open ground, they can fly high and scan the cold ground below them. They pick up herds of animals obviously, but also poachers. I'm pretty sure that we could use that kit too, but we'll need to find out if it will work through dense jungle canopy.'

'OK, I'll leave that one with your team.' said Max. 'Charly is tied up with sourcing the other aviation assets. See if you can find one. Start with neighbouring countries, speak to the operators. I suspect I'll need to ask the President to pull in a favour or two to get one organised.'

'Roger that, the other issue right now is competent operators. How many do we want? I was thinking twenty or so for the field op and about ten for the forward operating base.'

'Can we get hold of that many people on such short notice?'

'It's going to be tough. We already know that we're going to mobilise in two waves. At a push we have twelve here in Nairobi already. They can all go on the first transport the day after tomorrow. The rest will have to mobilise from elsewhere: the UK, the US, France, Israel. I suspect Australia is one step too far, but there are some good people there. They don't have to bring any sensitive kit with them, as we can take care of that, so they can all fly on commercial into Accra.'

'That's logical, then we can either drive them by road, or use a helicopter to ferry them up to the forward operating base, wherever that is.' Max thought a moment before continuing. 'I think on my call with the President I need to get the approximate part of the country where this is all happening. It may have real bearing on the logistics. Then I'll ask Glenn, as his priority, to find us a base location. It doesn't need to be fancy, just a waterproof hangar will do. He can start to get the basics in there, a couple of vehicles, water, food etc.'

'It's turning into an expensive start up. What are we going to ask for as our upfront fee?'

Max had a twinkle in his eye. 'Well, I think we go in with a good rate. A few percent of the recovered total will be the completion bonus, and then all the other elements billed at cost plus ten percent.'

Tom, who was also a major shareholder in the business, was right to ask the questions. He mentally did a bit of maths. Aviation resources, mobilisation and kit was probably going to budget towards a million plus, and by the time the project was over, costs would likely be a couple. The big question then was, what was the value of the gold. 'Well, it looks like we need to ask for a couple of million up front, I would suggest.'

'Exactly my thoughts, partner! Now, before we get carried away and start booking beach holidays on exotic islands, let's go and meet with the team again.'

Chapter 40

September 25th, Kayoro Mine. Ghana.

Inside the mine complex, most of the fires had died out. There were still some stubborn plumes of smoke though, one or two of the buildings were still smouldering. At the main gate, where the majority of the police officers had been killed, stood a military officer. He was trying desperately not to throw up in front of his men. This Colonel of infantry was a career desk jockey. He was wearing his jungle combats, but his boots were shiny and polished like glass. His gold braid lanyard was hooked over his shoulder under his gaudy epaulets. It was attached at the other end to a shiny silver pearl handled pistol in his hip holster. He was young for a Colonel, the son of a powerful politician. Raised to rank by his father's ability to get him onto one of the rare foreign attachment officer training courses as a recruit. As a result, he had spent a year at The Royal Military Academy Sandhurst, in the United Kingdom. It produced some of the best officers in the world. But not all that attended came out as good officers.

That was a few years ago now, but his father's power continued to propel him upwards. He was sitting pretty in a rank probably three above his level of competence. It was pure coincidence that this incident had happened in an area that he was responsible for. But, he felt, done right, this was his opportunity to achieve General rank. All he needed to do was track down these petty thieves, recover the gold, and life would be gravy from then on. And, he mused, not all of the gold would be brought back. Those naughty thieves would have hidden some in the jungle somewhere, wouldn't they. Wealth and power, all available to him now at the roll of the dice.

He came out of his reverie and looked back at the scene around him. At least he didn't feel like throwing up anymore. Day-old bodies in the heat and humidity of the jungle didn't do well. Especially ones that had died in battle. The smells rapidly attracted a surprising number of animals, predatory birds and insects. This Colonel had never been in battle with anything more dangerous than a teenager's bra when he was going through puberty.

115

Looking at this grisly spectacle wasn't pleasant, so he walked on through the main gate. He passed the burnt-out hull of an armoured vehicle, still plinking as it cooled, and into the main mine site.

There were a lot of people inside the complex. Mine personnel, police, medical responders. All were there either removing the dead or tidying up. He and his headquarters staff were met by someone from the mining company and given a guided tour of the facility. The tour ended with them being driven to the point where the robbers had left the site, through the berm, and escaped into the jungle.

As he stood there with his small team, he was getting excited. They had driven up today knowing that they were going to start a chase. He had about thirty men with him. The reports from site said that only about fifteen robbers had left with the gold, and he was delighted that the odds were in his favour. It was a bit top heavy, a full Colonel leading a platoon, but there was no way he was going to trust a simple second lieutenant on a job like this. Sure, other forces were mobilising too. The hunt was on. But he was closest, and he was fastest. The robbers had only left yesterday afternoon. How far could they have got in a day?

'Lieutenant. Get your men ready, we leave in half an hour. We'll follow them that way.' He pointed theatrically, directly into the jungle. A little part of him wished that he had brought the Regimental photographer with him, so that he could have captured that moment.

Chapter 41

September 25th, Nairobi. Kenya.

Max was in his office. The window behind his desk looked out onto the airstrip, which was mostly used by private aircraft, but which occasionally hosted something a little larger. Max paid a fair share to the members-only flying club for maintenance, so they didn't mind too much. It was getting into the late evening for him, but for once the time zones worked in his favour. Three hours behind, it was early evening in Accra. 'Mr President, good evening, it's Max. Thanks for taking my call.'

The deep, ponderous voice at the other end didn't waste any time. 'So do you think you can assist me, Max?'

'Yes, Mr President, I know we can. We have almost everything we need in terms of people and resources. There are a couple of things I need to ask from you, sir.'

'OK, go ahead.'

'Sir, I need to know more details about the incident, where we need to start the search and where we can set up a temporary operating base close to the location. We'll bring all of our own equipment.'

'OK. It was the Kayoro mine to the North and the thieves left camp shortly after mid-day yesterday. They stole six tons of gold bars and have escaped into the jungle in a number of pickup trucks.'

'Has anyone had any contact with them since?'

'No. As you would expect, we're flooding the area with military but so far we're only following tracks.'

'Sir, I need to ask, will you give us permission to use force, including up to lethal force in the pursuit of these criminals? I'm assuming that if they attacked a well-protected mine, they're heavily armed?'

'They have RPGs, heavy machine guns and a number of assault weapons. If you provide the necessary assurances on appropriate rules of engagement, then yes, I will allow you to use force in an offensive capacity. You may also bring your own weapons. I suppose you'll need some paperwork for them?'

'Yes, please sir, and a written letter with the use of force approval as well.'

'OK. What else?'

'We'll be bringing a lot of equipment that may raise eyebrows with your customs officers in addition to the weapons. Body armour, night vision equipment, radios and satellite phones. Perhaps if your note could cover that too please. And then finally, we might need some influence on getting hold of a particular type of search helicopter from one of your neighbours, but I'll let you know. It's equipped with sensing technology that will help us find them under the jungle canopy.'

'Yes, I understand. That sounds like a good idea.'

'Great, well the final thing is contracting. I appreciate the referral, and of course that you have asked us personally to support you. We are a small organisation though and so will need a reasonable deposit to help pay for all of the upfront items.'

'OK, what are you thinking?'

Max didn't like talking about this part of things, he enjoyed being creative, developing and then most importantly delivering solutions. But money was of course the grease for the wheels. 'We would like to ask for a $2 million mobilisation fee. The structure is very simple. We provide all the resources needed, at cost plus ten percent, without any withholding taxes. That covers the basics. Then we ask for a success fee. We can agree the specific definition, but we usually ask for three percent of the value recovered.'

The President, the expert diplomat, paused, letting the silence grow uncomfortably. 'Max, I agree to the mobilisation fee requirements. But let's talk about success. For you, success is a full recovery, and your reputation gains another endorsement. For me success is recovering as much of the gold as possible, and re-election in a few months' time. Between us I feel we have some middle ground.'

'OK, sir, what do you suggest?'

'Given that we're talking several hundred million dollars' worth of gold, I'll agree to the following. A three percent success fee is what you invoice. But you'll receive one percent.'

Max, a little uncertainly. 'Okaay.'

'The remaining two percent will be a referral fee, which will go to an account that I nominate.'

Max wasn't surprised. Cooked books, dodgy invoices, corrupt politicians. And here was this guy, busy stacking up the money for his campaign funds, or his mistress. It didn't matter really. What Max was not going to do was agree to it over an insecure line. 'Mr President I will be in Accra in a couple of days' time. Perhaps we can finalise that discussion then. In the meantime, if we can agree on the mobilisation fee, then we can get things moving.

'That's all good, send me the contract and the banking details. I'll get that organised this evening.'

'Thank you, Mr President. I look forward to meeting you soon.' Max hung up. For fuck's sake he thought. It was never easy. He texted Tom as he fumed. "It's a go. Deposit to come tonight. We'd better set up a project code name. M."

Max had another call to make now. As he brooded, he unpacked a new burner phone and inserted a new sim card. He had a strong suspicion that his personal phone was monitored by the intelligence agency in Kenya, and he was always careful when he used it. Of course, speaking to the President of another country would normally only help his case for legitimacy. That had gone a bit wrong on that last call though. He certainly didn't want any of the next conversation to end up in the wrong hands. He was about to call Glenn and get into the details of some of the tactical planning. The issue was the scale of the problem. Six golden tons' worth of scale was far too tempting a target.

Chapter 42

September 26th, Damana Forest. Ghana.

The Damana forest was vast: thousands of square kilometres, a huge expanse of green, breathing life, which extended down most of the West of the country. Large parts of it were forestry reserve, protected where possible from cultivation and much of it had been untouched for thousands of years. It wasn't all rosy though. In parts, the forest had been devastated, sometimes by natural causes, but mostly by man. Towns and even cities had been built within its borders but most of the damage came from farming, industrial timber and fire. Over the past forty years or so, with conservation efforts, large parts had been reclaimed and allowed to regrow. This had led to textbook examples of the classically-named primary forest and secondary forest. Primary was the oldest, so old that the canopy was a complete, thick blanket of gorgeous branches with voluminous leaves. That blanket was so thick that virtually no light could penetrate. Floor dwelling leafy plants therefore couldn't get the energy they needed to grow. So, the forest floor was fairly clear, except of course for the vines, dangling down from above, or stretching up from below. A thousand years of leaf mulch made it a paradise for insects, bacteria, and fungi. Underexplored, the future of modern medicine lay in its moist depths.

Secondary forest on the other hand, was like the jungle in the movies. Much younger trees, gaps between the branches, lots of sunlight reaching down to the forest floor. Here, explosions of leafy green undergrowth burst forward, roots delving deep and feasting on the abundance of nutrients. Secondary forest was a bastard to move through if you were anything bigger than a rat. For man, this was the territory of bloody and calloused hands, thorns and brambles, snakes and spiders. Machete-wielding, achingly slow movement.

The odd thing was that you could be moving easily through primary forest and then come across the results of some past event. Perhaps a fire had scorched its way through. Or a logging company had been in and stripped out hundreds of acres of valuable hardwoods. To get there, they may have cut a road. The scars of the activities had long since grown back, leaving thick bands of secondary forest for the explorer to find unexpectedly on their journey.

Abdi and his convoy of vehicles had just discovered one of these as they headed South. Movement had been slow so far, the convoy needing to travel slowly enough for a scout to walk ahead of the vehicles. The gloom of the jungle meant that even during the day the vehicles were driving with headlights on. The beams of light constantly jumping up and down creating crazy shadows in the distance. In the primary, whilst the tree trunks were widely spaced, roots, rocks, streams, and boggy patches meant that extreme care was still needed. The vehicles, low on their suspension, were constantly jinking, avoiding obstacles, trying to drive as straight a line South as possible. Go too fast, and you ended up with a vehicle getting stuck, needing to be towed out. The weight of the gold and the supplies risked terminal damage to the vehicles and more delay.

That hadn't happened yet, but as they had just found out, driving blind through dense vegetation wasn't a good idea. They had tried it and shattered the windscreen of the lead vehicle in moments. They discovered that it needed two men to hack a path through, clear enough to make sure that a vehicle could then nudge its way, knocking down the remainder of the undergrowth. They still needed to avoid rocks, roots and fallen tree trunks, and you would only find them when you had cleared the undergrowth. It was a painstakingly slow task. But once done, there would be a clear path for the long snake of vehicles to follow.

The thickness of this increased patch of vegetation was unknown, but what was obvious with this patch of secondary, was that it was very wide. Beyond line of sight in both directions it was perpendicular to their path. They had spent half a day so far, cutting and hacking, and the men were exhausted. To begin with, it was just the non-drivers cutting their way through. Given there were only seven of them, even Abdi and Azrah had taken their turns. Eventually the drivers had been included as well.

Tempers started fraying. The grumblings and groanings, the curses as people cut themselves or picked up splinters. There was also a lot of time for people to think as they rested weary bodies. A lot of the team had died on the assault of the mine. Friends and even brothers. As it happened, it was most of Abdi's assault team that had died. Cheko's had been the last to arrive. It was also the case that Cheko had chosen many of his own men to be in his group. He still had loyalty and support. Abdi as the foreigner didn't have many strong relationships. He was in a weak position and realization was dawning for all that this was not going to be an easy escape. Capture meant life in prison at best, but most likely, the death penalty.

'This fucking jungle!' a man shouted, when he cut his hand yet again as he slashed through the prickly foliage.

'Yeah, man, what the hell are we doing here!' shouted another.

'Ask the Somali!' exclaimed another 'He's the one that brought us into this fucking place!'

The vehicles were backed up, hundreds of metres of cleared vegetation were behind. A dark green tunnel, pressing right up against their sides. Palm fronds, vines and spider webs dangled from above. It was a claustrophobic hot and humid environment. No good at all for keeping tempers cool. At ground level, the fresh-cut vegetation left large stumps that would trip a tired man, and they were all tired. The only ways to change over from hacking on the front line to resting at the back were either to find a fortunate gap, or to climb up over the bonnet of the front vehicle and then over the cab.

'We shouldn't have come this way,' whinged the first man as he sucked at his hand.

'I know that. You know that. Who the fuck takes pickup trucks into the jungle? A filthy, ignorant desert dweller, that's who!'

'Actually, I live by the sea.' came Abdi's dangerous voice. He was standing on the back of the front vehicle, a weapon casually by his side. He was still wearing the bandage on his head, tied under his chin. It was grubby and smeared in mud. His face still had coagulated blood on it, the sweat pouring off him unable to wash it away. He was showing exhaustion, but he knew he couldn't risk sleeping. Too many people were unhappy and bad things could happen in the night. The complaining men were only carrying machetes right now and were not in the right place to challenge him physically. They knew it, but that didn't stop them from shouting up at him, venting.

'How the fuck are we going to get out of here?'

'Well,' said Abdi, 'If you stop bleating like goats, and keep working, it will happen faster than you think.'

'How do you know that?'

'Because I know where we're going. I have the contacts to get us out of this shit hole. Not only that, but I'm the one who'll make sure you get paid. However, if you don't hurry the fuck up, then we're going to get caught. Haven't you heard those helicopters? D'you think the military aren't looking for us?' It was the calm way that Abdi gave his speech that gave the men cause for thought. Here he was, on his own, and he was as cold as ice.

Grumbling, the men kept on hacking their way through the underbrush. It was only ten minutes later that they finally broke through, back into pristine, clear, primary forest. A cheer went up from the men as they were able to re-mount their vehicles and take a rest. The drivers could do the work for a bit. Unexpectedly though, Abdi called a halt. He told the men to make camp for the night. He called Cheko out to the side and they had a discreet conversation.

'Abdi, why have we stopped! Surely we should keep going? They'll be following us!' Cheko was looking tired too.

'Cheko, how long do you think it'll take us to get South at this rate?' Abdi needed some confirmation of his thoughts.

'Perhaps a week?'

'Exactly. And how much time do you think we've lost getting through that whore piece of jungle?'

'About a day?'

'I agree. I can't tell you why, but I feel that the army are close by. They'll be following our tracks and eventually we'll need to deal with that.'

Cheko was incredulous. 'You want to fight them! But there are so few of us!'

'You, me, fifteen men and one woman. You don't think we can beat an army?'

'I know we can't.'

'We're in agreement there too. The problem is this. In the open spaces, we have to choose our routes, around the trees, waste time. Then, in that crap,' he said pointing, 'We have to spend time cutting our way through. The people following only have to follow the tracks. They'll come ten times faster than us. That means at some time tonight, or tomorrow morning, they'll find us.'

Cheko paled. 'You want to make a stand here?'

'No, I want to ambush the goat fuckers here. It's a big difference. We use that piece of ground that we've just cut through, to channel them down a single path. We get Azrah to do her work. You and your men use the tricks that you know. We prepare the battlefield to be what we want. And then we kill them all. If we survive, we win. We'll be able to get away cleanly, to fight another day.'

Cheko's hope returned a little. It was logical, but it also indicated how bad a situation they were in. 'But what if the force following us is too big?'

'If that's true, then we've already lost. But, and it's a big but, I think they'll have split their forces. The jungle is a big place. Now, how are we going to do this?'

Chapter 43

September 26th, Nairobi. Kenya.

It was late in the evening in Nairobi and Max's team had spent the whole day checking equipment and loading it onto pallets. The small electric forklift, which would travel with them, was now busy moving those pallets onto the back of the large, civilianised Hercules transport aircraft that had arrived a few hours ago. This Herc was the civilian version of the well-known C130 that was in service with many Western countries. It had recently completed a contract in Ethiopia, delivering food aid for the African Union. This wide-bodied, high-wing, four-engine turboprop aircraft had no frills, no fancy gizmos or even airline seats. It was a workhorse plain and simple. What it did have was a huge lifting capacity and lots of space. While that work was going on outside the main hangar, inside in the main briefing room the team were having a final briefing.

Mike, who was sitting in the front row of the small cinema-like briefing room, was highlighting the main issues on the equipment side. 'Four of the quad bikes are all good, and their trailers too. We can take the other two as well and see if we can get them maintained in Ghana. If they don't make it into the jungle, then we can still use them around the forward operating base. We have plenty of other stores that can also move forward to the FOB. I think without any support at all, we can exist for at least a week, as long as we can get a water supply. My main concerns are weapons. We have about half of what we need. We're using our usual suppliers and we hope to get the rest here within the next 48 hours. They'll need to come on the flight with the main party. Raj, over to you, mate.'

Raj, who was sitting next to Mike, was wearing blue jeans, caterpillar boots and a checked linen shirt. He came straight in. 'I have one issue, and that is demolitions. We don't have enough explosives, det-cord or detonators for what we'll need in the jungle. I'm trying to get the supplier here in Nairobi to sort us out quickly, but the licensing regulations are completely nuts now. As a precaution, I've also ordered from the main supplier to the mining companies in Ghana. I know it's excessive, but we can't operate without it. If we end up having too much, I'll run a refresher course for the team, when the project is over.'

Max nodded his assent. 'Ok, anything else? Charly, how are you doing on the Chinook?'

Charly used a hand to brush a strand of hair behind her ear. 'Not sorted yet. I've found one, but it's a long way away. The mobilisation is going to take days, and it's going to be really expensive.'

'Do you still feel it's the best option?'

'Yes, in fact I'm certain now.'

'OK, sign the contract and get it on the way. Tom, how about the search aircraft?'

'That's sorted, it's mobilising tomorrow to Accra. We just need to tell it where to go afterwards.'

'Excellent. I agreed that just before this meeting started. We have permission to use an old military airfield near Tamale. That's a city pretty central in the North. The good news is that we can most likely get the Herc in there, though Glenn is going to take a look tomorrow. The advance party will take off tomorrow morning as planned, and head for Accra. If Tamale is good, then you'll refuel and head straight on.'

Mike asked a question. 'Max, I want to put a challenge into the room. Don't you think this is moving a little too fast? The fact that we don't even know where we're landing before we take off. Isn't that indicative that we're behind the curve here in planning properly?'

There were several nodding heads in the auditorium, as Mike had voiced what many were thinking. Max saw that and was grateful that the team felt they could challenge. It was healthy and professional. He spoke thoughtfully. 'Well, I'm not going to blow sunshine up your arses, but in this room is probably the only group of people in the world that could do this. It's a good challenge and I absolutely understand the concern. We pride ourselves on being able to respond to unusual requests and this is perhaps more unusual than anything we have dealt with before. Let's see how it goes over the next 24 hours. Tom will be leading the advance party, and if for whatever reason you all feel that you need to put a battle rhythm pause in, when you get to Accra, then I would absolutely support that. Does that work for everyone here?'

126

There were noises of consent around the room. 'Excellent, well as you all have an early start tomorrow, I suggest you get home, pack your personal kit and get some rest.'

As the meeting broke up, Raj turned to Mike. 'That was a fair question, mate. It does feel a little fast this one, doesn't it?'

'Yep, you know me, I don't have an issue with combat, but I like to choose the terms. I have a feeling that if we don't check this at the right place, we'll charge headfirst into a firefight that we could lose.'

'I know what you mean, buddy. I really do.'

Chapter 44

September 27th, Damana Forest. Ghana

The glowing hands on the Colonel's Omega said that it was dawn. Everything outside that immediate narrow vision was still dark, almost pitch-black in fact. He had only had a few hours' sleep and even that couldn't be called sleep. They had kept driving for as long as they could but eventually, at about midnight, he had called a stop. Everyone had settled down on the forest floor, or if they were lucky enough to have one, on their camp cots. Mosquito nets pulled around them like a shroud to keep the pests at bay.

Unfortunately, the location that he had chosen for the camp had turned out to be filled with army ants, vicious, aggressive biters. It started as though someone had pushed an electrical switch. Almost to a man there were grunts and shouts as some pheromone in the air told all the ants to bite at once. With the limited light, soldiers stuck under their mosquito nets were rushing around, smacking themselves, bumping into each other, banging into trees. It would have been comedic, except for the fact that the noise would have woken the dead. Then, the amount of light that was needed to get everyone sorted out and moved a couple of hundred metres further away, added to the lack of professionalism. Finally, they had settled down again, though this time, the Colonel had moved his bed onto the back of one of the military green land cruisers. His thoughts of a better night's sleep soon evaporated as the bites that he had received began to sting, and the ever-present buzz of mosquitos filled his ears.

As dawn came, groggy, he sat up and removed the mozzi net, absently scratching at the swollen mounds on his face. Somehow, he had pressed his face up against the net during the night, giving the insects a feast.

One of the soldiers brought him a cup of tea, and he could hear the rest of the camp stirring. In half an hour or less they should be on their way again. He reflected, as he sipped his sweet tea, that they had made excellent progress throughout the day before. Despite the immediate physical discomforts, he had a good feeling about today. He was certain that by the end of the day, they would catch up with the thieves. A short, sharp action later and they should have the gold in hand. He wondered what posting he might get first, when he was made Brigadier.

Chapter 45

September 26th, Damana Forest. Ghana.

Abdi and his men hadn't had much sleep either, but for very different reasons. He didn't know it, but he was following the mantra of drill instructors everywhere. Keep 'em busy, stop 'em from grumbling. The release from the thick jungle had helped release some of the frustrations, but the fear of failure was still in the cloying air. With Cheko by his side, he had tried to get everyone back onside and explain what he needed everyone to do. They had all stood at the exit to the green tunnel of foliage. It was carpeted in bruised ferns, and crushed palm fronds. From above, vines hung down, dripping with white sap from their wounds. The tunnel stretched away into the darkness for hundreds of meters, a reminder of how bloody hard it had been to hack through.

He had asked for, and been given, many ideas by those experienced jungle warriors and between them all they had come up with a plan. With lookouts posted at the very far end of the tunnel, he and his men had started to prepare the ambush location. They had to throw caution to the wind and rely on using a lot of vehicle headlight to help them.

Azrah prepared some of her surprises, high tech and deadly. Some of the very gnarly old jungle fighters prepared some of theirs too, using lessons handed down over hundreds of years. Deadfalls, pit traps with excrement-covered spikes, and spring-loaded spear traps. It was amazing what you could make with a machete, some twine, and bits of wood.

When one of the men suggested that they had to cut a path back into the vegetation alongside the original track, but offset by twenty metres or so, there had been a lot of groans. That man was respected though and so a hundred metres of path was cut back down the line in double quick time. Several brave young men volunteered to be that part of the ambush group.

Finally, before telling everyone to get some rest, Cheko placed the two remaining technicals as far as possible away from the exit of the tunnel, but where they were well in range and still had clear line of sight. Piles of undergrowth and branches had been piled up beside them as a simple camouflage. Particular attention was made to hiding the reflective surfaces of the lights. The .50 Cal weapons range was longer than most of the small arms that the soldiers would have. It would be like shooting fish in a barrel.

Chapter 46

Cheko was positioned on the newly cut ambush line with six of his men. Two more were at the furthest point along that path. They didn't have the discipline of a well-trained force and so they were sitting on their haunches chatting quietly. Being part of the ambush party was an odd experience for them. Their position was only a simple, narrow-cut path perhaps a metre wide. They had virtually no visibility, a combination of lack of light and the fact that the bush was right in front of their faces. When they tested their positions, lying down on the floor, their main torso was in the open gap, their legs stretched back into the undergrowth, and they needed to clear a small space in front so they could move their weapons. To be honest, they didn't know exactly where the main track was, but they knew that they would be able to work it out, when the enemy started to walk along it and the attack began. They were naturally worried about that. Alone in the dark, uncertainty started to creep in. Had they made a mistake in setting up the ambush? Were they really being followed, or had they just wasted even more time, when they could have been getting out of there?

Cheko had to bring himself out of the self-doubt that all leaders felt before combat. They didn't all show it, but the good ones all felt it, deep in their hearts. That questioning, searching: was everything prepared as best it could be? Would everyone do their jobs properly? Would he? The men sat for a little while longer before finally, they heard running feet. Urgent whispers of, 'They're coming, I see the headlights. Perhaps six vehicles!' and then the runner had gone, heading towards the technicals.

Cheko and his men settled down in the places that they had chosen to lie. Testing their positions, making sure there were no spikes, or obvious biting insects to distract them. Cheko patted his pockets, confirmed where his magazines were and with adrenaline flooding, tried to wait patiently.

Abdi and Azrah were near the two technicals and were hiding behind large trees. They had a good view all the way down the tunnel.

The other pickups had been parked several hundred metres further on, but the drivers had been called back. Everyone was needed to fight. In the darkness that surrounded Abdi's men, it was obvious when the military convoy started coming. Overconfident, they had full headlights on. Through the tunnel, the lights started as a distant glow and then grew stronger, like some oncoming train. The beams highlighted the emerald and olive greens of the backlit undergrowth, making aesthetic shadows from natural branches. As the first vehicle entered, the full beams hurt the eyes of the technical gunners. As they adjusted, using a hand to shield the worst of it, they could see more vehicles following on closely behind. The convoy covered the few hundred metres in seconds, undoing a days' worth of cutting work yesterday from Abdi's team. A part of Abdi's mind acknowledged the fact that had they chosen last night to keep moving, then by the end of today they would have been caught, most likely in the open, and killed. Of course, that could still happen this morning.

With the silhouette of the front vehicle lit from behind, showing that it was also a technical, Abdi was happy with the plans that had been put in place. That vehicle was probably driving at about forty miles an hour, as it reached the exit to the tunnel and smashed abruptly in to the first unseen obstacle. A three-foot-deep pit had been dug, with steep sides. A covering of branches and fresh green leaves covered the pit, hiding it seamlessly. With a metallic crash and last rev of the engine, the vehicle stopped dead, nose down in the hole. The vehicle commander and the driver both flew through the windscreen. The gunner smashed his head open on the gun mount collapsing in a heap. The loader was thrown clear of the vehicle, forward onto the open ground, smashing arms and ribs as he cartwheeled to the ground. The immediate vehicle behind reacted, veering to its left, smashing through the final few feet of bush and shrub. It too hit a trench, elongated for that purpose. Not nearly so deep, but enough for it to thump to a stop. No one was wearing a seatbelt and they paid the price. The third vehicle went right instead, plunging blindly through the undergrowth, only to find as it came clear, a huge tree trunk felled for that purpose. Three vehicles down, several men killed, and not a shot had yet been fired.

At that point Abdi's technicals started to open up. Tracer rounds, red and bright, arced through the forest, languid enough for the eye to see. The crossfire from both vehicles focused on the military wagons remaining in the tunnel. The rest of Abdi's group of men, coming out from behind the trees, added to the weight of fire. Metal, glass and bodies were shattered and shredded. The firing was relentless, a brutal assault on the senses. The gunners couldn't see so well, so they focused for a moment on the lead vehicle's headlights. With them destroyed, and the light from the rear vehicles providing backdrop, they began engaging the moving targets.

At the rear of the tunnel, there was a dull and slightly wet sounding boom. The two thieves at the far end of the ambush line had pressed the button on one of Azrah's boxes of tricks. A giant tree fell over the back of the tunnel preventing any vehicles from escaping back out the way they had come. At that point, even those with the slowest reflexes started to move. Azrah's other bombs went off in the middle of the kill zone, fragmentation shredding all those nearby; the foliage savagely blown apart by some unseen, violent cough of wind. The soldiers in the remaining vehicles jumped out and started firing or running. That was all that Cheko and his men needed, to know where they were. They started firing rapidly towards the sounds. Cheko shouting out above the noise. 'Aim low. Don't shoot too high!' The ambushed soldiers started falling in droves. The remaining pickup drivers tried to clear the area, driving straight into the dense foliage. No one knew what was in there and two vehicles ploughed into trees and rocks. The last turned into the ambush line and drove through it. There was a moment of shock as they cleared the line with the ambushers staring up at them as the vehicle drove past. Having heard it coming, Cheko's men turned and fired up at point blank range. They killed them all.

From the middle of the kill zone, a wounded man stood up, disorientated, confused, trying to move out of the lethal fire. His gold braid and shiny black boots shouldn't have been in the jungle on that day. He died on his very first day of combat and on his face, as he fell, was an expression of privileged outrage.

Chapter 47

September 26th, Damana Forest. Ghana.

With the firefight over, Abdi and his men quickly looted anything useful that they could: water bottles, ammunition, rations. They kept it simple because they wanted to move out quickly. None of the troop vehicles were usable, but as they went, the men destroyed any radios that were visible. Some unfortunate souls were still breathing. They were finished quickly, almost apologetically. There was no point in leaving them to suffer in the jungle.

Not a single one of Abdi's men had been injured. The ambush had been completely effective but, as the adrenaline of battle wore off, men reacted differently to it. Some created a sense of bravado with their friends, laughing and joking around. Some sat under a tree and cried, the emotional waves flooding through them, as they realised that they were still alive. There was no loss of respect for them. In whichever way the individual chose to show it, all of them would be haunted in their dreams in the future, because of the carnage they had seen and caused. Perhaps the worst for wear were the drone pilots. Still there, still alive, this wasn't Call of Duty. There was no reset button on this game.

Abdi noticed a change amongst the men. Those who had been so against him yesterday had a newfound respect. When he passed them, they gave an odd half smile, apologetic.

With one of the water bottles Abdi had picked up, he took the cap off and rinsed his head, soaking the bandage. His head was throbbing, his face still covered in blood. It was attracting the flies and that, he thought, wasn't good. It stung like hell when he pulled it off, breaking the scab, and it started bleeding again though not as much as it had previously. He had a clean field dressing already prepared and as he tried to put it on his head, Azrah came up to help him.

'You did well there, Abdi.' she said, as she helped him tie it on.

Abdi was a little non-committal, eyes watering somewhat with the pain. 'Thanks.' He used more water and, using his hands, tried to wash his face as best he could.

'Seriously, you did well. You probably saved all our lives. Everyone else was for carrying on straight away. But, if that force had found us in the open woods, we would all have been killed, or worse, captured.'

'I just needed space to think, we got lucky, that's all.'

Azrah looked at him very seriously, her brown eyes stared deeply into his. 'Oh no, Abdi. Luck is a fool's dream. Work hard enough, follow your instincts and luck, as you call it, comes to you.'

Chapter 48

September 27th, Nairobi. Kenya.

Dawn at Orly airfield, and the sun was rising over the Nairobi national park to the East. Animals grazed, eating as much of the dew-covered lush green grass as they could. Predators prowled, hungry. Scavengers like hyena and jackal chewed on yesterday's bones.

At the airfield, closer to human dwellings, a couple of warthogs used their tusks to rootle around for tender grass roots. Hairy backs caked in mud; tails pointed straight up into the air.

The Hercules was packed and ready to go. The team were having a last cup of coffee and some pastries. All of it laid on and spread out on the picnic tables at the rear of the house. The area was usually used for post-project BBQ's and team building days, but Max knew that an army marched on its stomach. It was such a small effort to feed people well, and they appreciated it. Inside the cavernous hull of the aircraft were cool boxes of iced soft drinks, generously made sandwiches and snacks. Herc's were not particularly fast aircraft, and the flight was going to take about ten hours. The team would get hungry.

Raj, who wouldn't eat sandwiches and physically recoiled from sugary pastries, had packed his own meals for the journey. Protein bars, vegetable sticks, whole grilled chicken breasts, chickpea salads, all in colour coded plastic Tupperware boxes in his day sack. His body was the proverbial temple. He had been standing having a glass of fresh orange juice, chatting with Charly, whilst Mike devoured some high calorie confection.

Charly, who was going to sit in the co-pilot seat for this flight, left the breakfast area to go and get on with her job and Mike, seizing his opportunity, told her that he would accompany her to the plane. He grabbed his day sack and caught up with her. As he did so, he reached down and held her hand. Raj giggled to see barrel-chested Mike, all muscles and testosterone, who towered above Charly, walking alongside the petite slim figure of the woman. Raj saw her turn sideways slightly and look up oddly at Mike, as they kept walking. He noted with a laugh that they weren't in step, so the hand holding would have felt awkward too. Raj kept smiling as he saw Charly recover her hand and put it in her pocket. Did he also see Mike's shoulders slump just a little bit?

Chapter 49

September 27th, Damana Forest. Ghana.

Abdi's luck was continuing to hold, no matter what Azrah thought about the subject. They had finally come across a gap in the tree canopy above, and not one so old that it had sparked an explosion of growth below. A gigantic tree had fallen, for reasons that they couldn't see, but it must have only happened in the past few months. As it had fallen it had pitched into a couple more trees, leaving them at abrupt angles and increasing the view of the sky above.

Undergrowth was already springing up from the springy brown mulch, but Abdi was able to climb up the branches and there he could pull out his satellite phone. He spent several minutes waiting for the screen to show him that he had a lock on enough satellites, and then he sent his GPS location to another phone halfway around the world. With the message sent, he dialled a number that he knew by heart.

Very few people had that number, and all those that did have it felt nervous if they ever had need to call it. It was answered at the other end by the man simply known as The Associate. The accent was difficult to trace, partly central African, sometimes with a far East twang, but definitely refined and highly educated. 'Yes?'

'Sir, it's Abdi.' There was no answer, and the pause went on longer than was comfortable. 'I am calling from the middle of the jungle. I have the gold, but I need some help to get out.'

With confirmation that the gold was in Abdi's hands, The Associate changed pitch a little. 'Tell me what happened. Why couldn't you get out on the transport plane?'

'Everything was going really well.' Abdi told only part of the truth of course, 'But as the plane came into land, it was shot down by the police.' That too was a lie, but a reasonable one Abdi thought.

'What police?'

'A whole great big group of them arrived, as we were emptying the vault. They had an armoured vehicle! I lost a lot of men.'

'That shouldn't have happened. I had made plans for any responses to be delayed, giving you time to get away. What did you manage to salvage?'

'Six tons. Everything that was in the vault.'

'What! How did you manage that? You just told me you are in the middle of the jungle!'

'Well yes, we loaded all the pickups we could find, and we drove it out.'

The Associate laughed heartily, the tone clearly changing now. 'Abdi, I knew you had balls, but I thought you had intelligence too! Aren't you being followed?'

'Yes, the army came to us this morning, but we ambushed them and killed them all.'

The Associate was serious again. 'You're telling me that the Army were so fast that they caught up with you this morning?'

'Yes. It's hard work to cut through parts of the jungle. Anyone following only had to follow the tracks that we made.'

'OK, and where are you heading to?'

'Well, that's where I need your help. I have nowhere to go. I'm just heading South at the moment, trying to get out of the area. I don't have any other escape plan than that.'

'OK, Abdi, stay there for a moment and I'll call you back in less than half an hour. Chin up. Rest assured, with the amount of gold you have, you're valuable to me!'

Chapter 50

September 27th, Damana Forest. Ghana.

It was actually twenty-seven minutes later when Abdi's phone rang, and he listened carefully to what The Associate told him. He hung up and then, feeling really quite relieved, he gathered in all of his people.

He stood on top of the fallen tree trunk, being careful not to slip on the moss and lichen. At this height he was well above all of his team, even though they had pulled the vehicles up into a semi-circle around him and were sitting on them. As he looked down, he could peer into the back of them, and he saw the ridiculous quantity of gold. It had lost its lustre for the moment though. There was no point in having it, while they were all still at such risk.

With the abundance of light in this part of the forest, he addressed the faces that were turned up to him, making his voice carry. 'The past few days haven't gone as planned. We've lost friends and brothers, and we'll take time to mourn their loss. But we cannot do that right here and right now. Firstly, we must find our way to safety, and we must take all of that gold with us. If we don't manage to do that, then this will have been in vain, and none of us will profit from the hardship and pain that we're feeling right now. I do, though, have good news! We're now on our way to a boat. It's still a long way away, perhaps six more days travelling like this. We have enough fuel; we have plenty of water and food. We even, thanks to our amazing success this morning, have plenty of ammunition!' There was a small cheer, but only a small one.

One of the fighters called out. 'But what about our wounded?'

'I am thankful that none of our wounds are serious, as you know,' he said tapping his own head gently, 'many of us have small wounds.'

'But this is the jungle, and wounds rot very quickly in here.'

Abdi reflected the fact that his own head was throbbing again, and if he was honest, it was feeling hot too. 'We managed to get some first aid kits from the soldiers. Let's have a look and see if we have the right antibiotics and bandages. We'll have to make do. If we get really worried, we'll send one of the pickups out with the wounded to go to

141

a settlement. Obviously, we can't do that with the gold. But we can find a way to work that.'

It seemed to appease the group, though in his heart Abdi knew that there was no way that was going to happen. There was too much at risk. He caught Cheko's eye and saw that Cheko understood that too.

Chapter 51

September 27th, 30,000 feet over DRC.

The team had been in the air for about five hours, and each member was passing the time in their own way. Tom, as usual, had his head buried in his laptop, catching up on paperwork and drafting emails. He was the only one sitting on a seat. All the other men had laid out roll mats and sleeping bags on to the floor, some were sleeping, some were just stretched out, headphones on. Raj liked listening to podcasts and Mike was plugged into an audiobook. Miguel was listening to Latin American music, eyes closed, a world away and almost swaying his hips as he lay there.

The Herc was in cargo configuration. Orange strap seats along the sides to comply with regulations, and all the pallets with kit on were down the centre of the aircraft. Thick latticed cargo nets, with strops hooked to the floor rings, covered them and kept the loads in place. All six quad bikes were parked head to toe, again strapped down. As the bikes were relatively narrow, there was lots of space beside them for the men to stretch out. In total there were sixteen passengers on board which, given the short notice, was a good size for the advance party.

They had agreed that they would try and have meals at about the same time. It helped keep the drinks cool, and cut down on the movement back and forth up and down the plane. As lunch time came around, people started to stretch, remove headphones and a bit more banter started to appear.

Raj was in a playful mood. 'Hey Mike. If you're abducted by aliens and "probed", does that make you a member of the mile high club?'

Mike grumbled back, unfocused 'What kind of a question is that? I'll fucking probe you, buddy!'

'Well, each to their own I suppose, but I don't think Charly would approve of that?'

'Approve of what?' she said as she appeared from behind a pallet.

Raj was suddenly out of his depth, his jaw dropped like a goldfish, but you couldn't keep a good man down. 'Well, Mike was offering to help me join the mile high club!'

'Really,' Charly replied, raising an eyebrow. 'Are you not a member yet?'

Raj couldn't quite work out how the conversation had switched to focus on him. 'Um no, actually I am not.'

Charly became very sincere, but with a twinkle in her eye. 'Oh, of course, is that because you only ever fly Virgin airlines?' There were guffaws of laughter from all the guys in earshot, and Mike looked especially pleased that Charly was giving as good as she got. She was on a roll and continued, the audience putty in her hands. 'So how many of you lot have joined the mile high club?'

About a third of the guys nodded knowingly. Raj tried to recover some of his honour, talking pointedly to Mike. 'What the hell are you nodding for buddy? I know you were a Navy Seal an' all, but she means with a woman!'

More laughter followed but Charly came to Mike's rescue yet again. 'Mike, do you see that door up there near the cockpit?'

'Yep.'

'Well, that's the aircrew rest cabin, for long haul flights. It has a bed in it.' Charly batted her eye lashes. Mike was incredulous. Everyone else, except Raj, was beginning to smirk as Charly continued. 'I'm on my lunch break, and right now we're at thirty thousand feet.'

'OK, and….' Mike stopped uncertainly.

'Well, that means we're over five miles high at the moment. Feel like renewing your membership?'

Mike was grinning, Raj was apoplectic, 'What! No fucking way! I take the piss out of him, and he ends up getting laid!'

Charly had one more shot however, 'Raj. Darling. Go suck on a carrot stick. Mike's coming to have some dessert.' She grabbed Mike by the hand, pulled him up off the floor and they walked up to the cabin with cat-calls following them all the way.

Chapter 52

September 27th, Damana Forest. Ghana.

It was night-time but Abdi and his men were still driving. They were moving at walking pace still, with a guide in front, and the vehicles using side lights only. There had been a lot of scrapes and dinks, and very few of the pickups had windscreens that were still intact, but morale was still OK. The battle yesterday morning felt a long way away now, but throughout the day the group continued to have their nerves tested, hearing helicopters flying above them. Abdi couldn't be sure, but he felt as though the overflights were getting less and less often. Certainly nothing appeared to be focusing on their area.

Where they could, men were sleeping in the back of the vehicles, or in the passenger seats. Both were uncomfortable, but their level of fatigue helped overcome the bumps.

Cheko and Abdi were sitting in the back of one wagon chatting quietly. Holding on to the sides when needed, as vehicles tested their suspension to the max. It felt completely normal now, that they were sitting on about fifty million dollars' worth of lumpy metal.

Cheko was feeling anxious and didn't want the conversation to be overheard. 'Abdi. Do you really have a plan to get us out? Is there really going to be a boat?'

Abdi knew that this was a dangerous conversation. If Cheko didn't have any faith, then he would simply kill Abdi, and take full command. He had enough men with him for that to be a walkover. Cheko could just split the vehicles up, send them all in different directions and guarantee that at least some of them wouldn't get caught. He sat there for a moment, in his dripping wet, dirty clothes, thinking. His throbbing head made it difficult, but he focused. 'Cheko, it's been a hard couple of days. Those bastards in the mine had more fight than we thought they would, and if the police hadn't come so quickly, we would have dealt with that problem before we lost our airplane.'

'Could of, would of, Abdi.' Cheko was looking serious. 'I don't want to hear that there "might" be a boat…'

'I know there's a boat. The boss told me he would organise one. He sounded really cross that his government contact hadn't done his job and delayed all the security responses. Personally, I'm more pissed at the mine manager. He didn't tell me about that armoured vehicle. That nearly killed us all.'

'That's true.'

'Actually, I don't think I thanked you for saving my life. It was a great shot. Thank you.'

'That's alright, you would have done the same for me, I'm sure. But that doesn't change the fact that it feels like we're on our own here.'

'But that's the whole point,' said Abdi with feeling. 'We are on our own for now, and that's how I prefer it. Everyone else that we've had to rely on for this job so far has let us down. We're back in control of our own destiny. We have a couple of choices. We can either head for the river, and the boat that the boss is organising, or we can do our own thing. Your opinion is important to me on this.'

'Do you really think there'll be a boat?'

'Yes, I'm certain of it. But even if there weren't one organised. When we get to the river, one of us goes and buys a boat there and then, for gold. That has to be a better option than driving on the roads, where there'll be roadblocks and security checks. Alternatively, we could try and get to an airfield, but I just don't see how we could load all that gold onto a plane with no one noticing. With a boat, we can load it up on a quiet riverbank somewhere and then we can go all the way downstream to the coast. At the coast we can find a ship, and then we're away. Then we'll be wealthy men!'

They sat in silence for a while. Abdi let Cheko come to his own mind. It was important that he did so and felt that he was a key part of the decision. Cheko would have to keep his men in line, or not, if that was Allah's will.

Chapter 53

The old military airfield at Tamale was a ghost town. The tarmac of the airstrip was crumbling, and the long slow process of nature reclaiming it had started. Small tufts of stubborn weeds were beginning to break through the runway like a sporadic green rash. Concrete buildings were coming apart, paintwork, long neglected was peeling away under the pressure of some kind of white mould. The hangars, large, brick sided, with rusting tin roofs, were mausoleums to a long dead air force. Six sad looking 1950's fighter jets were entombed there, tyres perished and flat, cockpits cracked, fuselages covered in guano. Birds or bats, it didn't matter, it was all the same shit.

Tom and his team had arrived a couple of hours before. The Herc had refuelled in Accra, and they had received a message that they could fly directly to Tamale. The small city of Tamale was seven hundred kilometres away from Accra, and the airfield was tucked into the jungle about thirty kilometres outside the city. The whole site was discreetly hidden and only those in the immediate area knew that it had ever existed. The Herc had made a bumpy landing as it came in low over the surrounding jungle. The plane had pulled up on a wide dusty dispersal, parking near one of the hangars where a nearly new, blue 4x4 Toyota Landcruiser was parked.

As the rear ramp came down, the guys took deep breaths of moist jungle air, and then stretching their legs, walked out to take a look around at their new home. Tom had gone straight over to Glenn, leaving Mike and Raj to supervise the unloading. The quad bikes and trailers came into their own, as did the portable pallet truck. All the big-ticket items were easily moved into the hangar and were parked in an area that had obviously been recently swept and slooshed with water.

The near end of the hangar appeared to have the best roof above it. At the far end, roof panels had fallen to the ground, leaving tooth like gaps in the ceiling. The hangar doors were rickety but, with a bit of effort, still worked and so they could be closed. At minimum, the doors would keep out the rain if needed. Glenn had obviously been able to rig up a generator in the short time he had been there. The huge flood light bulbs in the roof high above them had long failed, but a new string of smaller bulbs hung all the way around the walls at head height. They created a low halo in the living space, which faded slowly as you looked further up towards the high roof. There were extension cables that hung from the bulb strings down to the floor, with UK plug sockets in, so that the team could power its devices.

With some simple organisation, all the stores went on one side of the hangar, and all the camp cots and personal belongings on the other. An area between two of the old jets was set up with some trestle tables and some field kitchen equipment. Pilots of old would be horrified to see the wings being used as umbrellas to keep the bird crap off the food tables. With the newly-arrived aircraft unpacked and parked up for the night, the team got on with some personal administration: getting sleeping bags out, charging phones, making a brew.

Mike and Raj had put their camp cots adjacent in the line and were sorting their kit out, sitting on their beds, rummaging in their bags. Mike, who still had a grin on his face, kept adjusting his crotch, scratching absently.

'Dude, have you got to do that in front of me!' exclaimed Raj.

'What, ah, well, I was just thinking that that was the best in-flight entertainment I've ever had on a Herc.'

'Shut up, man.'

But Mike continued, 'I was thinking that normally, on a Herc, with all that vibration and stuff, you just get a bit of convoy cock, but man, that was the real deal.'

Raj couldn't help but bite. 'Convoy cock! What's that?'

'It's a phrase I picked up from the Brits. You know when you're doing a long-distance drive in the back of an army truck, the vibration, the bumping around. You can't help but get a boner. Hence, convoy cock!'

'Seriously dude, sometimes I worry about you. First you're talking about probing me and then you're admitting that every time you got in the back of a truck with a whole bunch of British dudes, you kept getting a hard on!'

'Ha, ha. Well, you asked.'

Throughout the conversation Raj had been getting a little more agitated, rummaging around in his bag. 'Fuck, I think I forgot it.'

'Forgot what, buddy?'

'My CamelBak!'

Mike gave a great big grin. 'You forgot your... Are you kidding me? We are going into one of the hottest, sweatiest, environments in the world and you forgot your drinking water system!' Mike laughed his head off.

'It's not funny, dude!'

'Yeah, it is, it's hilarious. Hey guys! Raj forgot his CamelBak!'

There were lots of laughs, but Raj was fuming. One of the men at the back shouted. 'Raj, you're going to have to use plastic water bottles, man. You're going to crinkle all the way buddy!'

Mike added to the call and in mock seriousness added. 'Raj, you know I love you mate, but I am not going to go into the jungle, and even potential combat, next to a guy whose kit is going *crinkle crinkle* every time he moves!'

As Mike continued to laugh, Raj, in the full knowledge that he was going to be the butt of all jokes on this trip, quietly told him to piss off.

Chapter 54

September 27th, Tamale. Ghana.

Whilst the team were getting the hangar sorted out, Tom was having a chat with Glenn. They hadn't met before, so there were the usual introductions. Glenn had originally served in one of the Scottish Regiments and had retired as a Warrant Officer. He had a talent for logistics and had rapidly gone on to a career with a mining consultancy, working in Ghana. He had learned the ropes there for several years before setting up on his own. Glenn was now in his mid-fifties with a bulldog-like face. He didn't like to admit it, but he had also developed a bulldog-like belly too, and some of the jowls.

Other things you noticed, that were really obvious when you met him, were that he had a very strong Scottish accent and that he was ginger. Offensively so. He was obviously proud of that fact and had long ginger hair, tied back in a ponytail and a ginger goatee. For temperament, he was the kind of guy you wanted on your side in a bar brawl. Amiable, slow to anger, but ferocious when riled.

Tom had already thanked Glenn for the rapid response and setup, and Glen was in the process of updating Tom on the progress from the last twelve hours. Tom had been in the air for most of that time and hadn't been able to download his emails in Accra because of some data roaming problem or other. Tom hadn't come across someone who spoke in such pronounced Scottish slang, in so long a time that he was having to really concentrate on what was being said.

'Reet man. The Turdis's wi' all arrive tomorro'.'

'Sorry, the Turdis's?'

'Aye man, the Turdis's. Ye ken? Fro' Dr Who! The bogs, the lavvies? Oh, man,' putting on a false English accent, 'the Toilets!'

Tom nodded, 'Got it.'

''Till then, tha boys 'll ha' te tek a dump oot thar in the bush.' Glenn paused making sure Tom understood before continuing. 'Ahm also expectin' satellite internet, the fud caterin' company, sum large wata' tankers, sum tents, and sum shuwa systems.'

Tom looked confused again.

'Showaa systems' grinned Glenn. 'Noo, 'ere's a bunch o' burrners wi' sim cards an' a couple o' dongles fer data.'

Tom nodded his head, bemused.

'Tha caterin' cumpnaay is gonna bring loadsa snacks, sum pop' an' a cleanen' leddy or two.'

Tom didn't get all of that, but let Glenn continue as he was obviously highly competent.

'So that teks care o' tha logistics. D'ya ken?'

'Aye' said Tom getting into it now.

'Oh! Dae ye talk Scots!' beamed Glenn, clearly enjoying himself.

Tom had the measure of him now though and replied, staring him in the eye, 'No, and do you speak any English?'

Glenn roared in laughter. 'Yool do, pal! Tha's funny! Noo, aboot yer helicopter. She's due in tomorro' mornin' an' will be based 'ere throo oot. Ye ken brief tha' pilot tomorro' mornin' after ye have ha' sum kip.'

Tom's head was spinning a little, especially after a long flight, but he was bright enough to have one clever idea. 'That's all excellent, thank you. It's really good work. Tomorrow I will introduce you to Raj, one of my team leaders. He will be the main interface with you on the remaining camp logistics.

'Nae problem. Oh yes, an' won more thang. Max ask'd me ta gi' ye' a wodge o' cash in local shreddies.'

'Shreddies?'

'Aye. S'actually' Cedi's, boot we all call 'em Shreddies. Anywho, this is ten thoosand quid's worth as requested.'

Tom took the offered holdall full of cash. It was large and bulky, not helped by the fact that the largest note in it was two hundred Cedis, about twenty British pounds. Still, he thought, after he had said "Bye fer noo" to Glenn. They had managed it. One of the fastest and largest mobilisations that they had done for a while. Tomorrow the work would really begin.

Chapter 55

September 28th, Tamale. Ghana.

It was mid-morning in Tamale and the team had been up since just after dawn. Mike had a mug of coffee and Raj had made some kind of herbal brew. They had sat on a wooden bench outside the hangar door eating some fruit left over from the flight yesterday. They had watched the sun come up over the trees that surrounded the airstrip and heard all the chatter of the birdlife, as it woke to a new day. During the night, the humidity had settled down a little, as had the heat, but it was still very uncomfortable and a rapid climate adjustment was needed.

All sorts of kit and equipment had been arriving throughout the morning and Glenn had been busy getting the camp set up. He was in his element as a former logistics manager and was highly efficient, except for when the local suppliers couldn't understand what he was saying. Even though the official national language was English, in the remote areas, a lot more local dialects were spoken, so there was plenty of space for confusion. Certainly, none of the locals spoke Scots. Luckily, Glenn had the right temperament, and treated everyone with respect, so with a laugh and a joke here and there he got the job done. Tom had liked what he had seen, and made a mental note to mention to Max that Glenn was obviously the kind of operator that the company wanted on its books; even if he was ginger!

Charly and the Herc pilot had left first thing, heading back to Nairobi to pick up more kit and personnel. The search helicopter had arrived about half an hour ago in a swirl of dust. It had come into the hover near the hangar, but not so near that its downdraft would upset things. The helicopter was a twin-engine Eurocopter AS350, painted black and yellow and with a large pod, mounted on a protruding gimble under the nose.

Mike had started getting busy with his role of pre-deployment preparation. He had a group of the men sorting the equipment into piles. The hangar floor looked like a bomb had gone off. There was kit everywhere. Boxes were being unpacked, kit checked again, radios being tested. Basically, now they had time, the equipment was being sorted into must haves and nice to haves. Everything had to be completely portable, or at least portable on the trailer of one of the quadbikes, which couldn't carry a huge amount.

In the near distance was sporadic gun fire. The far end of the airfield had been allocated as a weapons range and a couple of men at a time went up there to zero their weapons, longs and shorts. From then on, they felt much more comfortable. There wasn't a huge amount of surplus ammunition though, so it was no free-for-all. They used just enough to confirm a good grouping.

Raj, on the other hand, had been working with Glenn, organising amongst a host of other things, how to get the two remaining quad bikes serviced properly. Tom had observed at least a couple of occasions where he saw Raj looking completely flummoxed at something that Glenn had said, and Tom had laughed inwardly. Now, though, it was time for a quick team meeting. Tom wanted to have a chat with the new helicopter pilot and needed Mike and Raj with him for it.

David was from South Africa, the rainbow nation. He spoke with a distinct Afrikaans accent and called everyone sir or ma'am. Not necessarily out of respect, but because it had been beaten into him as a child along with every other student at public school. He had paid his way through university by working part time, and his hard work had been rewarded when he was offered a flying scholarship with one of the airlines. David had qualified on a number of rotary types, but after a few years found that something of the passion just wasn't there anymore. He had become disillusioned with flying politicians or wealthy businesspeople from A to B. Fortunately, his line manager at the time had recognised this. She had offered him an opportunity to qualify on their newest piece of kit in support of a new anti-poaching contract in the Ivory Coast. So, David had learnt how to use one of the most modern sensors available and was flying on behalf of the government, looking for poachers that were decimating the African forest elephant population.

The four men were sitting in the shade of the hangar, at one of the trestle tables. Tom had unrolled an ordinance survey map of the North of the country. He also had a laptop open with Google Maps on screen. Using a marker pen he had circled the location of the mine on the paper map, and the location of their forward operating base. Other than those marks, there was a lot of green out there.

Each of the men had a plastic one litre water bottle in front of them, which doubled up to keep the map flat. They were talking through how the search side of the project would go. Tom had opened the meeting with how finding the thieves was going to be crucial and that there were probably only a few days within which to do it. He asked David to talk through the aircraft's capability and his ideas for the search.

David's Afrikaans accent was strong. 'Let's start with the good news, brothers. That dome on the front of the aircraft is a multi-function sensor. It has both a thermal imaging camera and a seriously cool new prototype LiDAR sensor.'

Raj was impressed, 'Really? But that's only in research papers at the moment.'

'The benefits of working in the counter-poaching space. We have some very serious grant money, great scientists, and really good sponsorship. This kit is being trialled by our team to see if it does what the designers suggest.'

Tom asked, 'What? It's got good enough resolution to find people in amongst the trees?'

'No. But it is good enough to find vehicles, and you tell me that the thieves are all driving pickup trucks, right?

'Correct.'

'Well, elephants are only a little larger and we're having success in locating them.'

Raj continued, a little dubious. 'And it can see through the tree canopy?'

'So that depends. Thin leaves, etc, or rather the tiny gaps between them, then yes. If it's very dense, then no. And that's the same problem with the thermal kit. We've found that the thermal kit works best at night, when the top tree cover has cooled down a little. If we try and use that thermal during the day, we get a lot of heat blooming.'

Mike hadn't said much so far, and he drained his water bottle, squeezing it tightly as he went, making perhaps a touch too much noise. Raj looked at him suspiciously, before asking David, 'So basically you're saying that you should do most of your flying at night, but you have confidence that your equipment can detect them?'

'Yes, if, and it's a big if, we can actually fly over the part of the jungle where the thieves are moving. Do we have any idea where they're heading?'

Tom replied, 'We think they're moving South from the mine. They left in a hurry under fire from the Southern side and we don't think that they had the capacity to do that as a decoy. But, simply put, we don't know where they may be going.'

Mike finally contributed, in his deep base. 'If I had that much gold there's no way I would try to take it North from there. Burkina Faso is having a really tough time at the moment. Too many insurgents and too many security forces hunting for them. A convoy of pickups would stick out like a turd in a swimming pool.'

David reflected for a moment. 'OK, so let's assume South. We have to select a direction for the first part of the search anyway. Next question. How far could they have gone through the jungle, in heavily-laden vehicles in a period of what… a couple-plus days? My best estimate, thinking about the poachers I track, is perhaps a hundred kilometres, but it could be as much as a hundred and fifty, or as low as eighty or so. It all depends on how much secondary there is for them, and if they have the right kit for pulling vehicles out of difficult situations.'

There were nods around the table. Mike was still fiddling with his water bottle. Raj leant over and gently pried it from his fingers, before getting up and putting it in the bin. 'So, let's bank on a worst case of one fifty. I think I'll fly an East to West grid pattern. Starting at the maximum distance and then slowly moving it North. With the kit on, I'll fly at a couple of thousand feet and that will give me a good scanning distance with the LiDAR. Then if there's anything interesting, I'll come down and try and get a better image on thermal.'

With the basic principles agreed, David left to go and do his flight planning and to program his search pattern into his systems. He was then going to try and get some sleep before flying for most of that night.

Chapter 56

September 28th, Tamale. Ghana.

Tom, Mike and Raj remained at the table continuing the conversation further. Tom had picked up some salt and pepper shakers and was using them as simple icons. He had laid a long bread knife at the one-hundred-and-fifty-kilometre mark from the mine, and a wooden spoon at the eighty-kilometre line. Therefore, if they were correct that the thieves had gone South, then they had to be somewhere between the two brackets on the map.

Tom asked an open question. 'Thoughts, guys. Everything hinges on us getting this search right. What do you think about them having come South?

Mike had the stronger military planning mind between him and Raj and he started first. 'So, looking at the terrain. There are a couple of obvious obstacles. For a start this long river to the East. You can guarantee that the police will be on the few bridges that there are, and if these guys have got any sense, they'll stay well away from roads and bridges. Those rivers look too large for pickup trucks to get across and too small for boats to get up. We've already discounted the North, for good reasons. That leaves West, or South.'

They paused for a moment all looking at the map and Mike continued. 'On the West, there are so many roads, so many built up areas, and then you hit the border with Ivory Coast. My gut tells me they wouldn't go that way. Raj, mate, what do you think?'

Raj was nodding his head, 'Me, I think that they'll be doing one of two things. They'll either wait it out in the middle of that huge national reserve there, Moyale Forest by the look of it. Or they'll be making a dash for the South.'

'Good,' said Tom. 'Now, we know that they didn't have this as their main plan. They left camp in a hurry when the plane crashed. So, they can't have a lot of supplies with them. I think that discounts living it out in the jungle for a month. Unless of course they're going to make a lot of noise and steal from local villages. Let's focus on the Southerly exit. The big question is, where are they going and what are they going to do when they get there?

This time it was Raj's mind to the front. His more dubious past meant that he had probably spent more time running and escaping from a hunting force than the others. 'I think they're making for the sea. Once on a boat they can get clear. A boat has lots of places to hide it and a boat can take the weight. They might have planned to fly it out originally, but that was when no one would have even been aware, and the plane would have been long gone. Now, they can't get a plane into an airstrip, park up the trucks and just unload. It's too conspicuous. The other way is out by road, and you can bet your bottom dollar that all border checks are going to be in overdrive. Again, they could just get it somewhere and hole up, perhaps a safe house, an old warehouse, but without much food my money is that they'll try to get out quickly.'

Mike sucked his teeth, 'Surely they won't try and get it to a big port? They'll want to avoid the roads.'

'Agreed, but I think they'll try and get onto a river as soon as possible. Float it down to the coast, get rid of all those pickups. Then when they get down to the sea, they'll find somewhere discreet and transfer it all onto a much bigger ship. Then they just sail it away.'

Tom looked at the map in detail. 'If that's their plan, then there is one really obvious place where they'll try to do that. Look at that.' Tom pointed to the vast Lake Volta which filled almost the entire Eastern side of the country. Hundreds of kilometres long, and a hundred kilometres wide at its widest point, it was an obvious route.'

'But there's a huge dam at the Southern end isn't there?' asked Raj.

Tom looked at Google earth and zoomed in to see that it was indeed the case. There was no way a river boat could get past that dam. 'OK,' he adjusted. 'Perhaps they use the river and the lake for a few hundred kilometres and then cross-deck the gold onto vehicles?'

'I think we're reaching too much,' said Mike. 'I like the idea of them trying to get to the lake, where they can meet a boat, but what they do after that is just too hard to guess at this point.'

'You're probably right. Let's focus on the nearest objective, them coming South, and potentially making for the nearest point of the lake. Let's use the photos and images we have and see if we can identify any potential jungle drop-off points for us. We'll need to drop into the Jungle ahead of them to have the best chance of success. When we find them, it should give us a good confirmation of where they're heading.'

157

'Assuming that they aren't lost and actually know where they're going.' grimaced Raj.

Chapter 57

September 28th, Damana Forest. Ghana.

If Abdi really thought about it, there were fewer helicopters flying overhead now. The past twenty-four hours had been mostly uneventful, and good progress had been made heading South. That had just changed though and now Abdi had a problem. They had come across quite a wide stream. For such a simple obstacle, there had been much sucking of teeth before they had decided how they wanted to cross. The stream bed was deep, and in places rocky. Abdi had sent one team downstream to the East and one upstream to the West. Both had come back quite quickly. The Eastern team said that the stream only widened out, became boggy, and made a crossing even less likely. The Western team said that there was a place where a crossing was possible, but some work would have to be done.

Abdi had taken the whole convoy ten minutes upstream and looked at the site. Here the stream was perhaps two metres wide, steep sided and quite fast moving. There were a lot of boulders and rocks nearby and it looked like it would be possible to make a crossing point. Everyone disembarked and started to collect materials. Sturdy tree branches were hauled into place, rocks and boulders were shunted, but ultimately there was a problem. The faster they made the dam, like children everywhere, they discovered the higher the water rose. The dam they were building had to be wide enough, and sturdy enough to carry the weight of fully laden pickups. It would be catastrophic if one attempted the crossing and rolled whilst doing so. In order to take the weight, the construction had to be really solid. But if it was made solid, then the water filled up faster above the dam and made the riverbank, muddy and slippery. The water had to go somewhere. They had tried several times to build a dam wall sturdy enough, testing it even just by walking on the top. They couldn't build anything near solid enough. In his frustration Abdi became even more irate. 'Cheko! This isn't working. We need to do something different.'

Cheko, who was standing in the stream, up to his waist in cold water looked at him. 'Eh man, what do you suggest?'

'That's just it, I don't know! All I do know is that this isn't working. Does anyone have another plan?'

Surprisingly, it was one of the drone pilots who came to the rescue. 'Actually, I do.'

Abdi looked at him coolly. 'Go on?'

'Instead of building up, I think we should dig a ramp down to the riverbed, and then a ramp up on the other side. The stream itself looks like it is down to the bedrock. So, we make a gentle slope and then just drive across.'

Cheko pushed his feet downwards in the cool water. 'It feels solid to me. And we have lots of shovels in the vehicles. Let's do it.'

After that, it took less than an hour. They moved a little upstream and the slopes were built. As the mud was dug, it was thrown into the water to wash away downstream. Tree roots were the main problem, interrupting the digging. The men had to hack them away using both shovels and machetes. Hands became even more blistered and sore. Eventually though, when all was ready, the stream bed had been widened considerably, which helped to reduce the height of the water. It made the slopes treacherously muddy underfoot though. A technical drove across first, the water coming up to only just above the tyres. With the heavier vehicles, carrying the gold, it was a nerve-racking moment that simply evaporated as the first one breezed across. The last pickup slid a little on the climb back out of the river, as it mounted the muddy bank made wet by all the vehicles before it. However, with a bit of a push and a shove, with the wheels spinning mud the vehicle made it. With a cheer of a job well done, Abdi and his team were quickly on their way again.

Chapter 58

September 28th, Tamale. Ghana.

Inside the hangar, it was pandemonium. Men were shouting, running around, tables and beds were upturned, food had been thrown everywhere. It was only when someone fired their pistol that order started to return. The problem? Baboons.

The troop of baboons had been watching with interest the humans take over their home, for the last day or so. When the smells of food, and the sight of shiny things had become too much for them, they bravely ran into the hangar, when they felt there were no humans around. In fact, the men had all been sitting at the far end of the hangar having a briefing and at first no one noticed when the primates arrived. These baboons were muscular monkeys, up to a metre and a half from nose to tail, and the big males weighed up to thirty kilograms. The lead males and the matriarchs would happily charge at the front of their pack, yellowing fangs bared. A big male, if hungry or diseased, would charge a human, no questions asked, if there was food available.

The troop of thirty or so monkeys had charged straight towards the kitchen area and started grabbing whatever they could. It was the crash of tin plates which made the team suddenly aware of them. Screeches and calls, tails raised above bare, pink and diseased-looking arses. Every monkey for itself, trying to grab what it could and escape.

When the shot was fired, the noise was deafening inside the hangar and the monkeys started to run. On the way out, one that hadn't yet grabbed any food saw something on Raj's bed. It grabbed a couple of items and legged it.

'No, no, no, you fucker!' shouted Raj as he ran towards his bed. 'Agh, you bastard!'

Mike caught up with Raj at the door of the hangar, where they both watched the baboon in the distance examining his loot.

'What did he get, buddy?' asked Mike.

'That little shit, he stole my protein bars and a packet of wet wipes!'

Mike looked at him trying not to laugh. 'Your wet wipes?'

'Yes! And my protein bars.' Raj was indignant.

'So let me get this straight. You haven't got your water system, and now you don't have any wet wipes either?' Mike was trying really hard not to laugh.

Raj turned to him, saw the smirk. 'It's not funny!'

As they watched, about a hundred metres away, the baboon was attacked by a larger male. The screeching battle lasted a few minutes, with the original thief battling hard to keep hold of one of the items. When the battle was over, after the mauling, the thief was left, sitting on the tarmac. He was holding the wet wipe packet in one hand, and with two fingers on the other, was pulling them out of the packet one at a time. He gave each one a sniff, and then let go of it to fly away in the wind. The baboon with the protein bars sat there eating one smugly.

Later that evening, well after dark, David took off in the Eurocopter flying on NVG. Mike and Raj were standing by the hangar doors as they watched the aircraft lift into the hover, and then tilt forward transitioning down the runway, before flying North.

Once the noise of the rotors died away, Raj said, 'I do think, that if I hadn't had a mis-spent youth, I would have liked to be a helicopter pilot.'

'It's probably quite a good job,' said Mike, 'though there is no way I would fly millionaires around. Too many demands, and flying from A to B with passengers, it just wouldn't be my thing. The guys I used to work with said that if you were going to do that job, you needed to do something with the platform.'

'You mean like combat, or search and rescue?'

'Yes, or even air ambulance, or police work. I think that would be quite interesting. The flying is second nature, and you use your skillset to solve problems.'

They turned away from the doors and started to head towards their bedspaces. Raj reflected as they walked. 'I like the fact that as a pilot, like David there, you're completely in control of both yourself and the machine. Off he goes now, to do his job. It's his plan, his equipment and his experience.'

They stood for a moment, beside their camp cots. Most of the other men were lying down, reading a book, or listening to music. Mike commented, 'Yes, he's completely in control. If he forgets anything, its entirely his fault, his responsibility.'

'Yes! Perhaps that's it.' Raj sat down on his bed, only to suddenly leap up again when it made a loud crunching noise. 'What the...' He picked up his sleeping bag and turned it upside down. 'Oh, you bastards!' he shouted as a pile of empty water bottles fell to the floor bouncing in all directions making a racket. All those innocent men who had been ignoring them suddenly started laughing.

'Crinkle, crinkle, buddy.' Mike grinned.

Chapter 59

September 29th, Tamale. Ghana

The following morning and the airfield was a hive of activity again. The cargo plane, arriving mid-morning, had brought an inflatable medical clinic and a medical team, fully capable of stabilising serious trauma. That team had been given an adjacent hangar and they were busy unloading their equipment and setting up. The simple fact that it was there was a huge reassurance to everyone on site. Irrespective of the potential for combat, working in the jungle was dangerous and knowing that a doctor was on full standby was a considerable morale booster.

The inflatable clinic really was just that. It had several low-pressure fans that constantly pumped air into the structure, like a kid's bouncy castle, but with several rooms. All the equipment and machinery that went into it came in high quality foam-lined, hard-shelled Peli cases. Everything from portable X-ray machines to complete operating systems were unpacked and carried inside the structure.

At the same time, out on the dispersal, David was doing a walkaround of the Eurocopter combined with some basic maintenance. The black and yellow helicopter had been out all night. David had come back twice to refuel, noisily waking those in the hangar, but the ground party had been highly efficient. A couple of jerry-rigged flood lights had helped shed light on the large drums filled with aviation fuel. A small electrical pump, plugged into the aircraft systems had helped transfer the fuel quickly into the fuel tanks. In total, David had flown more than seven hours, much of it on NVG, and he was tired. He hadn't seen anything of the thieves, but his equipment had picked up several elephants as he overflew the Moyale National Park. David felt that he had covered the area between the mine site and the thieves' expected escape route thoroughly. He was disappointed not to find them but knew that he would get up again tonight to keep searching. He wanted to check everything was in good order with the aircraft in daylight, before he went to get some sleep.

With the camp mostly coming together, Raj had taken a moment to himself. He felt he was losing his grip a little with all the piss-taking and he was after a little revenge. Off to the side of the hangar there was a crumbled old building. It was so old and run down that it had started to collapse in places. The walls had fallen in one corner and there was a considerable pile of rubble. Raj was poking around with a forked stick, whilst in a tree above him several baboons were watching him interestedly.

It didn't take him long to find what he wanted. A beautiful sand racer snake hiding in a crevice. It had a bright yellow belly all along its one-meter length. Then, a number of tide lines where its markings switched through several shades of brown, until along the spine it was a deep chocolaty colour. The snake was only a few centimetres thick, but it was long, elegant, and fast. Raj had to work quickly, gently trapping the head of the snake with the fork of the stick, watching the body writhing, unable to break free. He stepped in closer and deftly picked the snake up around the back of the head. Once under control, he released the stick and let the long body curl around his forearm. The snakes mouth opened wide, all pink and moist. Small sharp fangs pointed backwards from the top of its mouth. It looked like a fearsome, but beautiful creature, but Raj had been reading up on them and he knew that this one was only mildly venomous. With the snake secure around his arm, and careful not to hurt it, he went off in search of Mike.

Mike was standing chatting with Tom. Tom with his Desperate Dan jawline, already showing five o'clock shadow, was standing leaning his thin frame against the hangar wall in the shade. Those who knew Tom well, knew that he didn't smile very often with his mouth, but his eyes always told a different story. Mirth hid in there waiting to be let out. He saw Raj approaching with a snake around his arm, and to his credit he hardly paused his conversation with Mike. Raj with a finger to his lips approached from behind, while Tom kept speaking.

"So, it's still touch and go on the Chinook. The office is really trying hard to get it here tomorrow, but it's a long way away. I want it here immediately, but more than that, I want it here without fail, so there is no point in the crew risking everything and ending up crashing into the jungle somewhere.'

Raj was right up behind Mike now and he held the snake, with its mouth open, right up to the back of his head. Using a moist finger, he gently wriggled it into the back of Mike's collar. Mike idly scratched as Raj pulled his hand away. Raj did it again. Mike spun around, uncertain, to find himself eyeball to eyeball with the sand snake. He let out a very unmanly yelp. 'Yaaaah!'

Those who had been in the hangar and who had seen the play, started laughing whilst Mike recovered. 'Dude, you fucking know I hate snakes!'

'Really buddy? No, I had no idea,' said Raj innocently, waving the snake towards Mike as he tried to back away.

'Oh man, take it away will ya. You've proved your point.'

'Of course, no problem, I'm just going to go and find a nice place for it to sleep. Is your sleeping bag free?'

'What! Why would you even say that?'

'Well, now every time you put your feet into your bag you're going to wonder if I've put a snake in it.' Raj was grinning as Mike shook his head and rolled his eyes.

Tom nearly cracked a smile too, as Raj continued, 'You know, in the bush, in Australia they say that if you don't want a poisonous snake to enter your bed, you should keep a non-venomous one in there.'

'What? No friggin' way am I doing that! Anyway, haven't you been bitten by one?' said Mike, still unhappy but morbidly interested.

'Well, there was one time way out in the bush in India, when I got bitten on the end of my thumb. I wasn't even messing around; I was just careless. I reached down to put my boots on in the morning and a juvenile saw-scaled viper bit me. The problem was, I was in the middle of nowhere, no anti-venom, no doctor. I was very worried, but luckily, because it was the end of my thumb there was very little flesh so not a huge amount of venom. The guide I was with, quick as a flash, tied his belt around my arm, took his knife out, and sliced my thumb wide open!' Raj held up his thumb for Mike and Tom to see. He did all the things that the first aid training says not to do. 'He popped my thumb in his mouth and sucked. Blood, venom, you name it. Suck, spit, suck, spit. Anyway, after that came the weird part. He sat me down on the ground, bandaged my thumb up and put a blanket over me. Then this little man built a fire, all the way around me in a big circle. He made me stay inside that circle for two hours, cooking me I tell you! I was so dammed hot and sweaty and all that time he was dancing and chanting around me. The only time he stopped was to pass me another cup of boiling hot tea. But it was the oddest thing! I got no paralysis, no shortness of breath in all that time. Oh, man, but there was some pain though and I was really afraid, delirious. Anyway, eventually he let me out of the circle and told me to drink lots of water. Sure, I felt a bit ill for a couple of weeks, but given how serious it all was, I consider a small scratch on the end of my thumb a small price to pay.'

Mike was still cringing, so it was Tom that spoke, 'Raj, that's a great story. Really glad that you told us that one before we go into the bush.'

Chapter 60

September 29th, Damana Forest. Ghana.

As David sat in the cockpit, going through his start-up routine, he paused for a moment to adjust his posture in the seat. He shoved his backside deep into the beaded seat cover and readjusted his feet on the foot pedals. Dusk had fallen, but he knew it would be fully dark by the time he reached the start point for his search tonight. It was only about fifteen minutes' flying time to the North and tomorrow night the search area would be even closer. As he started the rotors, and allowed them to spool up, he double checked his instrument display. He trusted inherently the glass cockpit in front of him and the onboard computers. Well, almost trusted, but not completely. Helicopter pilots that flew for a full career, successfully, had an inner trait that was always expecting something to go wrong. A suspicious mind that was constantly alert and ready to intervene. Unlike fixed-wing aircraft, pretty stable flying platforms, helicopters were inherently unstable. Take your eye off one thing and another thing started to veer out of normal limits. A helicopter pilot was constantly dancing, always adjusting the controls, with the input made on one having an impact on another. What you couldn't afford to do was switch off. If something went wrong in a helicopter, rapid reactions and the right drills would save your life. It was part of the fun of flying.

David reached up to the top of his helmet and lowered his Gen-4 night vision goggles so that they fitted correctly in front of his eyes. If he looked under them, he could see his aircraft systems and if he looked into them, he saw the world around him in a green speckly hue. At that moment, his goggles had shut down a little. There was still too much ambient light. The very last residues of sunset, and leakage from the lit hangars. The goggles would soon settle down though. With a gentle pull of the collective and a slight play with the cyclic, he lifted into the hover. His feet worked the pedals to keep his heading without any conscious thought. There in the hover he did systems checks and, after a quick tail check, turned into wind and pushed the cyclic forward. With a gentle pull of the collective, the aircraft moved faster and faster into forward flight. With a slight surge of lift, like a racehorse responding, he applied more power and gained height and speed.

Once he had cleared the treetops at the end of the runway, he turned North onto the heading shown on the display by his navigation system. As he gained height above the forest, on his way up to two thousand feet, the lights of the city of Tamale were off to his right at the two o'clock position. It was a clear night, the moon was about three quarters, and there was not a cloud in the sky. He looked at Tamale through his goggles and again, the light pollution contributed to less visual acuity through his goggles. He flicked the goggles back up onto his helmet, electing to fly using the mark one eyeball. As he did so, the world changed colour again. Inside the cockpit, the computer screens gave a clear image of aircraft systems. But outside it was now black below, the jungle was ominous beneath him and yet every small village or town gave off a dome of yellow light. Plenty enough for him to navigate at this height.

David stayed in the cruise until he reached the start point for his grid search. Tonight, he was flying fifty-kilometre legs, then offsetting five kilometres North and flying the return leg. The result was that he ended up five kilometres North of his original position. His sensors covered the arcs below him as he flew. They were set to give a tone if anything interesting was detected. He was going to keep that search pattern up all night, only pausing to refuel. He double checked his surveillance system, ensured it was working in dual LiDAR and thermal mode and turned onto his first heading. He flicked his goggles back down over his eyes as he turned away from the town and settled into the routine. It was going to be a long night. David briefly reflected that realistically he needed to be successful either tonight or tomorrow. After that, with the distance the thieves would be travelling each day, the net would be spread too wide. Like looking for an ant in a cornfield.

Chapter 61

September 30th, Damana Forest. Ghana.

It had been a couple of days since Abdi had spoken to The Associate, and when the opportunity came, with another break in the trees, Abdi pulled out his satellite phone. Truth be told, Abdi was getting a little worried again: vehicle fuel was going to be tight. There was still a long way to go and whilst they still had some fuel drums left, there was only so much available. He was close to leaving the two technicals behind. He wanted the weapons, but he could reduce his fuel usage by a third if he could leave them. Currently, they were still carrying lots of supplies, but they were not carrying any gold. Abdi had pretty much concluded that when their use as pack mules was over, then he would transfer any remaining items of worth to the other vehicles. Then they would be left to rot in the jungle. Sometime in the future a random traveller might come across them and wonder where the hell they had come from.

Aside from the vehicles, he was also beginning to feel ill. His head was throbbing unbelievably and when he changed the dressing Azrah told him that thick yellow ooze was forming. The humidity wasn't letting a good dry scab form. It wasn't smelling yet though, she had told him, as though that was a good thing. Abdi had a tiny bottle of Bactroban, a powdered antibiotic that he was applying liberally each day. It helped dry the wound temporarily and he hoped that it was helping with the infection too.

He was conscious that others were also beginning to suffer from their wounds. Cuts and grazes were getting red and sore, people were getting grumpy and short tempered with each other.

The phone up against his ear rang and was picked up fairly promptly at the other end. 'Sir, it's Abdi.'

'Yes.' More of an acknowledgement than a greeting.

'I just sent our location as an SMS on the phone.'

'One second.'

Abdi waited for considerably more than a second as he heard the typing of a keyboard at the other end. 'OK, I see where you are.

Hmm, I thought you might travel a little faster than that. Are you having problems?'

'The biggest problem is this fucking jungle.'

'No need to be crass. Just tell me what you need.'

Slightly taken aback Abdi considered his reply. 'Well, the jungle is hard to travel through, we're not going very far each day and we use a lot of fuel. It will be touch and go with the vehicles.'

'Abdi, you're telling me that a fortune in gold is going to end up sitting in the forest somewhere in the middle of nowhere.'

'Well, no, I was just saying it would be tight.'

'So, stop worrying. Tell me when it's no longer possible, and we'll work out another plan. In the meantime, I've confirmed that a boat, in fact a couple of boats, will be at the place we agreed last time. Once you get there you'll have extra help.'

'That's good news, but I need one other thing. Many of us have injuries or wounds that are turning nasty. We'll need lots of antibiotics and anything else a doctor says we'll need for deep, infected jungle wounds.'

'OK, I'll see what I can do. It looks to me like you have another, perhaps, four days to go until you get to the boats. Unless you're able to speed up a little. Either way, the boats will be there in two days' time and will wait for you.'

Allah have mercy, thought Abdi as he finished the call. Four more days in this unpleasant hell hole. Time to get everyone moving faster, he thought, and that wasn't going to be popular.

Chapter 62

September 30th, Accra. Ghana.

The Presidential palace in Accra was a vast imposing building, built in neo-colonial style, all marble columns, huge square windows and flourishing gardens.

Max had been collected from the commercial airliner as soon as the doors were opened, escorted down to a waiting limousine and whisked out of a back gate of the airport. It was only a brief journey to the residence, police outriders making short work of the snarling traffic. Cars, trucks and hand carts were forced out of the way, up onto the kerbs. Nothing stopped the irate honking of horns though.

The protocol aide spoke pleasantries, banal conversation, how was your flight, what's the weather like in Nairobi? Nothing of materiality. Max was polite back, but inside he was rehearsing his lines. He had been expecting to get his own transport, change at the hotel before the appointment later that evening. He reflected that it was a classic negotiation move. Put your opponent on the back foot, fight on your own turf and in your own timeframe. As they entered the palace building, Max was searched by security. His bag whisked away to an X-ray machine just inside the front door. He was expertly frisked by a stony-faced man in a white shirt and cheap black suit, the obligatory earpiece coiled up to his ear.

After the groping, Max was told to put all electronic devices into a box by the front door and was taken to an anteroom. It was a real power play. Portraits on the walls, shelves of imposing looking leather-bound books. Red leather sofas and mahogany coffee tables. He was asked to sit and wait, but a waiter took an order for coffee and then left Max in the room to himself.

Having sat all the way on the flight, Max wanted to stretch his legs, so he stood up, walked over the plush beige carpet towards the bookshelves. He started to read the titles, Hemmingway, Tesla, Bronte: an eclectic collection. The bottom shelves were more modern, autobiographies of western Presidents: Thatcher, Obama, Merkle. These were well worn, obviously read. Max took down a copy of *A Promised Land* and was surprised to see pages with the corners turned over, paragraphs highlighted. He took it back to the sofa, sat down and skimmed through it, noting with interest the highlighted sections and trying to guess the mind of the man who had done it. His coffee came and went, and he became thoroughly engrossed. He didn't notice the soft footfall as someone entered the room, until the person was standing over him.

'That's my personal copy.'

Max looked up astounded to see the President. 'Oh, hello, Mr President, I'm sorry, I didn't know.'

In his deep melodious voice, the President replied. 'Most people who come into this room and who are told to sit, will do so. But my staff tell me you went straight to the bookshelf?'

'Well, sir, I have a lot of experience of waiting for senior members of government.' Max was being tactful. There were times when he had flown all the way to a country to meet someone, to find the person either kept him waiting for days, or in one particularly memorable case, had actually left the country on a business trip the day before. That minister's aide hadn't cancelled the meeting.

'Yes. I'm sure you do. How was the trip from the airport?'

'Well sir, it put me on the back foot a little, but I'm sure that was your intention. I thought we were meeting later this evening.'

The president laughed. 'I do like a man who speaks his mind, who isn't afraid of all this pomp and glamour. It's… refreshing.'

'Quite. I find that diplomatic language at times of crisis can lead to misunderstandings, mistakes even.'

'Yes. I suppose you're right. Now, who else have you spoken to about this little project?'

'No one other than my team. There are a few externals, who think we are doing a survey project, but none of them really know why we're here.'

'Good. And all your equipment got in?'

'Yes, I'm told there was a bit of an intake of breath at customs when they saw the quantity of weapons and explosives, but the team called the number you gave me, and it was quickly resolved.'

'Well, it wouldn't have done for a plane full of mercenaries, guns and explosives to have all been arrested, would it? What was the name of the company that tried to initiate a coup a few years ago?'

Slightly evasively, Max said, 'I don't recall.' Of course, he did recall perfectly, and some of his old mates had been involved in that catastrophic project.

The President looked at him shrewdly for a moment. The threat of potential arrest had been clearly made, though perhaps unnecessary. Time to talk money. 'I'm grateful that you mobilised so quickly. The deposit obviously helped getting wheels moving?'

'Yes, Mr President.' Max waited for what was coming.

'Now, regarding the success fee we spoke about on the phone. As discussed, I need you to invoice me for three percent. But your expectation needs to be that you will be paid one percent. The remaining two percent will go through your accounts and then you will pay the two percent balance to an account that I designate.'

'Sorry, Mr President, but respectfully that is a hard no.'

Silence grew. The presidents' eyes narrowed. 'I am not paying you nine million dollars as a success fee. That's outrageous.'

'That's OK. I will accept a one and a half percent fee. What I cannot accept is the, shall we say, *over-invoicing*. I have staff and businesses around the world that work in a number of jurisdictions. I cannot risk some future investigation resulting in the imprisonment of my staff under either US or UK corruption law. Though I am sure of course,' Max went on quickly, 'That the commission is anything but....'

The President continued to weigh Max up. He decided he would go to plan B. 'Very well. You can have your one and a half percent. I will find an intermediary to bill the project commission fee.'

'Great, but that is, I believe, entirely none of my business.'

'Good, well, with formalities concluded, why don't I have a driver take you back to your hotel to change. We have a state dinner tonight. If you can get hold of a suit, you're welcome to attend.'

Max's mouth watered, though not because of the food. A huge number of international senior diplomats was a business development wet dream. 'I would love to, Mr President.'

Chapter 63

September 30th, Damana Forest. Ghana.

David had already refuelled twice during the night and was just coming to the end of his current search plan. Running constantly through his mind, whilst the sensors did their jobs automatically, was that inherent nervous uncertainty that all search and rescue pilots knew. You based your search on a whole lot of variables, normally trying to use the best estimates of terrain, winds and tides. In this case, of course, he was trying to guess what a criminal opponent was doing and that made it harder. He had made a lot of assumptions and they had led him to believe more than anything else, that the criminals were heading South. Had he missed something? Was there some fundamental piece of information that he wasn't aware of? Even if he had got the broad direction of travel right, had he chosen the right search pattern? There were plenty to choose from, spirals, clock patterns, creeping search lines. All had different purposes, and all worked differently, based on the terrain: so many assumptions. He pulled himself out of that particular pit and kept doing his job. He would talk to Tom in the morning and see if he wanted to adjust anything.

Knowing that he was soon to be heading home, he started to increase his water intake. Nothing worse, being a pilot, than needing a pee in the middle of a flight. Plenty of pilots had tried, to varying levels of success, peeing into the narrow top of a water bottle whilst flying. Most of the time it resulted in spraying a mess, or dribbling down your flight suit. If you weren't flying solo, you needed to have a good mate as a co-pilot. Someone who wouldn't mind the smell or the splashes, and who would take the piss literally. Assuming of course that both pilots were blokes as well. Not quite so easy for the female pilots.

He was just putting his water bottle away, when his sensors pinged. His head immediately turned to see the LiDAR image on the screen. Clearly shown were three obviously fabricated rectangular shapes, a few metres long, and they were moving across the jungle floor under the canopy. Pressing a button to lock the sensor in place he flicked to the thermal picture. Not nearly as clear, but there were obviously a number of heat sources moving in a line. He counted five, no, seven heat signatures. Feeling relieved, knowing that there was no way anyone else was driving in the jungle at night, other than perhaps a military convoy, he marked his GPS system with the location. He flew North a little more, loitered for about five minutes before turning back South. He wanted to see the overall direction of travel, and the easiest way to do that was to record two GPS points over a reasonable time interval.

As he flew back over the top, he marked their new location, and then turned to head home. As he flew, he called the night watch on the radio, told him the location and that he was one hundred percent confident. With an hour or so to go until dawn, it was time to wake up the team.

Chapter 64

October 1st, Damana Forest. Ghana.

The Chinook had arrived yesterday afternoon, just in time. Its elongated khaki-brown body, bulbous nose and twin rotors showed it was designed for one thing. Carrying heavy loads from A to B. In service all around the world, it was known to be a reliable and robust workhorse. It sat there now on the apron, with blade ties added as a precaution against gusting winds.

The early morning call from David had been very welcome news, and after briefing Tom and replaying exactly what he had seen, he had retired to his bed. Tom, Mike and Raj had spent an hour discussing the next part of the plan; finalizing really, as most of the planning had already happened. All they had needed was a location and direction of travel for the thieves, so that they could identify where they would insert themselves. They needed to get well in front of the thieves, if they were to have a good chance of intercepting them. The problem was that in dense, thick, impenetrable jungle, there weren't any places that they could see from the imagery, where they would be able to set down.

What they did have, though, was a plan on how to either find one, or make one. First, they were going to fly to the approximate area where they wanted to be. Then they would either find a spot visually to touch down, or they were going to send a couple of the team members down by abseiling. They would then create the space needed. That was always the most dangerous option though.

The Chinook crew had taken off early, to go and try to find a suitable open location in advance but despite a long time searching, they had come back empty handed. Abseiling it had to be.

Mid-morning, with just a few of the team on board, they had taken off again for the thirty-minute flight to the drop-off area. The loadmaster in the back was doing some basic checks on the stores, making sure that they were secure. Tom, Mike, Raj and Miguel were all sitting strapped in. Only three of them were going in at this point. Tom was along for the ride, making sure everyone got in OK. In transit, the team were all wearing headsets. It helped with the noise reduction and they could all talk on the intercom. 'I spoke to Max just before we took off. He met with the President last night, apparently went to some fancy dinner.'

Miguel, who would rather stick pins in his foreskin than mix with a bunch of diplomats, rolled his eyes. 'Hey man, better him than me.'

Tom continued. 'Well, he said he finally got agreement on all the contracting stuff. Not bad, considering we started the project nearly a week ago.'

'So does that mean we finally have a project name now?' asked Raj.

'Yes, Project Inca'

'Well, that's not very subtle.'

'It was a close call between Sovereign and Croesus apparently.'

They were interrupted by the loadmaster coming over the intercom. 'Ten minutes, gentlemen.' He then moved to the door at the rear of the aircraft where he proceeded to double-check the abseiling rope and its fittings yet again. Mike joined him, walking a little awkwardly, with the tight harness between his legs. He was wearing jungle combat clothing and a Kevlar helmet with an integrated radio set. He was also wearing a chest vest, packed full of the essentials and he had his weapon on a sling over his shoulder. His rucksack and a chainsaw were attached by a short length of rope and carabiners connected to his harness.

Clipped onto his right hip was his Glock and clipped to his left, with an additional cord around his left thigh, was his machete. Raj and Miguel, similarly equipped, waddled up beside him. Miguel had a lighter South American frame, making the equipment weight harder to carry. All three carried AK-47s but they were not their weapons of choice normally. However, with limitations on planning, and the 7.62 calibre round, which had more stopping power than 5.56, it was the best available option for the jungle.

The loadmaster checked that all three were hooked on to a safety line and with five minutes to go, he opened the rear door. The ramp lowered gently, a mechanical mouth opening wide to show the vast expanse of the jungle racing away down below.

The aircraft came into the hover, a slight nose up attitude causing all those in the back to adjust their balance. The pilots in the front spent a moment manoeuvring, the downwash blowing the trees excessively. Mike spoke to the loadmaster, shouting that he would rather gain a little more height, to reduce the effect on the trees. He saw the message passed on and the aircraft raised about fifty meters. With the rope length known to be one hundred and twenty-five metres long, Mike was hoping that the tree height was well under seventy-five. The loadmaster walked down the ramp and, leaning out precariously, looped the abseiling rope through an installed hoop on the ceiling. He looked down, holding the remainder of the rope which had been very carefully fed into a special bag. Beckoning Mike, he gave a 'what do you think' kind of look. Mike also walked forward, still clipped on by his safety line and peered down. He spent a moment looking at the environment below him. There were no obvious gaps, so he gave the loadmaster a thumbs up. Mike connected his figure of eight to the rope and then attached that to his waist harness. While the loadmaster double checked for him, he gave a nod to Tom, who replied with an OK sign. The loadmaster nodded and handed the bag with the remainder of the rope to Mike to hold in his right hand.

With gloves on, Mike held that in his right, and the lower portion of the rope in his left, adopting a classic abseiling position. By moving his left hand down, he created a braking mechanism through the figure of eight, which stopped his descent or sped him up depending on the friction applied. With full brake on, he sat briefly, dangling in mid-air, testing his weight on the rope and the hook on the ceiling. Perhaps more importantly, he was making sure his meat and two veg wouldn't get trapped in his harness. It was a long way down and he thought Charly would appreciate that. Using his backside, he forced more rope out of the bag, and released the brake on the rope, as he stepped all the way out. He gently began to lower himself, controlling bag and brake, until he disappeared below the ramp. The noise was incredible directly below the aircraft: the double whomp of the blades, the bass pounding through him. The sweet smell of the exhaust fumes forced down at him in a barrage of wind. The fifty metres down to the canopy was the easy bit, but he couldn't quite tell where he would touch down, until he actually got there. At this height though, he was committed. He needed the pilots to maintain the hover on an absolute dime for the next ten minutes or so.

Using the rope and his feet, he paid out more until he was in the best possible place. He almost walked through the top branches.

He had to let the chainsaw and rucksack hang through first. Both hands were fully occupied with the rope, so he couldn't stop the branches from flicking into his face as he breached the tree canopy. A green tree snake, which hadn't seen sense to escape, when the helicopter arrived, started to dance away through the treetops as Mike punched through. He didn't see it though, as he was too busy trying to navigate his way down. Once through the thin twiggy top layer, it became easier. He could set a path then and he carefully continued to lower himself. It got darker and darker as he descended, passing thicker and thicker branches as he went lower. Far below him was the leafy jungle floor, but suddenly he had left the branches above him and was dangling clear again. He risked dropping the rope bag now and it fell to the jungle floor, spooling out the rope as it fell. A minute later, and with gloves having protected his hands from the friction on the rope, his feet hit the ground. He unclipped and he breathed again, great lungsful of moist, musty air. Already he was sweating, and his heart was still thumping from the excitement of the drop. Mike was truly on his own right now. A master of his own destiny.

On his radio he called, 'I'm down.'

'Roger that.' replied Tom, 'Do you want to drop a tree, or can the others make it through?'

Mike thought about it before replying. 'I think it's better to drop one. Can you give me ten minutes?'

'Will do, clearing the area now.' And with that, the abseil rope disappeared upwards, pulled in by the loadmaster whilst the helicopter flew a couple of kilometres away to loiter. Calm began to return, no helicopter noise, just the sounds of jungle birds and monkeys calling out to each other in fear and anger.

Mike dropped the rucksack and the chainsaw on the floor of the forest and paused for a moment to look around. Certain he was on his own, he walked briskly around the immediate area looking upwards at the trees. He couldn't find any that would drop easily. He was worried that the branches were so intertwined above, that even if he tried to bring one down it would stay standing upright, suspended, supported by the others.

Well in that case he was going to have to drop a couple he thought. From the side pouch of his rucksack, he pulled out three explosive charges, each one prepared so that it could bring down a large tree. They had been placed inside ammunition bandoliers. The long straps that were attached, and the pockets sewn into them made them ideal for tying around the base of trees, keeping the explosives tight against the trunks. Mike quickly selected three medium sized trunks, he couldn't tell what type of tree they were, and attached the devices. He had a moment of conscious thought that those trees were probably twice as old as he was. Whilst it was to be regretted, it needed to be done. Remembering to move his rucksack out of the line of any blast or falling trees, he jogged about a hundred metres away. There he found a bit of a depression in the ground, and a large tree to hide behind. Efficiently as soon as he was safe, he pulled out the remote trigger, braced himself for the noise, armed the device and pushed the button.

The three charges went off simultaneously, forming one loud blast. Mike lifted his head up, to watch the effect. The charges had sheered the trees at their bases, knocking them sideways off the root structures. Raw, pale, timber splinters arced lazily, visible through the misted water vapour. It took an age for the trees to fall. The multitude of thin branches above trying so hard, clinging to each other. But, with the inevitability of death, the three massive trees started to topple. It started as a crashing sound in the branches high above, groaning, creaking, cracking. There was a fuller background rustling of a billion leaves sounding like the heaviest downpour. Smaller branches and debris from above fell first, hitting the soft ground, and then with a massive thump and a shiver the trees lay flat on the floor.

Almost angelic, light flooded the newly formed space, streaking through the mists and the dust. Mike, ignoring the spectacle, his eyes adjusting, went to pick up his chainsaw.

When the Chinook came back a few minutes later, Mike was already standing on top of one of the tree trunks. With his chainsaw he was chopping off the topmost branches. His intent, to create clearance above, so that when the rest of the team arrived, they could fast rope down easily without the risk of snagging. He paused briefly in his work, because the down draft of the rotors was blowing all of the sawdust back up and into his face and hair. It stuck to his sweat and even blew down the open collar of his shirt. He looked upwards, shielding his eyes, awestruck as always at the massive platform hovering just above him. As he watched, firstly Raj and then Miguel abseiled down. A mere forty or so metres for them, compared to his much longer and more complicated descent. Then, using the radios for confirmation, the loadmaster started to send individual packages down the ropes, using a clever mechanical gadget that self-managed the loads' speeds as they descended.

With the loads complete and the rope coiled back in, the helicopter turned, showing the men its rear end where they could see Tom waving as it departed. They had a few hours now to bring down lots more trees and clear a space. They needed to prepare for the remainder of the men and all the rest of the supplies to come in, and that needed a lot of work. Mike started up his chainsaw again, whilst Raj and Miguel prepared more demolitions.

Chapter 65

October 1st, Damana Forest. Ghana.

At four in the afternoon the Chinook was back, this time with some stores and a full load of men, led by Tom. Max had arrived earlier at the airfield, and he would now command the project with the few support staff, the medics and the helicopter crews.

Slung under the aircraft were two of the quadbikes, with their trailers, one set under the aft hook and one under the fore. As the Chinook came into the hover, the pilots marvelled at how much of a clear space the three men had created: well, them and a shedload of explosives.

The Chinook was able to come down into a high hover, gently touching the quadbikes down on to the ground and then releasing the strops that held them. The down wash caused vast amounts of sawdust to fly into the air like a swarm of insects. The pilot was a little concerned at one point as visibility reduced and chunks of the stuff must have been going into the engine intakes. There wasn't enough clearance yet of the rotor blades from the treeline, for the aircraft itself to put its wheels down. So, with the aid of some thick fast ropes, the twenty or so fully kitted-up men abseiled down, one after the other. Touching down onto the ground, they doubled away before the next man descended on top of them.

With the sudden surge in labour force, preparation of the landing zone would be much faster now. They could also use the winches on the quadbikes to help drag large branches if needed. The aircraft was going to make one more run today, with fuel, water and the remaining quadbikes, before it got dark.

Not all of the new labour set to work on the LZ though. Despite the noise, the project had turned tactical, and several men were posted as sentries. No point in getting caught unawares after all.

Mike and Raj took a breather and a drink, Mike sipping from his CamelBak, Raj from a canteen bottle which he had scrounged from one of the other guys. 'You know, Mike, the last time I was in the jungle, I saw a lizard standing on its hind legs, telling jokes.'

Mike looked at him not understanding.

'Yes, seriously it's true, buddy. When I saw it, I turned to the tracker I was with and told him that the lizard was really funny. Do you know what he said to me? No? He said it wasn't a lizard. It was a stand-up chameleon!' Raj waited, smiling, but Mike deadpanned him.

'You're such a dick, Raj. Some of your jokes just aren't funny, dude.' Raj didn't really pay attention; he was too busy laughing to himself.

The rest of the day passed quickly, the remaining equipment arrived and then the men got into their evening routine. They were not going to risk moving in the jungle at night and were going to wait to get a further fix on the robbers, before heading out early in the morning. David would be out again tonight and would hope to locate them again. That new fix, combined with the one from last night would really lock down the routing and provide the best chance of an intercept.

With the last of the light, men started to get their hammocks sorted. Easily stowed, taking up very little space, the hammock was the best sleeping system by far to use in the jungle. Used properly, you could get a good night's sleep. You just had to find the right trees. All of the activity in and around the landing zone had caused mayhem amongst all the insects. Leaf mulch had been scuffed and scored, homes to billions of them had been disrupted and as dusk came, they were all on the move. Miguel, an old pro for living in the jungle because of his cartel days in South America set his bed up quickly. He hung his hammock first, taut as a bow string. Then he hung a square of waterproof fabric above that, a roof from the rain and for any small items, insects or animals that might fall from the trees above. It sat in an upside-down V shape about a metre above the hammock, and with a couple of rubber bungee ropes was made taut, by connecting it to deeply buried tent pegs on each side. From that roof, he hung a mosquito net, which ultimately when he went to bed, he would tuck under himself so that nothing touched the floor. The only remaining task now was to coat the ropes with a heavy-duty insect repellent cream. The stuff the military used would literally melt the plastic on your weapon. God knows what it did to your skin, but the added benefit was that it melted the legs off any insects that might decide to join you in your bed in the middle of the night. After a brief meal of boil-in-the-bag food, heated using chemical cookers, the men began to go to sleep. Everyone would take turns 'on stag' as the Brits called it. At least one hour each throughout the night on sentry. With four men on duty, that meant that each man would do at least two shifts during the night, getting four hours of sleep in-between.

Chapter 66

October 1st, Damana Forest. Ghana.

Just before midnight and David was in the air again. He had spent some time that evening doing some basic planning. He had plotted the locations where he had spotted the robbers on a paper map and measured the distances that they had travelled. With the timings known, and the approximate time of the initial robbery also known, he was able to calculate the average speed that they had been travelling through the forest. It was only a rough guide, but with that, he was able to project, forwards in time, the approximate area where he would expect to find them again. He marked the map with arcs using a pair of compasses, his best guess, and his worst-case scenarios. He then did the same again, but this time drawing a complete circle around the last known point. He would start with a search pattern based on the opinion that they were still heading South. If he didn't find them, then he would be in recovery mode and would search the larger circle. Perhaps for some reason, they might have completely changed direction.

As it happened, when he found them, it was because of obvious headlights in the jungle that were pretty much where he had extrapolated them to be. Though, perhaps the robbers hadn't travelled quite as far as he thought they would. He flicked across to thermal view on the sensor but could only see a couple of vehicles. What was obvious was that the forest had been damaged here somehow. There was some kind of gap in the canopy, a lot of low vegetation, and a great score across the ground where many of the trees had fallen or burned or something. The fact that he couldn't see all of the vehicles worried him. He elected to continue North for a bit and then he was going to come and do a low pass. See if he could pick up anything else. He called in the location of the sighting to the team at the airfield and began a descending turn.

Chapter 67

October 2nd, Damana Forest. Ghana.

Just after midnight and the sound of the not-so-distant helicopter had come for the third night in a row, bringing with it frustration and fear for Abdi and his team. He didn't know that it was the same aircraft, but it certainly sounded like it and they hadn't heard any other helicopters at all during the day. Cheko and Abdi had discussed it earlier, both of them worried. If there was a helicopter, and it had worked out where they were, then there must be troops close behind it. They had been debating what to do as they continued their drive through the jungle, but then late in the evening they had come across a thick patch of secondary jungle. The difference here, compared to the last one, was that whatever had caused it, had happened in the last couple of years. There hadn't yet been time for the trees to regrow fully and so as they left the treeline of the primary jungle, they had been able to see clearly upwards to the sky.

They had sent a vehicle in each direction to explore if there was a way around it. In the meantime, they had set the men to starting to hack their way through, in case it was another vast patch like the other day. As night fell, they used vehicle headlights to help the team that was cutting. When they heard the helicopter though, all the lights were promptly turned out. Cheko made a rapid decision. He got the two technicals, with the heavy weapons, and any man available, out on to the path that had been cut. They stood out there, waiting, wondering if the helicopter would come back. Only a few moments later with the sound suddenly roaring over the top of the trees, the helicopter appeared. Travelling fast and low without running lights it was obvious from the sound and the blank space in the sky that it was right over head. The two .50 Cals opened up dwarfing the noise made by the AK-47's that had also started firing. At only a few hundred metres away the helicopter had no chance. With several hundred rounds of ammunition fired at such close range, the civilian Eurocopter stood no chance. There was no fiery explosion mid-air, no sounds of bullets hitting metal, just a very obvious swerve as the helicopter suddenly came off course, banked sideways and smashed into the trees perhaps a mile ahead.

Chapter 68

October 2nd, Damana Forest. Ghana.

At dawn, Tom had checked in with Max on the satphone. Tom was standing in the middle of the newly cleared helicopter landing zone and had clear line of site to the satellite many miles above. Max had broken the bad news that the search helicopter hadn't returned and was now well overdue. The Chinook had just taken off to search for it, starting with the last known location that was reported in. The aircraft's operating company had also been contacted by Max's operations team in Nairobi, asking for details of the satellite transponder system. All efforts were being made to find the potentially lost aircraft.

That said, Max had been very clear that there were plenty of other resources to continue with that problem, and that Tom and his team's job now was to get moving and rapidly. The last known position sent by David in his last call had updated where the thieves were, and their heading was now obvious. They were making for a wide river, which was a tributary to Lake Volta. Having looked carefully at imagery, Max had seen that the river was obviously navigable by large river barges for quite a long way away from the lake. He had to assume that the thieves were going to meet up with some kind of boat. He needed Tom and his men to get there well ahead of them and ambush them before they got there.

Tom hung up the sat-phone to hear firstly the sound of screaming, and then laughter in the camp. Noises that were totally at odds with the sombre thoughts he was having about a potential lost pilot.

He walked briskly back to the camp to find out why the hell tactical discipline had broken down so badly. As he arrived, he saw Mike and Raj rolling around on the floor. Mike furious, Raj laughing his head off whilst defending himself against half-hearted blows from Mike. Several of the other members of the team, some of them new and who didn't know Mike and Raj so well, were standing there a little bemused.

189

Tom had to raise his voice to break up the scene. 'Guys, what the hell's going on? What happened?'

'I'll tell y'all what happened,' said Mike as he grappled with Raj on the jungle floor. 'This asshole put a snake in ma' rucksack!'

'What?' said Tom. 'A real one?'

'Oh, it was so, so, funny!' giggled Raj. 'You should have heard him scream!'

'Nah, it wasn't a real one, just a fuckin' rubber one. An' now I am gonna shove it right up his ass and make him scream too!'

'Guys for fucks sake, cut it out.' said Tom. 'Everyone! Listen up. We move out in ten minutes! The thieves are ahead of us, and we have to get in front of them before they get to the river.'

Mike and Raj stopped messing around immediately. It was suddenly game time, but this was a different type of game.

With the professionalism of the type of people that Max employed, they were all on the move within nine minutes. The quadbikes taking everyone's rucksacks in the trailers meant that everyone else was just in their fighting order: webbing, helmets, and weapons. Setting a punishing pace, Raj led on point with Mike just behind him. Tom was about three men back and navigating. After everyone had warmed up a little, with sweat pouring off them, Raj started a loose jog. He was going to keep everyone moving. Jogging, then walking, then jogging again, a rhythm that they could keep up all day. Once they were well underway, Raj called back gently to Mike. 'Buddy. What's your fascination with my ass, hey? Have you ever served any prison time that you haven't told us about?'

Mike, who focused more on upper body strength than running stamina, was already concentrating on his breathing. He managed a quick 'Fuck you,' before tucking his chin down and along with everyone else, he ran.

Chapter 69

October 2nd, Damana Forest. Ghana.

Luckily for Abdi, that new stretch of secondary jungle hadn't been very thick after all. They had cleared their way through it quite rapidly after they had shot down the helicopter. Abdi was seriously worried that someone somewhere knew where they were now. If the pilot had radioed their location back, then surely people would come looking? Was there any kind of emergency transponder on the aircraft? Was there a debris field? Was the pilot talking to troops nearby on the ground? How the hell had it found them, and how much time did they have left before those soldiers arrived?

The more he worried, the more he came to realise that he had been heading in a straight line for the past couple of days. If anyone was tracking them, then it wouldn't take a genius to work out that they were heading for the river. Abdi had spoken to Cheko, agreed a plan, and then spoken briefly to all the men and Azrah. They were so close to the river now and to getting away. They were going to keep going through the day, no stopping, no breaks. When it got to night-time, they would see how far they were from the boats and then they would plan. Either get some rest or keep driving through the night.

There had been another problem first though. Fuel was running out. There was so little left that they would definitely have to leave the two technicals behind. Abdi organised a work party and all the essential stores, some water, ammunition, and food, were transferred to the remaining vehicles. Those technicals were literally left where they were parked. The last of the fuel drums had been shared equally between the remaining six pickups. That was it now, they were committed. Either they reached the boats with what they had, or the whole convoy would grind to a halt somewhere in the jungle.

As they had moved out, they hadn't seen the helicopter, nor a sign of any crash. Did that mean that it was so light that it was literally sitting there on top of the canopy far above? The thieves left the location far behind and drove on all day, endlessly swerving between trees, but thankfully not coming across any more obstacles that delayed them. The drivers made such a good distance over the day that

Abdi decided that they would go for it. Keep moving, even as the darkness came. The risk of driving with night-time lights on was weighed against the risk of getting intercepted. With luck they would get to the river early tomorrow morning.

Chapter 70

October 2nd, Damana Forest. Ghana.

At about the same time, with a brief halt for a drink and something to eat, Tom was talking to his team. 'Sorry, guys, but with that terrain we went through earlier, we just aren't covering the ground as fast as we should be. We have to speed it up. Move faster.'

There were groans all around. They had been tabbing all day including through some really rough patches of 'wait-a-while'. The prospect of going for twelve hours more, whilst not impossible, was still challenging.

Tom continued, 'What other options do we have?'

Mike said, 'We could call in the Chinook, blow some trees and winch out, then get it to drop us closer to the new route?'

'That might have been possible in the middle of the afternoon, but now that it's getting dark, I don't see how we can re-insert safely. What else?'

Raj contributed, 'How about some of us take all the quad bikes and zoom ahead. We can get at least eight of us there faster?'

Tom thought for a moment. 'It's an option, but a high risk one. I don't like the idea of zooming through the jungle on quads at night, even with our night vision kit. Someone's guaranteed to get hurt, rolled, and then we'd have to do a night medevac. Add to that, this crew just attacked a heavily-armed mining installation. Do we really want to hit them with only eight of us?'

Mike grumbled, 'Urgh, it's so frustrating. We're so close. If we still had that chopper, we could find out exactly how far away those assholes are.'

'Dude, you're on about someone's buttocks again. What is it with you these days?'

Despite the pressure they were all under, there was still time for a bit of grim laughter.

It was the break that Tom needed. 'Let's go guys. Let's up the pace, keep running for as long as we can. Then we'll reassess in six hours' time if we should split the patrol and send some ahead on the quads.'

Those who had been sitting or leaning against trees picked themselves up, adjusted their webbing straps over their sweaty shoulders, and moved out. As the light truly faded, night vision devices, a mixture of thermal or NVG were lowered to help them move through the inky black forest.

Chapter 71

October 3rd, Volta River. Ghana.

Abdi was nodding off in the back of the pickup when the driver suddenly slammed on the breaks and started to bang the side of the vehicle with the flat of his hand. He was shouting excitedly. 'The river- Abdi, the river!'

The vehicles spread out, no longer driving in a long line. They gently nudged through the ten to fifteen metres of thin foliage to find, as they all breached the treeline, the edge of the river. There was no road, just a thin belt of light bush, then a drop of perhaps a metre down to the slow moving, turgid brown, silt-rich river. The river was perhaps a hundred metres across and the bank on the far side looked exactly like the bank they were now resting on. It was well past dawn and with the river flowing West to East, as they looked downstream, they had to shield their eyes from the bright sun.

Azrah and Cheko were already out of their vehicles, anxiously scanning up and down the river, as Abdi jumped down to join them.

With the excitement palpable, and expectation high, there was a little disappointment in Azra's voice as she said, 'But I don't see any boats?'

Abdi fished for his satellite phone and stabbed at the power button. As it connected to the satellites above, he received a text message. "Boats still at original location, Check in when you can." Abdi used the GPS fix and sent his location back to The Associate. Then after pressing a few buttons, he pulled up the onboard map. 'We're not far, only two kilometres away, around that bend in the river.' He pointed West, 'We must have drifted off course when I was asleep. Sorry about that.'

'That's OK, Abdi,' said Cheko, 'as long as the boats are there.' Then louder to everyone. 'Nearly there, men! Just a short drive around that corner! Let's go!'

If anything, the excitement made everyone a bit reckless, they started to speed a little too much as they followed the river bank up stream. The discipline of the last six days evaporated. They were tired, they were bored of the jungle and they just wanted to get out and get paid.

With their overexuberance and limited skill sets, they were fortunate that no one got hurt. As they came around the bend, Abdi rejoiced to see two medium-sized river boats. Those boats were not going to win any glamour contests, but to Abdi they were the most gorgeous floating palaces he had ever seen. Their peeling hulls were low in the water, their paintwork a matt black and the flat cargo cover hatches on top a dull green. At the rear of each barge was a simple wheelhouse, with enough room for perhaps a three-person crew to live. Originally purposed to move freight up and down the country, there wasn't so much need for them these days, as roads had been developed and railroads had taken on the brunt of that work.

As the vehicles approached, the crews lazily roused themselves from their bunks. They had been waiting for a few days, and the arrival of their client meant that they could get underway soon. The old skipper of one of the barges was wearing filthy faded blue shorts and a t-shirt that might once have been green. He stood up, stretched, scratched his balls, and spat over the side as he looked with a frown at his new passengers. The cars had been hammered, virtually no glass left that wasn't cracked, the wing mirrors had all been lost days ago, paintwork already scratched was now smeared with long-crushed greenery, turning brown.

The skipper's face lost some of its frown when the men got out of their trucks, armed to the teeth with both light and heavy weapons. To his credit, the skipper hardly blinked though. He wasn't much of a talker and had very little English. 'Abdi?'

'Yes, that's me, good to meet you. We're glad you're still here. What's your name?'

The man looked blankly. It took Abdi a while before he pointed to himself, 'I am Abdi,' and then pointing at the skipper, 'You?'

'Ezekiel. We go now.'

'No, first we load.' Abdi pointed at the vehicles.

'Cars no fit. We go now.'

'We take cargo.'

'Cars no go. No fit in boat! We go now!'

Abdi was tired, his patience at an end. But he still had some sense. 'Cheko, come and talk to this man will you, see if anyone speaks his language?'

Fortunately, with a little translation, it transpired that the man hadn't been told about a cargo. The first time he actually perked up was when he saw the first gold bar. He couldn't comprehend that such a vast sum even existed, let alone that it would be put on his boat.

Cheko and Abdi quickly agreed that they would rather keep all the gold with them on one of the boats, and that the second boat would lead down the river, with the majority of the fighters on it. That way, there would be little temptation for any funny business in the night. Azra and the drone pilots would stay with them and the gold and a very few of Cheko's most trusted lieutenants. Abdi was almost beyond worrying about a double-cross now. If Allah willed it, then it would happen. Cheko however, preferred to keep the dice loaded in his favour if he could.

The next problem was how to move so much gold. Six tons, no winches, and only a rickety old gangplank stretched from the barge to the shoreline. The fighters all lined up forming a human chain and one by one, just under five hundred gold bricks were passed into the hull of the boat. With much-needed breaks, it took most of the day, the skipper worrying about the weight of the load. He didn't want it stacked up, pressuring his hull. Instead, he wanted it spread out over the entire floor of the hold. When they had finished, there was a solid gold carpet covering that damp mildewed planking, and the barge was the most expensive ever to float on the Volta.

Chapter 72

October 3rd, Volta River. Ghana.

Tom and his team had been slogging through the night, and through the day. They had had to pause for breaks, but those were short and infrequent. The team had been moving now for nearly thirty-six hours and were exhausted, filthy, sweaty and hungry. In the later part of the afternoon, they had come across obvious tyre tracks. So fresh that the mulch was still moist. In places, where some insect nests had been disturbed, jungle birds were pecking up an unexpected meal.

Of course, tyre tracks meant the team had missed the opportunity to get in front of the thieves. But the tracks were fresh enough to give a glimmer of hope. It was time to throw caution to the wind. Tom quickly commandeered the four quad bikes and selected seven other men to hop on. The remainder were instructed to follow on at best speed, following the tracks. No matter what, as they were so close to the river, they would meet up again at night fall.

Tom, Mike, Raj and Miguel drove a quad each. Other team members rode pillion. The path through the forest made for an obvious routing and so the team drove rapidly, twisting in and out of the trees. As they approached the riverbank about twenty minutes later, the forest started to lighten up. The clear left hand turns in the tracks left no room for doubt as to which way the thieves had gone.

It was only moments before Tom called a halt to the drive. He could physically see in the far distance, two barges in the water, and the white sides of pickups through the trees. He couldn't see any people though and he was concerned that they had made too much noise in the approach. As the quadbike engines stilled, he could hear the low throb of the barge engines. And then, with a sinking heart, he saw the barges pull out into the centre of the river. There were expletives all round as the men saw what was happening. Needing space to decide, Tom told everyone to pull the quads deeper into the forest. He concealed himself in the vegetation on the edge of the river. Should they attack? Reveal their presence? He could see all the thieves now, lounging about on the decks of the barges, looking decidedly relieved. There were a lot of them, and they had some

0.50's. There was no way, he thought, that eight men could ambush the boats effectively. He would wager that those barge timbers were a foot thick. The barges were drifting with the current towards him. Time to decide. Fuck! It was all going wrong, right at the last minute. What would happen if he did attack? Best case, he might sink a boat but with his puny weapons, odds were that it would keep heading down stream for a lot longer and then it would settle into that deep muddy brown soup. A vast fortune sunk. Worst case, he and his team would get cut to shreds, a massive weight of fire coming back at them. Any attack would also give them away. Remove any element of surprise.

Lost in his rapid thoughts, he didn't notice that Miguel had crept up beside him. 'This ambush position stinks.'

'I know,' whispered Tom. 'It's not an ambush, this is a death trap.' The barges were coming level with them now, and all along the riverbank, Tom's team had snuck up to the edge, using the thick grasses and shrubs as cover. Men turned to look at him, prepared to do their jobs, weapons ready. Tom closed his eyes again. Trying to picture the map of this part of the jungle. There was about a seventy-kilometre stretch of river to go before it widened out into Lake Volta. He didn't yet have a full plan, but he knew the best course here was to hide, stay quiet. The barges were less than fifty metres away, sitting ducks, slowly gliding past in a throb of marine diesel smoke.

The team continued to stare at Tom, waiting for the command, safety catches off. If it was going to happen it had to happen now. Tom closed his eyes, cleared any perceived pressures and bias and made the decision. He shook his head. Stand down. He was letting a vast sum in gold float away from them. All that hard work from the last week, all that planning. Tom lowered his face into the crushed bracken in front of him. Started to take deep breaths. The scents of the freshly-crushed greenery filled his nostrils. His heart was sinking, and uncertainty was creeping in. That self-doubt in leadership ability that all great leaders felt sometimes. Had he made the right call? Tom could hear across the water the laughter of the thieves. Were they mocking him? The thieves were happy. They had gotten away. As he watched the barges float away, Tom was stunned to recognise the face of the man standing at the stern near the wheelhouse. He had seen that man only a few months before, standing on the deck of a highjacked supertanker. What the fuck was Abdi doing here?

Chapter 73

October 3rd, Volta River. Ghana.

Once the barges were out of earshot, Tom pulled out his Sat phone. 'Max, they got away.'

'Ahh. What happened?'

'They got to the river before us, they had a couple of boats waiting for them. They have obviously loaded all the gold onto them because they have left the vehicles behind. Frustratingly, the thieves are all now drifting down the Volta in a couple of knackered old barges. If I was a betting man, I would say that all the gold was on the rear one.'

'What makes you say that?'

'A few things. The rear one was much lower in the water. The front one had the majority of armed men on board it. And if it was me, I wouldn't want all the hired help next to me at this point of the journey. And finally,' Tom paused not believing what he was about to say, 'I just saw Abdi on the rear barge.'

'What! Pirate Abdi?'

'One and the same. I was the one who took his photo on the Hibernia III. I would know that face anywhere.'

'Good lord, well we need to think about what that means, but not now. What d'you want to do?'

'Well, you'll think I am nuts, but I want the Chinook, and I want it ten minutes ago.' He heard Max mumble to someone next to him to get the Chinook crew to start up in a hurry'

'I want it to collect us from the river bank, and pivot us down stream about thirty clicks. Then it's going to drop us off again and we are going to ambush those bastards.'

'OK, and how are you going to recover the gold?'

'I'm still working on that. What I know for certain is, I want that Chinook to bring every underslung load cable that it has and lots of shackles. I am sending you my location now. But, and this is important, tell the crew to stay well away from the river until they get to my location. I don't want them flying over the thieves or giving the game away with noise.'

'Right. Anything else?'

'I think that's it. Please text me an ETA when you have it. If it takes longer than an hour we're buggered.'

After he hung up, he looked around. The team had gathered around him and had heard the conversation. They could see he had some kind of plan but were not sure yet what it was. He was still in command mode. 'Right, you four. Take the quads and go and pick up the others. Bring them back here. You have less than an hour.'

'Raj, Mike and everyone else. I want a ramp into that river, strong enough to drive the quad bikes over. Blow some trees, do whatever you need to do to clear a landing zone. The Chinook is going to come down hovering over the river and we're going to drive all of our kit straight onto it. Make sure there's enough space for the blades on this bank. You guys have,' he looked at his watch, 'about fifty-five minutes.'

Chapter 74

October 3rd, Volta River. Ghana.

'Dude, are those logs gonna hold?' Raj was looking down at the small trunks of trees that the team had just felled into the river. They couldn't risk explosives with the barges having only recently passed, so good old muscle power and axes had been needed. Using a combination of gravity, brute strength and the quad bikes, which had made their return trip quickly, there were now several smaller tree trunks up against the riverbank. Behind him, several of the men had done their best to clear a wider area for the Chinook to be able to come down to the hover.

'Yeah, I think so, buddy,' said Mike, giving them a solid push with one foot. 'They're wedged into all that mud.'

'I think we'd better check, dude; we have to get four quads on to that bridge.'

Mike looked at him, then he looked back at the mud below, thick, dark and glutinous. There was no avoiding it. He was going to have to jump down there and test those logs properly. He shook his head a little and jumped. At that moment, a large frog, which had until then been hiding in the riverbank, was startled. It leaped down onto the mud, but before it could jump again, Mike landed. He tried hard to adjust the landing zone of his size eleven boots. All he ended up doing, though, was hitting the mud, feet wide apart. Then, with nothing to hold onto, he fell forward into the gloop and on top of the unfortunate frog.

Raj burst out laughing. A sound so unnatural in that place at that time that the other men came over to see what was happening. Mike was trying really hard to get up. He was face first into the muck and when he put his hands down, he had nothing to push up against. His struggle was epic for a few moments, like a landed catfish. Tom grew concerned and was about to jump in to help him. Finally, Mike managed to roll himself over and draw a massive lungful of breath in through mud-covered lips.

'Dude, you killed a poor little frog!' Raj was still laughing. Mike was so shocked at his sudden fall in stature. He knew that he must look a real picture and he couldn't think of anything to say. Raj, though, had no mercy. He had pulled out his digital camera and was happily snapping away.

They were interrupted by the sound of the whump whump of the Chinook.

'Pull your fingers out, men!' shouted Tom. Then he got onto his radio and started speaking to the pilot, telling him what he wanted him to do.

As the Chinook did a quick orbit, Mike had no option but to get into the river. He spent several minutes trying to wash himself down as best he could. The mud had penetrated everywhere. His webbing pouches were full of it. His clothes caked. He scrubbed and he scrubbed, rubbing the brown river water all over his face and head.

The Chinook came into the high hover above him, its down draught forcing fine spray off the surface of the river. There was plenty of room and the aircraft turned to face away from the riverbank. The loadmaster had already lowered the rear door ramp and with infinite skill, the aircraft reversed all the way up to the bank until the ramp was almost touching. Its rear wheels were actually in the water, the hull mere inches above. The pilot kept it there, steady as a rock.

With the noise and the vibration buffeting all, the four quadbikes and their trailers were driven straight up into the aircraft. The men followed shortly after. Raj stopped to help Mike clamber up the bank and onto the ramp, whilst Tom did a final check to make sure there was no equipment left behind.

As the aircraft pulled away and everyone found a place to sit, Raj was still buzzing.

'Fun fact, Mike. Did you know that the River Volta has one of the highest leach concentrations in the world?'

'Raj, if a leach is brave enough to get into my jockey shorts, it's gonna get the fright of its life.'

They were interrupted by Tom, who needed them to rein it in a bit. 'Everyone, listen up. We have perhaps ten minutes to brief the plan. This is what we're going to do.'

Chapter 75

October 4th, Volta River. Ghana.

Abdi was resting, lying on top of the barge's green-patched cargo hold cover. He had taken his shirt off and was using it as a pillow. He felt the vibration of the barge through the hull and into his bones. He was feeling exhausted and the opportunity to rest was gratefully accepted. With the engines running, they were perhaps drifting down river at about four knots. Tomorrow morning, the skipper said, they would reach the very Northern tip of Lake Volta. Then they had a slow cruise down to the very Southern end and that would take a few days.

The tree line was drifting lazily past. The light chocolate brown river flowed smoothly, with the occasional diving kingfisher providing light entertainment. Abdi had taken all the phones off the crew, with a promise that he would give them back at the end of the trip. The skipper hadn't been too phased by that, and had explained in his poor English, that they were in such a remote area that the phones wouldn't work anyway. Abdi had managed to glean some other knowledge too. There were no roads in this part of the country, certainly not by the river. There were some small fishing villages: ancient tribal homesteads where life continued without wide screen TVs and refrigerators. The First Mate had a battery-powered radio and Abdi listened carefully each time a news bulletin came on, trying to understand how much of what they had done was in the news. None of it, appeared to be the answer.

Once they were underway, the skipper had pulled out a bag filled with medical supplies, and pointed at Abdi's head, grimacing. Abdi had no idea what he looked like, but he was sure it wasn't pretty. He had to soak the bandage on his head, to get it to separate from his scab. He looked at the stinking mess of yellowy green, septic gunk that flowed freely as the scab tore. Wrinkling his nose at the smell, Abdi threw the stinking bandage over the side and into the river. The cut hurt like a camel's kick, but he used a couple of bottles of drinking water to rinse the wound and to wash his scalp. He was sure if he pushed too hard that he could actually feel the bones of his skull. He swallowed a couple of antibiotic pills, poured antibiotic powder over the wound and then just let it breath for a bit in the sunshine. He put both the pills and powder into his trouser pocket for safekeeping. They were literally going to save his life, until he could get to a doctor.

Abdi had spoken to The Associate earlier and had been updated on the plan. Abdi now had a location to get to, and a timing to meet someone who would help with the next piece of the escape. Until then, he and his team needed to keep their heads down but stay alert. With that in mind, Abdi had made sure that there were always at least two guards awake and on deck, but with their weapons hidden. Any more than that might look suspicious for a simple river barge. The rest were all in the holds, sleeping as they lay, recovering.

Chapter 76

October 4th, Damana Forest. Ghana.

The Chinook had taken twenty minutes to get to the drop-off point. Tom didn't have an exact location in mind, so he was doing a recce on the fly. They found a point where the river narrowed considerably to only about sixty metres wide. The forest pressed right up against the banks on both sides. The next bit wasn't as easy because it was rapidly getting dark. The team had to create an ambush location that didn't look as though it had been touched, but they didn't have time to fly somewhere else, drop trees and march in. Instead, they were going to swim. With the helicopter back in the hover, just above the river, most of the team jumped into the water as close to the near shore as they could get. They had borrowed all of the lifejackets that the Chinook had to help them stay buoyant. A fully grown man in fighting order and carrying a weapon tended to sink very quickly otherwise. One after the other, they had jumped in and then swum to shore. Taking great care to all step out and onto the bank in the same spot, they were trying to dislodge as little foliage as possible.

The last man of this group to jump was Tom and he had tied off one length of abseiling rope to his webbing. He swam the short distance with the spray of the downdraft making it hard to see. Once on the bank though, he and a group of men began to pull on that rope. As they pulled, slowly but surely some great lengths of underslung load steel cables started to snake out of the helicopter and into the water. They kept pulling and pulling until several lengths, held together by shackles, fell out of the aircraft and into the water.

Mike, Raj and Miguel, with another length of rope, now jumped off the back of the helicopter and into the river too. They swam to the opposite bank, a slightly longer swim. This time as they got out, they had a quick hunt for the sturdiest tree they could find. It wasn't hard, those trees were ancient with huge trunks. As they pulled on their rope, two lengths of steel sling cable came out of the water. As the cables came ashore, their weight increased considerably. Two inches thick, those cables were rated to carry fifteen tons. They were not very flexible, and they were very heavy.

The helicopter departed, heading back to camp leaving the site silent at last. Using all their strength, they bent the cable around the base of the tree at ground level and then using the eyelet at the end of it secured it with a D shackle.

The second cable was a little harder. They needed it to stay at about waist height. Using his machete, Mike carved a deep notch into the back of the tree, then with a length of the abseiling rope, secured it around the cable on the front side of the tree. That he suspended from a sturdy branch about two metres off the ground. Wrapping the rope around and around the trunk, they did their best to keep the cable in place. With the task completed, they stepped back down to the riverbank. Having tidied up as best they could, keeping close together, they swam back to the other side.

Tom and his team had a similar job to do, but theirs wasn't easy. They had to spend a little longer finding the right anchor points because they needed to be able to leave the cables unconnected until the very last minute. The cables had to lie hidden under water until the barges came along. Those cables would be raised at the last safe moment so that the barges couldn't avoid running into them. The team had a couple of practice runs, until they found the right trees and then they laid the cables down on the forest floor.

There was one final, crucial part of the plan, which was perhaps the riskiest. Tom took Mike and Raj aside to discuss it with them and to prepare. With that done, the team set up their ambush positions. Cut-offs were out, both up and down stream, radios were checked one last time. The team had seen those 0.50 Cals, so they spent some time digging in slightly. They worked hard on their camouflage to make sure that they were invisible from the river, and finally, when that was complete, they settled down to wait.

Chapter 77

The MV *Red Stiletto* was a superyacht, forty metres long, Ferrari red with white swoosh trim. Inside, she was white suede with red embossing, cherry wood flooring and highly polished brass. She was one of those millionaire playthings where the crew were immaculate in white shorts, socks and polo shirts with red piping. She was opulence personified. She didn't have a heli-deck though, because the owner was afraid of flying, but she did have a specially built rear deck, and sea level aft door which hid all the toys. She carried a mini-submersible, jet skis, a tender and a whole bunch of diving equipment.

Clashing terribly with the smartly turned-out staff, and standing next to the captain on the Bridge, was Chris. Chris was in his fifties, tall, with short blond curly hair and a mousy brown close-trimmed beard. He was leaning casually up against a control console, wearing deck shoes, a brown polo shirt and black cargo shorts. Chris had been a promising Royal Navy Captain once, but a torrid affair with one of his female officers whilst deployed had seen him court martialled. He had joined the maritime security consulting industry, and he was Max's best project manager at sea.

Red Stiletto was on a charter for Max. He had hired it at the last minute after the previous charter had bailed. That billionaire had thought it would be romantic to take his girlfriend from Monaco to Cape Town, but things hadn't gone well. Firstly the woman, who was half his age, hadn't liked the Atlantic swell and had been seasick for a week. That had been a big turn off. Then as they entered the Gulf of Guinea a couple of ships had been hijacked and the billionaire had lost his bottle. He insisted that they be dropped off at the nearest available port and he and his girlfriend finished the rest of the journey by private jet.

The cancellation had cost him a fortune, but it was small change to that idiot. That man's misfortune was Max's good luck. When his team had started looking for a maritime charter, they were expecting to hire a fishing boat or a small cargo vessel. The yacht broker had offered *Red Stiletto* at a fraction of her normal price and, as she was close to where she was needed, Max had snapped her up. Chris and Bob, the other team member, had boarded yesterday afternoon after a quick mobilisation flight from the UK.

Red Stiletto was currently cruising gently along, about thirty nautical miles offshore from Ivory Coast. In about eight hours they would reach their holding area, just this side of Ghanaian national waters. There was a vast tidal sandbar that they were heading for and once they got there, they were going to wait for further instructions.

Bob was down below having a look at all the toys. In a cavernous rear compartment, with a vast portal to the sea that lifted like a DeLorean door, were all sorts of goodies; some on chocks on the floor and some strapped to the walls. The whole space was immaculately organised. The owner of the vessel was obviously into his marine life and exploration. The submersible was a two-person submarine, with a bulbous Perspex dome, two, long, slender, yellow mechanical arms, and a boxy energy pack and thruster system at the rear. There were a couple of jet skis, a doughnut, surfboards, and windsurfers. There were wetsuits, dry suits, a deep diving suit, simple oxygen tanks, rebreathers and harpoons.

Bob was an ex-Royal Marine senior non-commissioned officer and definitely wasn't used to the playthings of the rich. He was only about five foot six, but powerfully built in his chest and arms. He had short brown hair, a slightly ginger goatee and grey eyes. Bob spoke to the deck hand in his southern English burr. 'Right mate, so does all this kit work?'

'Well yes, sir, of course.'

'An' we can use it all whenever we want?'

'Yes sir. It's included in the charter.'

'Great, an' how long can that sub stay underwater for?'

'Well, how long can you hold your breath for sir?'

Bob looked at him, saw the gleam in his cocky eye and thought he would give the man some slack, though not too much. 'That was actually quite funny. Not as funny as me throwing you overboard and watching you swim all the way to shore though.'

Seeing Bob's deadpan face, the deckhand quickly went on. 'It all depends on the depth you want to go to, sir. We usually plan on hour-long trips down to thirty metres or so. Anything more than that and, to be honest, usually the pilot gets tired.'

'And I am allowed to drive it?'

'Yes sir, but I am a trained pilot on it and will have to go with you. As a safety precaution, if anything goes wrong, our captain is also qualified to pilot it remotely and bring us back.'

'That's pretty cool. I want to play with that next time we stop.'

'Very good, sir.'

'Now tell me, what's this kit here?'

'Well sir, the owner is passionate about exploring underwater, finding valuable artefacts. Those bags are flotation bags. You attach them to those cargo nets using the strops over there and fill them with air. Then whatever you have found rises to the surface. We then use the equipment crane and can bring whatever it is right on board.'

'Excellent. I want to play with that kit too.'

'Lovely, sir.' He said with a bright-toothed grin that a dentist would be proud of. 'We have all the toys.'

Up on the bridge, Chris had just finished talking to Max on his satellite phone. He had received a project update and it didn't sound too positive at the moment. A bit touch and go. The good news was that *Red Stiletto*, as garish as she was, was perfect for what they needed. Chris wasn't too sure exactly what that would be though at the moment. Last minute projects meant too much could go wrong.

Chapter 78

October 4th, Volta River. Ghana.

Azrah was sitting towards the bow of the river barge, cross legged and in a classic meditation pose. Her long black hair was loose and she was drying it in the breeze as the barge continued its ponderous journey down the river. In front of her, the other barge was about two hundred metres ahead. Its ancient old marine diesel engine spewed out black smoke from a blackened pipe that stood proud of the wheelhouse. Some of that smoke hung in the air as the second barge followed. It desecrated the pure jungle air and left a sour taste in the mouth.

Cheko and Abdi were at the wheelhouse of the second boat, at the stern, and they were relaxing a little more with each passing hour. They were hundreds of kilometres away from the mine site now, well away from any search area. 'How do you think she does it?' Cheko asked Abdi as he indicated forward to the statuesque Azrah.

'Does what, the bombing?'

'Well, yes, but I was thinking more about the killing. Her devices killed what, a hundred men when we attacked that camp?'

'I hadn't really thought about it. But now that I do, I only saw her actually kill the police when they responded. Sure, she made the bombs that killed the guards in the towers, and she laid the mine which got that armoured vehicle at the gate. But if you ask me, it wasn't her that killed the guards, it was those guys.' Abdi pointed at the drone pilots sitting just outside the wheelhouse, who could hear every word and who suddenly looked very uncomfortable.

'But did you see her face each time she set one of her bombs off? It looked like she had a fucking orgasm!'

Abdi looked at him, trying to see if he was serious. 'I didn't see that, my friend. Are you sure?'

'Yes! She obviously gets off on killing people!'

'Well, there was me thinking she was just emotionally devoid. But now you mention it, I wonder how many people she has killed. Does she have no conscience at all? Is she a complete psychopath?'

'I don't know. She obviously had a tough childhood, but what turns a woman down that path? What makes her tick?'

As the barge chugged along the great, brown, brackish, Volta River, Abdi and Cheko continued to discuss the pros and cons of having such a psychopath in their midst. They were completely oblivious to the fact that clinically, they were probably psychopaths too.

Chapter 79

October 5th, Volta River. Ghana.

Still waiting on the edge of the riverbank, with infinite patience, Tom and his men were doing what they had been trained for all those years ago. Oddly, with the dawn that morning, a thick mist had formed. It had clung to the river in thick swirls. At one point it was so dense that the far bank was almost completely invisible. The odd tree appeared and disappeared like some ghostly apparition. With the hours that had passed, the mist had risen off the river a little. But only as high as the treetops, where it continued to cling desperately, as though afraid of being blown into nothing.

Tom had been checking in with Max via the satellite phone's text message system. He was suffering from the natural uncertainty of waiting. Had the barges stopped? Had they unloaded the cargo upstream? Tom had no way of checking. It was too dangerous to send the Chinook out to look, as the noise would obviously give them away. Tom had been told though that this morning the Chinook had found the remains of the other aircraft. Sadly, it had confirmed that David was dead, and the loadmaster had winched down and recovered his body. David's body would be repatriated back to his family in South Africa once the paperwork was confirmed. They had to get around some local laws first though.

There was one other piece of critical information that had been passed down the phone. Max had been ordered by the President not to allow the gold to escape this time, under any circumstances. Max hadn't told the president where the gold was right now because he didn't want anyone to intercept his success fee. But the way Max interpreted that order was that it was better to destroy the boats in place, and get some diving kit up to the location, than to let it pass this ambush point. Finding the gold in a muddy river would be a nightmare, but it was so dense that it shouldn't go too far, as long as the boats were sunk and sunk quickly. The worst case would be if the boats were sunk slowly, perhaps dropping gold bars all the way down the river as their hulls burnt down.

Tom still had one plan up his sleeve though to try to capture the gold. He was gambling that all the gold would be on the boat with Abdi. He didn't like gambling on those odds, but they had been on the back foot since this project had begun. It was time to seize the initiative. Tom's radio earpiece came alive. It was the sentry he had posted several hundred metres upriver. 'Boss, two barges just rounded the bend. It's the same ones we saw yesterday. They're about two hundred metres apart and they will be with you in about five.'

Tom double clicked his transmitter to acknowledge and looked down the line of his team. Everyone had heard that through their earpieces and had perked up massively. Discreetly and with a minimum of movement, magazines were checked one more time, firing positions adjusted and safety catches were released.

Chapter 80

October 5th, Volta River. Ghana.

Miguel, Mike and Raj were not in the ambush line up. Instead, they were about a hundred metres upstream. Or, to be more precise, Mike and Raj were "in" stream. They were heavily camouflaged and hidden in the water in amongst a bank of bull rushes. There was a large branch of a tree with voluminous, thick leafy cover, floating in the river in front of them. The branch was like countless others that had drifted past the ambush line during the past day and didn't look at all out of place. The same type of leaves were deeply intwined into Mike and Raj's helmet bands, and into the shoulder straps of their webbing. They were submerged under water, except for their heads which were just above the waterline in the midst of the branch. Miguel was still on the riverbank, nice and dry. Next to him was another steel strop, one end tied around a vast tree, the other with a huge eyebolt on it, was hooked on the tree branch in the water.

Mike and Raj were holding onto the tree with one hand, and in their other they held their weapons, muzzles resting out of the water. With a prompt from Miguel, who could now see the barges coming, they kicked out slowly from the bank pushing the tree branch in front of them.

The ambush line consisted of ten men. There were two more men about a hundred metres downstream. All of them were heavily camouflaged and had had an opportunity to prepare their firing positions. Behind the ambush line, where the ends of the cables were resting on the leafy floor, four more men were hiding, waiting for the instruction from Tom.

Tom was watching the barges come plodding downstream. He looked on, in relief, tinged with disgust, to see how casual the security was aboard the front barge. It didn't look like anyone was particularly alert and only two people were visible on deck. The barges came closer and closer. With the river only sixty metres or so wide, the barges seemed impossibly close to the riverbank where the ambush party were hiding. Tom felt quite exposed lying flat on the ground, in a small depression hidden by thick grass. When the barge was only a hundred metres away, he gave a command on the radio for the cable operators to do their job. The four men started with the lower cable that would be on the waterline. Together they gripped it and heaved it into place, clipping it rapidly around the pre-prepared tree.

As Tom lay there, he could see the cable lift out of the water briefly, droplets cascading off it and making circular splash marks on the surface. He looked at the skipper of the barge, who had seen something, but wasn't totally sure. The skipper stepped out of the wheelhouse, looking forward, the barge ploughing on. It was when the second cable sprung up that he realised there was a problem. Out of nowhere a barricade had suddenly appeared and he had nowhere to go. The skipper leapt back into the wheelhouse, shouting unintelligibly in panic as he went. He slammed the engine into full reverse.

But this was no nimble speed boat. This was a great hulking barge, it had a lot of inertia, and the knackered old engine wasn't going to let it stop on a dime. It drove on forwards, almost in slow motion. All that shouting though achieved one thing. The thieves, who were all in the forward hold, sprang up to take a look at what was happening. Some had their weapons to hand, and some didn't. It was all the ambush party needed.

All along the line, guns started firing at point blank range. Short, calculated bursts, each one targeting a man. For the first three seconds or so, there was limited reaction from those on the barge. One minute, men were standing, the next they fell. They died not understanding what or how it had happened. As the barge drifted into the cabling, the lower cable was struck a moment before the higher one. The strain was enormous, the cables tightened rapidly, absorbing the shock. The barge still had momentum though and it had to go somewhere. The barge started to slew sideways in the water. Those on it who were still alive, found the barge lurching under their feet, twisting, turning. The bow started to slip along the trapped upper cable to the bank where the ambush party were. As it did so, the gunwale tipped down into the water, the keel rose to the surface. The ambushers had a clear line of site into the hold and quickly killed those who were hiding. The barge tipped beyond the point of no return and suddenly water was gushing into the vast hold as the barge slewed sideways. It was held there for a moment until with huge strain the cables pinged over the top of the hull, coming to a stop in their original positions, vibrating angrily.

The barge, slid sideways down the river sinking rapidly now. About a hundred metres downstream, its bow caught the bank as it went, forcing the barge to rotate and the stern to go headfirst down river. The river wasn't very deep though, and the barge lodged, stuck, causing waves to form around the partially submerged wheelhouse.

The ambushers had been firing for less than twenty seconds, and they switched fire to the second barge which was less than a hundred metres away now.

On that barge, it was Azrah who first reacted to the problem. She came out of her meditative trance to see the barge in front hit the cables, and they all heard the noise of the automatic weapons on the bank.

Azrah leapt off the hold cover that she was sitting on and jumped down into the hold. The barge skipper wasn't a military man and couldn't comprehend what was happening. This type of thing just didn't happen on the rivers in Ghana. Both Cheko and Abdi started screaming at him to react. He put the barge into full reverse, but all that did was slow the boat down in the killing zone. The few fighters on this boat were at least returning fire now, though what they were firing at they didn't know. They simply aimed as best they could towards the undergrowth on the starboard side where all of the noise was coming from. When the ambushers switched fire to them, it was the .50 Cal gunner that caught it first. A concentrated weight of fire shredded through the wooden hull of the vessel causing lead and splinters to scream through the cargo space. The drone pilots, also slow to react, were gawping but managed to jump onto the floor of the hold as the bullets started spitting over their heads. The vessel continued to slow right down. In full reverse it was almost abeam the ambush point. Suddenly, there was a massive graunching of metal at the stern. The barge captain looked fearfully behind him, not understanding. The propeller sheared off. The gearbox imploded and the engine screamed up to rapid revolutions as it shook itself to death.

Mike and Raj had done their job. They had taken the tree branch out into the middle of the river and simply allowed the cable to hook over the propeller. It had been dangerous and just a little bit exciting for a moment, but once the propeller sheared, they were able to recover the cable. With the barge now at almost walking pace, they were able to push forward with the branch. Raj now had his weapon up and covered their approach to the stern of the vessel.

Cheko came to the rear of the boat to see what calamity had happened to the engine. As he leant over the stern, he saw the branch. He peered at it and then his eyes locked with Raj's. Cheko reached behind him for his weapon, which was slung behind his back. Raj, who had already lined him up, put a short burst into his chest. Miguel, who had also been watching, started firing at the same time.

With the man falling backwards into the boat, Mike swam up and hooked the eyelet on the end of the cable over a mooring davit that was on the stern. This knackered old iron post, partly rusted, was the key to recovering a vast fortune in gold.

With the engine still screaming away, but with no thrust, the barge drifted with the current. As it did so, the far end of the cable, which was connected to a vast hard wood tree next to Miguel, acted as an anchor. Nature's forces meant that as the cable came taught, there was only one place for the barge to go, and that was drifting towards the bank where the ambush was.

Tom, seeing that the plan was succeeding, called back to the men who had raised the cables across the river, to release them. As they dropped back into the water the second barge drifted gently past, ending up bumping into the bank, on their side of the river. It came to rest about fifty metres beyond their position.

At that point, using dry fire and manoeuvre, some of Tom's team led a boarding party. As they crossed onto the vessel, they found four people in the hold. Three weedy-looking men and one woman. None of them were armed and as it turned out they all spoke English. All of them were busy protesting their innocence as they were roughly searched, plasticuffed and taken ashore.

Tom stepped up onto the deck of the barge. It had grounded out on the riverbed now, too many holes in its hull below the water line. But what was obvious, under the thin layer of brown water was the carpet of gold.

Tom was joined by Mike and Raj, dripping wet and grinning. 'I told you my physics was right. I knew if we could hook her that she would do this!' Raj was gloating a bit.

'Dude,' said Mike, 'No one likes anyone who says I told you so.'

'But I did, I did, I told you so! We're just like the A-team, buddy. Stuck in the jungle, a couple of ropes and an impossible mission.'

'Oh man, are we ever gonna hear the end of this? So, if we're the A-team, which character are you?'

'Well, it's obvious! I am B.A Barrakus.' Raj grinned.

Mike laughed. 'Dude, I'm the black man! How can you be B.A Barrakus?'

'No need to get racist with me. Just because I look Indian, doesn't mean I don't identify as black deep down in my soul.'

Mike leapt in with both feet, 'Are you fucking kidding me! If you're B.A, who the hell does that make me?'

'Oh, that's easy. You are Howling Mad Murdoch!'

Mike looked at him, paused, and then launched at him, knocking him down to the ground as Raj was laughing.

Tom had to intervene as they were rolling around amongst the leaves. 'Guys, for fuck's sake, the firefight finished about a minute ago, there might still be some of the wankers around here, including Abdi, cut it out!'

Raj was still struggling with Mike and said, 'Sure thing, Faceman!' They both started laughing like the children they were.

Chapter 81

October 5th, Volta River. Ghana.

When Cheko had collapsed backwards into the boat, his disappointment-filled eyes rapidly lost focus. He had managed one last connecting glance at Abdi, and then he had died. Abdi had pity in his eyes, for a moment. And then his own sense of survival kicked in. With bullets zipping across the deck, and the knowledge that someone was only metres away at the rear, he ran and leapt off the barge over the side away from the ambush. He took a huge breath as he did so. Blessing the fact that he had grown up messing around by the sea, he dove deep.

Abdi's dive into the muddy brown water was effectively blind, but that suited him. With the current and with powerful strokes, he swam downstream. He entered a water world, where the sounds of shooting became a blurred mush of noise. He had no idea if anyone had seen him dive, but he was taking no risks. This was a professional hit, and if it was professional then this ambush party would have cut offs downstream. He wasn't going to risk surfacing too soon. When he finally felt that he was going to suffocate, he let out all the air underwater, briefly put his head above and took in a massive lungful of air. Then he swam again, under water for all he was worth. The next time he did it, he sensed he was on the opposite bank. His hand caught the riverbed, and he didn't think he was very deep. He kept going. Several minutes later Abdi felt he was safe, and he raised his head above the water. The battle was way back behind him, the sound of gunfire had stopped, and he couldn't see the barges anymore.

Chapter 82

October 5th, Volta River. Ghana.

Over the next six hours, Tom and the team worked hard. The first thing that happened was that the Chinook came back. It still had nowhere to land, but it came right down into the low hover over the water. The loadmaster threw out several finely meshed cargo nets and some heavily reinforced canvas materiel sacks. Those sacks were similar to the kind of giant bags that builders' merchants use to deliver gravel or sand. The sacks had canvas strop hoops around the top and the intent was to lash them together creating an envelope around the gold.

Tom's men were up to their knees in the water, moving gold bricks aside so that they could clear a space to put the open nets down. It was heavy work, especially given how exhausted they already were, but the cool river helped. Working in shifts, with some on guard duty and holding a perimeter, the rest stacked gold.

The nets were placed down on the deck once a space was cleared. Then one of the sacks was placed on top. One and a half tons was placed into each sack, brick by brick. It was slow work, but after hours of hard work all of it was in the sacks. Those sacks were wrapped in cargo nets sitting solidly in the bottom of the hold.

A couple of the team members had swum across the river to go and release the other ends of the cables. They had then been pulled back to this side of the river. The cables had been carefully coiled up, one end attached to the cargo net, and the other waiting to be attached to the hooks under the Chinook when it returned.

The aircraft was away a little longer than planned. It had returned to the airfield to have a long-distance internal fuel bladder added. This internal rubberised fuel tank was going to more than double her fuel capacity, and that was going to be important for the next part of the plan. When the Chinook finally returned, it was low level. Flying fast up the river, blades just clear of the trees, fighting desperately to stay below the cloud which had formed rapidly throughout the afternoon. As it came into the hover, the pilot swung the back end towards the team. Some men were standing on the riverbank, some on the deck of the barge. The loadmaster threw out a handful of harnesses and connected a mechanical hoist to the same hook at the rear of the aircraft that Mike had abseiled off not so long ago. Two by two, with a lot of noise and down draught, the team members were winched up. They didn't have to travel far, but they swung a little, legs intertwined as they went.

As this was happening, Tom released the prisoners. He wasn't completely heartless. He made sure that they had plenty of food, some medical supplies and even some cash. But he wasn't going to leave them any weapons. If they had any sense, they would realise that they could probably find some in the river near where the ambushes happened. The drone pilots and Azrah didn't look particularly happy at this, but all they needed to do was stay by the river, flag down a passing ship, and pay for passage. If they were lucky, they could probably still get away, though not in time to interfere with Tom and his team.

Finally, with just Mike and Raj left on the ground, the aircraft adjusted its hover and came right down, its wheels almost touching the barge, blades so close to the branches of the nearest trees that its down draught caused a flurry of leaves and twigs. Conscious of static electricity, especially as they were standing up to their knees in water, Mike touched the cable to the hook first, dropping his hands at the last minute. Once it fell, Raj passed it back to him to connect to the giant hook.

There were two underslung load hooks under the aircraft and Mike connected two cargo nets to each using the recovered cables. Indicating to the loadmaster, who was peering over the rear ramp, Mike asked the aircraft to rise. Once it had taken the full length of cable, and he was certain that the loads wouldn't snag, he and Raj hooked onto the winch. The loadmaster raised them, as the helicopter continued to rise. There was a considerable increase in power as the cables went taut. Inch by inch the loads lifted clear of the barge. A little more power and the loads were clear of the tree line. The Chinook was able to transition clear, heading down the river, gathering speed whilst occasionally passing through the edge of light cloud. Mike and Raj reached the top of the winch line and stepped on to the rear ramp.

Looking up the length of the airframe, they saw everyone sitting and relaxing into the strap-based seats along both sides of the cabin. There were high fives, grins, and sighs of relief.

Mike and Raj turned towards each other and gave each other a high five that turned into a solid grip, elbows bent and leaning in to a bear hug.

As they did so, the aircraft lurched to the side, a very strong movement considering the value of the load. No sooner had it turned, it swung back onto its original course, swaying a little as the loads beneath continued their swinging. Mike and Raj recovered their balance, piling into the loadmaster who also grabbed them. The loadmaster was suddenly concentrating on his headphones listening to the pilots.

As Mike and Raj untangled themselves, the loadmaster looked out the back of the aircraft and pointed. Flashing past them, at the same height, but heading up stream, was a Z-9 helicopter, in battle green camouflage. This Chinese export was a light battlefield helicopter and Ghana had several of them in its air force. Even as they spectated, they saw the helicopter slow into the hover. There on the riverbank was a man, drenched, covered in mud and barely recognisable.

Tom came up to stand at the rear. 'I'll bet you all the gold that's hanging beneath us that that bastard is Abdi.'

Chapter 83

October 5th, Volta River. Ghana.

When Abdi had finally stopped swimming underwater, he let his body float for a while, allowing the silt-rich water to carry him for a couple more miles, before finally climbing out of the river and hauling himself up onto the bank. He lay there panting for a while, recovering. If he thought about it too much, he realised he was in very deep trouble. The fact that he was now stuck in the middle of the jungle, with no food, no clean water and no weapon was almost immaterial. He had lost the gold. The Associate didn't take that kind of failure quietly. No matter that the political support Abdi was meant to have received on the ground had failed miserably. Abdi had had the gold in his hands and somehow, in a way that he couldn't fathom, he had lost it all in twenty seconds of bullet-filled fury. He shook his head and tried to compose himself. Abdi started by checking what resources he had; at least there was his medicine. But then on reflection he realised that was the least of his worries. If The Associate let him live long enough, then he might live long enough for the antibiotics to work.

He put his hand down to his cargo shorts pocket. The one by his thigh in which he kept his satphone. The bulk of the phone was still there, but as he pulled it out of his sodden pocket, he had no hope that it was still working. He was staggered to find that it was. Its design and ruggedised case really were waterproof. He pushed a button and the screen lit up, just like normal. The power was down to only about one bar now, but the thing still worked! Allah be praised!

Abdi reflected for a moment. Would The Associate help him now that he had failed? Or, was there perhaps still a way of saving his skin and recovering the gold. It certainly couldn't go anywhere quickly. It was all in the bottom of that barge. Abdi was afraid of giving The Associate the bad news verbally. He was afraid of being left in the jungle to rot. He was just as afraid of ever making it out of the Jungle alive and getting back to his home town in Somalia. The Associate knew everything about him, had given him his first chance in life and was known to be ruthless with those who disappointed him.

He thought carefully what he needed to say and then dialled the number. When the phone was answered, there was no greeting, so Abdi just began. 'We were ambushed on the river. Everyone is dead and the boat sank. The gold is still in it, and we can get it back, but I need help right now.'

No reply, so Abdi kept talking. 'I don't know how they found us. I don't even know who *they* are. There were a lot of them, and they butchered us and won the battle in less than a minute.'

'And yet you are alive,' came the cultured voice in an accent that was impossible to trace.

'Only because I could swim!' exclaimed Abdi.

'I don't tolerate failure.'

'This was not my failure. I saw some of them! They were not Ghanaian security forces. There were white guys, black guys, Indians. Who the fuck were they?'

'That's the first thing that you have said on this call that I find interesting. And they are in control of all of my gold now?'

'Yes. We need military support; you have to bring in lots of it. That gold can't go anywhere quickly. It might all be sitting on the bottom of the river for all I know.'

The Associate rarely got angry, but his voice was ice cold now. 'I have spent a fortune in getting this project up and running, and right now I have nothing to show for it. I will decide what I have to do. I will talk to some people. Send me your location and I will decide. Either you will hear from me, or you won't.'

Well, that conversation went as well as he could have hoped, thought Abdi. His fate was resting entirely in another man's hands, and that was not a feeling he wanted to get used to. It took about ten minutes before his phone pinged with an incoming message.

"A helicopter will come for you today. Stay where you are."

Abdi hoped that that meant it was positive news. Surely The Associate wasn't sadistic enough to pay for a helicopter to come and collect him, if he then intended to kill him? Well, he would find out soon enough.

Chapter 84

October 5th, Volta River. Ghana.

The Z-9 helicopter was a Chinese military export. It was provided to countries that wanted something with a bit of firepower, in return for giving away influence tokens, to the not-so-sleeping dragon in the East. From a technology perspective it was pretty reliable. For once, the Chinese government had actually licensed the technology instead of stealing it and so it was effectively a French Dauphin helicopter, made under license in China. Trust the French arms industry to sell anything to anyone.

The one that arrived to collect Abdi later that afternoon was a utility version of the helicopter, painted in jungle camouflage. It boasted a door-mounted minigun and as it came into the hover above Abdi, the door gunner opened the rear sliding door to talk the pilots down.

Abdi, who had been standing on the bank, realised that he wouldn't be able to get into the helicopter from where he was. The blades would start striking trees if it came any closer. The door gunner obviously realised that too and so connected a thick knotted rope to a hook mounted externally above the door. He let the ten-foot rope drop into the water and beckoned through the spray for Abdi to get back into the river.

Not particularly impressed, especially as he had just dried out, Abdi did so. He waded out as far as he could, but had to swim that last few metres and reached the rope with some difficulty. A multi-ton noisy beast, hovering a few metres above his head, added to the difficulty. However, the really hard part came when he reached the rope. It was thick, it was wet, and even though it had huge knots tied into it, Abdi was not the kind of man who had ever worked out.

The pilot kept the wheeled aircraft in a very low hover, barely a metre off the water, but, as Abdi looked up, into the face of the visored door gunner, it could have been a hundred metres up. Abdi gripped the rope and then tried to pull himself up. His wet clothes, the moving river, the noise, it was too much. He simply couldn't haul himself up. He clung there like a drowned rat, not wanting to let go and be carried off downstream. He was too far below the door gunner for him to reach down and grab Abdi either.

There was a moment of indecision, and then the aircraft began to descend lower. Now even the wheels were in the water. Abdi, coughing and spluttering, adjusted his grip further up the rope. The door gunner was lying on the floor of the cabin, reaching down. Finally, he grabbed enough of Abdi by the scruff of his shirt and hauled him up and into the cabin.

Abdi lay there on the deck, floundering like a fish and gasping as the door gunner hauled in the now soaking-wet and heavy rope.

As the aircraft pulled up and away, Abdi had a set of headphones plonked unceremoniously onto the top of his head. It made him wince as it broke the scab on his wound. As he sat up, one of the pilots at the front turned to the rear and started talking to him.

'Welcome aboard. Now, who the fuck was flying in that Chinook we nearly crashed into?'

Abdi, still breathless, replied, 'How much do you know about me?'

'The only thing I know is that I got scrambled to pick you up by the deputy commander of the Air Force himself. He told me that this was top secret and that I had to do anything you asked.'

Abdi tried to look into the eyes of the pilot, but it was impossible because of the dark visor that was covering his face. Abdi turned to the door gunner who was on the same intercom. 'Have you got bullets for that gun?'

The gunner was a little surprised but said 'Yes, sir.'

Abdi turned back to the aircraft captain. 'Captain, that Chinook is here illegally and is part of an international organisation that I can't tell you about. I need you to shoot it down.'

If the captain showed any emotion, Abdi couldn't see it. There was a pause before the captain repeated back what was said. 'Sir, you're telling me that that aircraft is a threat to the state of Ghana and that it should be shot down. Is that correct?'

'Yes.'

'One moment, sir.'

It was obvious that the two pilots had switched Abdi out of the comms loop and were conferring up front. They pulled power as they spoke and started to accelerate downstream. The aircraft stayed low, well below treetop height, skimming the river as it flew. The cloud, or mist, or whatever it was, still clung to anything higher. It made for a rough ride. At speed, the pilot had to take the bends of the river like a racing car, steep turns forced the blades to such an angle that the tips almost beat the surface of the river. The forces of the air on the blades created a bop, bop, bop sound as the aircraft pulled tight turns, the engines at max power. Abdi had been strapped into a rear bench seat by the door gunner and he felt the g-forces from some of the turns. As he looked out of the windows, there were times when he was staring up unfathomably into the mists above him. And then there were the times, when he saw precisely how close to the river they were, and the branches that stretched out above them.

The intercom came back to life in Abdi's ears. 'Sir, I have the approvals I needed. We're going to do what you want. There's no low-level radar way out here in the bush, so I have to assume that the Chinook is heading down the river still, so that's the way we'll go. Good news is that with those underslung loads it was carrying, it'll be going relatively slowly. We should be able to catch it in the next ten minutes or so.'

'Can't we go any higher than this?' was Abdi's only reply as he looked down into the face of a fisherman in a dugout canoe staring above him in fear.

'Well, we could, but then we would likely not find your Chinook. This cloud layer extends for a couple of thousand feet. We can punch above it but getting back down to ground level would be too dangerous. This is an important question. Do you think the Chinook will risk going high and being detected by radar, or will they stay low and hide?'

Abdi was thinking about the great big sacks he had seen under the Chinook, when it had passed him. 'Oh, that's easy. They are going to be low. As low as they can be.'

Chapter 85

October 5th, Volta River. Ghana.

There was a debate happening on the flight deck of the Chinook too. Tom and the two pilots were talking. Tom had stepped up there after the crazy jinking manoeuvre to avoid the helicopter that had nearly flown into them. 'What was that, and what are the odds that it would have been in exactly the same place as us?' he asked.

The pilots were wearing blue flying coveralls, with matching navy-blue flying helmets. Their visors were up, and they were desperately concentrating on the task in hand. Flying with underslung loads as heavy as those concentrated the mind. Then adding in the appalling visibility, low cloud cover, treetop height and a lack of manoeuvrability to fly out of trouble meant that they were really working at maximum capacity. The captain's answers were short and sharp in his northern English accent.

'It was military, and incredibly unlikely.'

'Can they catch up with us?'

'Yes, and quickly. Watch the bend!'

Tom saw the delay between the pilots' actions, steering as best they could, and the aircraft effectively responding. The Chinook seemed to skid and slew around the corner. An alarm started sounding in the cockpit, and an orange light lit up on a display. It said 'Overload.'

'What does that mean?' asked Tom nervously.

The captain leant forward and pushed the button. It still flashed but at least the siren stopped. 'It means all that gold weighs too much and we are trashing my airframe by flying this fast and pulling G.'

To Tom, the helicopter was a massive solid beast, and he hadn't thought about that. 'What do we do if they do catch up with us?'

'Well, we can't outrun them with the loads on, but we could with them jettisoned.'

'Jettisoned! We can't do that!'

'Well in that case, they will catch up with us, if that's what they want to do.'

'Can't we hide in the clouds or something?' asked Tom.

'Too many movies, mate. We either break and head straight up, out of the clouds, or we stay here at low level and hope to God we can get to a place where this mist has cleared.'

Almost to command, the mist thickened right down to river level and for a moment Tom swore that he could see nothing ahead of them at all through a blanket of white. His face paled. It lasted less than a second before the pilot continued. 'Too much more of that shit and we'll break skywards anyway. Of course, we then increase the risk of alerting military radar and then we really will be in trouble.'

Another alarm called out suddenly, this time an audio. 'Terrain. Terrain. Pull Up.' It was almost robotic, and oddly female. It spoke using a tone that meant, listen to me for once, darling and do what I say, without actually screaming or shouting.'

The pilot again pressed the cancel button and adjusted a dial on the dashboard.

'What was that?' asked Tom.

'Radar altimeter. Very accurate. Told us we were too close to the ground.'

'But we must be well above the ground, aren't we?'

'We are mate, but those loads are on the end of thirty-metre strops. The nets add a couple more metres. And this radar is set to fifty metres.'

'So those nets are less than ten metres off the ground?'

'Yep.'

'And you're racking it around these corners?'

'Yep.'

'What happens if they hit something?'

'If it happens, we can't do anything about it.'

Tom went even paler. 'Do you want me to stop bothering you then?'

'Might be a good idea, mate.'

'Fuck. OK, last one. What do we do if that other helicopter catches up with us?'

'You guys have got all the weapons. If you want to keep these loads, you'll have to figure something out, pal.'

Chapter 86

October 5th, Volta River. Ghana.

Tom had quickly staggered back to confer with Mike and Raj. There were more than a couple of green-looking faces in the back of the Chinook. Being thrown about when you can see out the front window was one thing. But being stuck in the back of a flying bus as it did hairpin turns down a narrow river was quite another. To add to the vomit inducement, the extra-long-range fuel bladder, which was secure but wallowing on the deck, gurgled a little. There was a strong smell of aviation fuel from the recent refuelling. As Tom arrived, he was obviously interrupting an important conversation between Raj and Mike.

'Dude. How's that convoy cock thing working out for you right now?'

Mike, an ex-Navy Seal, wasn't looking too well. 'Raj, if you don't want me to yak all over you, I suggest you shut the fuck up.'

'You know, I was just thinking of that really fun project we did in Sudan. You remember that abattoir that had been hit by a rebel bomb? Man, that was something, blood, guts, and shit everywhere. All those bits and pieces of humans and animals all mixed in. Do you remember buddy? I can still see every...'

Tom arrived just in time to prevent another blood bath. 'Cut it out, Raj. Work.'

The three of them spent five minutes working out what they needed to do. Then with a quick warning order around the team, who were trying to switch off, they briefed everyone on what needed to happen next.

The loadmaster had been nominated as the lookout. He went to the rear of the aircraft and lowered the rear ramp, very slightly. Not enough to be obvious, but enough for him to see out and to the rear. His move was timely. No sooner had he started to look than the camouflage fuselage of the Z-9 appeared from around the bend to the rear. There followed a few moments of cat and mouse. The loadmaster relayed to Tom that the chase aircraft had instructed the Chinook via radio to follow them and land at the nearest air base. The Chinook captain had refused to even reply. The Z-9 approached much closer. This time the radio warning had stepped up a gear. "Follow us or be shot down." Again, no reply.

'Its rules of engagement stuff,' said Mike. 'Next one will be a warning shot, and after that they are going to hit us.'

Raj joined the loadmaster and peeked out. 'I don't see any air-to-air missiles. Just a mini-gun on its port side.'

Tom spoke out with a commanding voice to the whole team behind him. 'OK men! If we get to the warning shot stage, we will go for it as briefed. Everyone ready?'

The sound of any replies was drowned out by the burst of fire from the mini-gun on the Z-9. It had closed to only a couple of hundred feet away, right up the rear end of the Chinook. The Z-9 pilot had obviously wanted the Chinook crew to hear the sound of the weapon firing.

The loadmaster hit the button for the rear ramp, and it started to descend. On the rear deck of the Chinook, lying down, and clinging on through the turns, was a line of men, all with weapons up and aimed to the rear. Behind them, kneeling, were ten more. With all of the AK-47's there was an arsenal of firepower. As the ramp lowered to the stops, like a framed picture, in the middle of the kill zone, was a helicopter. As the team opened fire, there was a flicker of horror on the faces of the Z-9 pilots. For a moment anyway.

Chapter 87

October 5th, Volta River. Ghana.

When Abdi had first seen the Chinook ahead, wallowing along just above the river, he had been elated. There was a buzz of chatter amongst the crew and Abdi could hear the radio commands being transmitted to the occupants of the Chinook. Because there was no answer, there was a bit of a debate as to what they should do, but ultimately the decision to make the warning shot had been the captain's.

Abdi had watched the door gunner lean out of the open port side sliding door, grab the handles on rear of the mini-gun and cock the weapon. Even though he was expecting it, Abdi was shocked at the firepower. A simple few seconds' burst had sent more than a hundred bullets forward from the revolving barrels. Every fifth was a tracer and so those angry red wasps were visible as they raced past the Chinook on its port side. The pilots in front couldn't have missed seeing them.

The shots had at least created a response on the Chinook and Abdi and his pilots had all watched as the rear ramp descended, like a blackened mouth opening up. It was hard to see into the interior, even from this close range, but as the ramp opened fully, they could see the loadmaster standing on the ramp. Abdi couldn't understand why it looked like he was saluting though. When the firing started, it was horrifyingly obvious. The flame suppressors didn't dim the evil twinkling lights in the dark cavern of the rear of the Chinook. All of those flashing, winking, fiery protests. Each one betraying a bullets anger. And all those bullets were heading Abdi's way.

His pilots weren't even remotely fast enough to react. The glass of the cockpit shattered in front of them, riddled, as were the air crew. Alarms started howling. One of the pilots had enough control to jink the aircraft back and away. More alarms, curses, the gory door gunner thrown out of the aircraft, held on only by the safety line. Smoke filled the cabin now. Thick white smoke. The reeking smell of burning hydraulic fluid. The aircraft was falling and quickly. Abdi was frantically clinging on, miraculously unhurt. A pilot still alive? Yes! Screams of pain and panic through the intercom. A moment of terror as once again Abdi found himself in the water. The Z-9 hit with a thump and immediately turned over in the deep muddy brown depths. The blades smashed into the river, fracturing, splintering, and frothing the surface.

The white smoke was replaced by gushing silty liquid. It entered the cabin space like a tidal wave. Shock, incomprehension. Abdi, panicking and still strapped to his seat, was now upside down. Water flooding up to him. Air rapidly leaving the cabin. A last frantic, desperate gulp of air. Abdi fought to get free. He was gripped by something. What the fuck? Heart beating. Can't see a thing. Eyes opened briefly. Stung by the water. Really panicking now, the fucking seat won't let me go! Hands thrashing, found the buckle. Twist and free! Yes!

But now what? Where do I go? Eyes still closed, which way is up, or down? Lungs bursting! Am I twisting? My ears just filled, am I sinking? Allah be merciful, where is the door!

Getting dizzy. Heart beating faster. Hands grabbing. The gun? The door! Kicking! Pulling! I'm free!

Abdi's head broke the surface of the river gasping for breath. So weak and so afraid, but grateful just to be alive. He turned onto his back, allowing the current to take him with it. Great lungsful of air. As he floated gently down river, he looked up into the misty sky. The trees passed sombrely by, lining his passage, silent observers to his passing.

Chapter 88

October 5th, Volta River. Ghana.

There was no real celebration after they had shot down the Z-9. It had been cold blooded, brutal, point-blank killing. They had all seen the aircraft hit the water, quickly invert and disappear beneath the surface. Then just as quickly it disappeared, as they turned a bend in the river. The loadmaster informed the pilots that the threat had gone, and that there was no more pressure on them from behind. There was a noticeable slowing down of the aircraft at that point. Less need to take risk. No point in getting away a few minutes faster if you were going to smack into the treeline and not get away at all.

Flying in cloud had been the death of many a pilot over the years. That feeling that it wouldn't happen to you. Controlled flight into terrain, or whatever the accident board would call it after the fact. That was a polite way of saying the pilot had fucked up, and fucked up big time. It happened to the best and most experienced pilots too. They were found guilty of bending the rules, one roll of the dice too many.

The Chinook flew on for another hour, before finally it reached the vast expanse of Lake Volta. The river had gradually been getting wider and slower. It was probably two hundred metres wide at the point where it entered the lake, and the river traffic over this part of the lake was suddenly everywhere.

Unfortunately, something happened to the weather at that point and the mist descended right down to the lake level. It was simply no longer possible to fly low level and the pilots had to make a break up through the cloud. Technically, it was an emergency manoeuvre. No radar to guide them, fortunately, and no one to talk them through it. If the cloud layer hadn't been so thick it might not have been a major problem. However, as they continued to climb, they realised that they were up at three thousand feet, before they broke through to clear blue sky again. Up there, the long-range radars would find them eventually. That meant that, without a flight plan and not transmitting on their transponder, they would be highly suspicious and might be investigated. Add to that, they didn't know what the military pilots in the Z-9 had managed to broadcast before they had been engaged. There was too much outside Tom's control and he didn't like that.

Tom walked back up to the flight deck once they were out of the climb, and spoke to the pilots again. 'So how long before we get to the coast?'

'A couple of hours.'

'Are you worried about radar up here?

'A little, but inland there aren't many airports. It's when we get to the coast that we need to focus. Accra and Takoradi have overlapping radar zones. If we're still at this height at that point, they will definitely pick us up. If we see a break in the cloud, we'll get back down to ground level as quickly as possible.'

Not very reassured, Tom went aft again. He needed to make some phone calls.

Chapter 89

October 5th, *Red Stiletto*. The Ivory Coast.

The *Red Stiletto* was moored off the Ivory Coast, near a large sandbar about fifteen miles out to sea. The Ferrari red decadence bobbed gently in calm water. No other ships could be seen as the vessel floated there and the radar wasn't picking anything up either. The tidal sandbar was vast and as it was currently low tide, the fragile skeletons of ships of old could be seen rusted and embedded in the dunes. With every tide, speck by speck or splinter by splinter, those doomed ships would erode eventually to nothing.

For now though, those decaying vessels were being observed from under the surface. Bob and the deckhand were in the submersible. Stencilled on its hull was a wave motif and the name *Aquaholic*. The owner loved his toys with a passion and this rather expensive one was state of the art. Bob was piloting it, under the watchful eye of the deckhand. He was using the thrusters infinitely carefully, learning how to manoeuvre close in to the wrecks.

From only a few metres away in the calm sea, in the lee of the sandbar, the wrecks were teeming with life. The sandbar evidently sat on top of some giant undersea mountain that had never quite thrust up enough to become an island. It meant, though, that the beautiful underwater paradise was incredible. The sandbar stretched for miles, gently passing under the surface, where it extended further underwater, until it ended in an almost sheer cliff, which disappeared out of sight into the depths below. Bob had initially taken the submersible to look at the cliff face. Through the large viewing bubble, he had seen cracks and crevices, a living wall of seaweeds, corals and fish of every colour and size.

Heading back over the underwater sand dunes, Bob had seen several sand sharks, unsettled by the passing of the submersible. A pair of manta rays had glided silently over the top of the Perspex dome. Momentarily, their shadows left an eerie impression on the crew.

Bob's southern English accent came over the intercom. 'Right, let's try and use the claw.'

'Do you mean the manipulator arm, sir?' said the slightly smarmy deckhand, who still hadn't fully learned his lesson.

''As it got a claw on it?'

'Yes, sir.'

'Well let's use the claw then,' Bob smiled at him. A shark-tooth smile that put the deckhand back in his place.

'Lovely, sir. This is the controller for the... claw right here. How about I pilot whilst you try it out.'

'Awesome, let's go over to that wreck and see if we can give it a grope.'

'As you wish, sir.'

The bright yellow submersible beetled over to the mostly submerged wreck of what might have once been a fishing vessel. Bob spent five minutes playing with the claw, practising the movements needed to grip, twist and pull. He was interrupted by Chris' voice on the radio.

'*Aquaholic*, this is *Stiletto*. I need you to come back now please.'

'Roger that. Returning now.' Bob spoke into the headset and then to his crew member he said. 'Give us another play then.'

Fifteen minutes later Bob and Chris were on the toy deck of *Red Stiletto*.

'Sorry to cut your playtime short. I just heard from Tom.'

'How are they doing?'

'Pretty well actually. They'll be with us in about three hours.'

Bob looked surprised. 'Alright, better get sorted out then, hadn't we?' He turned to the deckhand. 'Mate, can you plug that baby back into recharge. We might be needing her again later.'

238

Chapter 90

October 5th, 5000 feet over Ghana.

The Chinook pilots had been more than a little shaken by the air-to-air combat. Preying on their minds were all the known unknowns. Had the military helicopter been looking for them? Did they know it was a Chinook that they were chasing, or had they come across them by sheer dumb luck? The military obviously had approval to engage an unarmed aircraft, so who authorised that? Did the Air Force know about them and were there fast jets racing to intercept even now?

This Chinook was a civilian version, so there were no fancy defensive aid suites on board. No chaff or flares, no infra-red defence systems and certainly no in-cockpit warning systems, that would tell them if they had been targeted by an air defence radar or missile.

When the pilots finally started to get ahead of the weather front, they began to see the ground patchy below them, through the gaps in the clouds. They were just beginning to breathe a sigh of relief, when over the emergency radio frequency came a chilling command.

'Helicopter at five thousand feet, thirty kilometres northwest of Takoradi defence zone, this is Ghanaian Air Force controller. Identify yourself.'

The two pilots looked at each other, double checked their navigation equipment and realised there was no doubt that the air traffic controller was trying to talk to them. As previously agreed, they didn't reply.

'Unknown helicopter, you are commanded to squawk 3592 and ident.'

The captain looked down to the transponder and made doubly sure it was turned off.

'Unknown helicopter, you are commanded to divert to Takoradi military airbase, or you will be engaged.'

That was a new one to the pilots. Could they really be engaged? It was suddenly getting very serious. After a very brief consultation, the captain put the aircraft into a steep dive, rapidly accelerating to maximum possible airspeed, conscious of the underslung loads but losing height as rapidly as possible.

The hairs on the back of their necks began to prickle. The descent was taking ages. If the radar system could see them, then they would know that they had been heard and that this was an aggressive evasion. Still, it was better than just plodding along high up with a target on their chests.

With a gap in the cloud all the way to ground level identified, the captain turned at ninety degrees perpendicular to the direction where the defence radar was. Some old manual popped into his head talking about doppler effects on radar guidance systems. A ninety-degree turn might help them mask, but just as importantly it might help confuse the radar operator of their overall direction of travel.

The drop from five thousand feet continued to take too long. The air traffic controller kept demanding that they identify. They just ignored him, but the threats continued. All the way down the pilots were expecting a missile the size of a telegraph pole to come flying up at them. Missiles were exactly that, *miss*iles. Rarely did a missile actually contact what it was being aimed at. But all it had to do was get in the vicinity and then explode. It was the explosion and subsequent fragmentation that did all the damage. Of course, there were kinetic weapons that did hit, and they flew so fast and hit so hard that the energy dissipated was catastrophic.

At about a thousand feet, the captain started to pull up on the collective again and adjust the attitude of the helicopter. He needed to treat the airframe gently. With all that weight underneath, he couldn't just stop on a dime. As they dropped under a hundred feet above ground level, they changed direction again heading back onto their course. There was no way that the radar station would pick them up again down here. The terrain was rugged, there were hills and valleys, lots of clutter to get lost in amongst. Feeling more confident again, the pilots started nap-of-the-earth flying. It wasn't so comfortable for those in the back, but if you were dead, that wasn't particularly comfortable either.

In the rear of the aircraft Tom was on the satphone to Chris. He had strapped himself into a seat near the comms console, so that he wasn't being thrown around and could focus on the conversation rather than holding on tight. 'Well, I tell you what, Chris, this bucket that we're being thrown around in right now is nothing like the luxury that you and Bob are having to suffer.'

'What? We are suffering! It's really hard to keep the ice in my Bloody Mary from melting!'

'My bloody heart bleeds for you. Now, tell me about the drop location.'

'It's a good one. A huge sand bar well off the coastline. Some volcanic uplift or other. I think you guys can manage it. We don't want to put the gold on top of the sand bar, simply because we can't get the ship in close enough to pick it up. What I suggest is that we drop a couple of buoys in the water, then release your loads. Then we can use the flotation gear and the ship's toys to bring the loads over to the ship's onboard crane.'

'That sounds too easy, what's the catch?'

'Yes, there is always a catch isn't there. Well, if you miss the marker then you will drop the loads over the edge of a volcanic mountain, and it will sink about a thousand feet. That's also a possibility if the equipment fails once we are trying to float it off the sand bar.'

'Lovely. That would be a bit… unfortunate, after what we've been through to capture it in the first place. And you're sure that the location is out of Ghanaian waters?'

'Definitely. It's five miles into the Ivory Coast's maritime zone.'

'Great, well, according to the pilots, we're about an hour away from you.'

'Bugger, you mean I 'm going to have to share these Bloody Marys after all?'

'It's alright, you can keep that rubbish. I'll settle for a cold beer.'

Chapter 91

October 5th, *Red Stiletto*. The Ivory Coast.

The *Red Stiletto* had dropped her anchor on the edge of the sandbar and had settled nicely with her bow into the gentle current. Off the starboard side, the vast stretch of white sands had shrunk with the rising of the tide. There were still hundreds of square metres of rippled sand dunes visible. The glare of the sun glittered brightly off the sand and sparkled off the lapping water. Bob had taken the ship's sleek tender and some snorkelling gear to choose a drop location. He and the deckhand had moored at a spot less than a hundred metres away from *Red Stiletto*.

Wearing fins and a snorkel, Bob had leaned backwards off the side of the tender, landing with a splash in the cool water. Aside from the occasional shell, and the odd brightly-coloured fish suspended as though in mid-air, Bob could have been above a snowscape. With a depth of perhaps three meters, a smooth sandy bottom and crystal-clear water, there was plenty of space to drop the loads. The chosen area was also a long way away from the cliff edge that Chris had been worried about. Surfacing, Bob pulled out the mouthpiece of the snorkel and spoke to the deckhand. He sounded very nasal as the mask still obstructed his nose. 'It's a great spot. Tie the buoy ropes off at four metres and let's drop one here, and the other in that direction, fifteen metres away.'

'Certainly, sir.' The deck hand didn't know what the plan really was but had looked after a vast number of eccentric millionaires. With an eye on a cash tip at the end of the charter, he was happy to help them with their weird requests. With the rope attached to a small sand anchor at one end and a bright red buoy at the other, he dropped the lot over the side.

Bob, floating in the water at the side of the tender looked down, breathing through his snorkel to see the anchor drop rapidly. The blue rope stretched taut upwards towards the buoy. He thought that perhaps he'd overcooked it a little with a four-metre rope, but it was no matter. There was a football field's worth of target to be hit. With a light tap on his head he looked up to see the deckhand motioning for him to stay clear. 'Starting', he heard, muffled through his water-filled ears.

Bob swam well clear of the tender and the deckhand pulled in its anchor. As it happened, he didn't need to start it up. He just drifted gently for ten metres or so and then dropped his anchor again. The next buoy went over the side and Bob checked that one too, to make sure that the anchor took in the sand. He put his head back up above the water again. 'Take her back to the ship, I could do with the exercise.' He got a thumbs up and the tender started up and gently went back to its mother.

Chapter 92

'Inca Six, this is Dragon Six over.' Tom's voice was coming over the radio on a pre-agreed and little used VHF frequency.

'This is Inca Six. Send.' Chris and Tom knew each other's voices very well and no further confirmation was needed.

'Inca Six, we have you visual, are you happy to proceed, over.'

'Affirmative. Two obvious markers a hundred metres north of our position. I have you visual now too, over.'

The sight of the Chinook coming low and slow over the ocean after so much planning and effort was a real morale booster for Chris and Bob. Both were standing on the bridge of the elegant superyacht. Behind the captain's console, the teak decking spread to a horseshoe-shaped open-air seating area, with cream weatherproof sofas and low tables. They had been sitting there having an ice-cold coke waiting for the arrival of the team, and as soon as the radio had squawked they had leapt up, binoculars in hand.

Just a couple of minutes later and the vast bulk of the Chinook was in the low hover. The staggering weight of the machine was suspended in mid-air. It rotated as the loadmaster, leaning out of the open side-door, looked down and verbally guided the pilot over the red buoy markers.

As the helicopter descended, the downwash started to create spray and a cloud of fine sand particles. In the strong wind, a fair storm of it was forced towards *Red Stiletto*. The deck crew, who were all watching the amazing spectacle from a lower deck, groaned inwardly. The mix of sand and water, mixing cement on the move, made them realise how much cleaning and buffing they would have to do to get the ship immaculate again.

This time it was the pilot's voice over the radio. 'Inca Six, this is Dragon. Confirm you want us to drop here, over?'

'That will do nicely.' Chris replied.

Bob and Chris watched as the Chinook descended further. She gently lowered her bulk, like a settling toad, until the cargo netted loads passed under the surface of the sea. Still the helicopter descended. The long strop cables, that had been so taut, suddenly slackened off as the loads touched the seabed. The loadmaster was obviously talking the pilot through the manoeuvre. A moment later, the front cargo hook released on its magnetic locks and the cables holding the front two load cables dropped undramatically into the sea.

'No! Not there!' It was Bob's voice on the radio sounding frantic. Chris turned to look at him, surprise on his face.

'What! What's wrong?' Tom's worried voice came back immediately. 'Is that the wrong place?'

'Nah, just shitting with you, boss.'

'You are such a tit!' Tom didn't sound amused, but Chris and Bob were having a good laugh. They were still giggling as the rear cargo hook released and the final two loads also dropped onto the seabed.

Chapter 93

October 5th, The Chinook. The Ivory Coast.

'I am going to kill that guy when we get hold of him.' Tom was tired and his sense of humour had deserted him temporarily. Raj, though, always the one to see the funny side, tried to calm him down a bit. 'It was a little bit funny, I thought.'

Tom gave him a look before giving in. 'Sure. Let's get this last part over with and then we can relax a little more.'

Tom, Mike, Raj and Miguel were leaving the Chinook at that point and had already prepared their kit. Anything of value was in the dry bags inside their rucksacks. In addition, they had put their weapons, comms, and some other useful items into a couple of large waterproof Peli cases. They would keep the kit dry as they swam across to *Red Stiletto*. The men were still wearing full combat rig, and they were smelling really quite ripe, given that they had been tabbing through the jungle and fighting for the past week.

They had already said goodbye to the rest of the team, who were all going to stay onboard to travel with the Chinook to Monrovia. There they would catch onward civilian flights back to the real world.

Tom's immediate team walked to the rear of the Chinook, saying farewell as they went, and then they walked out onto the rear ramp. The helicopter was in the ultra-low hover, literally a metre above the sea. Its rear end was facing towards *Red Stiletto* barely a hundred metres away.

'Jesu! Look at that gin palace.' said Miguel in his thick Colombian accent. 'That fuckeen sheep is ridiculous!'

'That is quite right buddy, and that floating mansion is going to be our home for the next two weeks.' Mike, as an ex-navy SEAL, had spent a lot of time at sea, but never in anything as plush as that.

'As long as they have a fully-stocked fridge, that's gonna be fine with me, amigo.'

The loadmaster had been a good sport throughout the whole project and Tom and his team shook him warmly by the hand. Then, dropping their rucksacks and the two Peli cases into the water, they stepped off the rear ramp into the sea.

It wasn't a long drop, but hitting that refreshing cold water was better than a breath of fresh air. As they surfaced, they immediately saw the Chinook was transitioning away towards the West. It rapidly cleared the area, staying low level. The loadmaster leaned out, giving them a mock salute as it went.

Chapter 94

October 5th, *Red Stiletto*. The Ivory Coast.

With the men in the water, holding onto their kit and the Peli cases, they floated, enjoying the sensation of buoyancy as the small tender approached. Driven by the deckhand and with Bob leaning out over the gunwale, it gently pulled up next to them.

'Good afternoon gentlemen. Fancy a lift? I tell you what. I'll take you anywhere you want, but the going rate is about three hundred million, plus change.' Bob was grinning like a Cheshire cat.

'I'm still not talking to you.' Tom said, a little grumpy.

'Really? Well, we don't want any sourpusses on our gin palace over there. Let me help those who want to join us on our pleasure cruise with their kit.'

'But I'm bloody well paying for that floating gin palace!'

'Well, you better start being a little happier about it then.' Bob grinned and lowered his hand for Tom to grab hold of.

Realising he was being a little childish, Tom relented and let himself be hauled into the tender. Moments later, they were all on board with their kit and heading towards *Red Stiletto*.

As the evening was fast approaching, there wasn't a lot of time to chat. There were four loads, with a vast fortune in gold sitting like some long-lost pirate treasure on the seabed. There was just a little more work to do before the men could relax.

Bob, Tom and Mike were by far the best swimmers, and they quickly got suited up into lightweight wetsuits and diving kit.

Raj and Miguel in the meantime, with the deckhand, were helping to load extra air tanks and the flotation airbags into the tender. Raj had of course done the maths and calculated that two of the airbags would be needed for each load. Miguel looked at him as he scribbled down some equations on a rough piece of paper. He knew that Raj had a brain on him, but that was a new one on him. 'Hey man. Why didn't you go to university, or some shit like that?'

'Me? I never got the opportunity. And then when I could afford it, I was already doing something that I liked doing. Your normal university graduate doesn't get to play with the kind of toys that we do!'

'Sure, but you could have really been something, if you'd had the chance.'

'Maybe. But what? A medical doctor. A businessman? For me now, it's all about the people, the adventures. Solving other people's problems.'

Miguel was thinking back to the forest. 'You mean, you like getting shot at and blowing shit up?'

'That's definitely got something to do with it!'

With the kit stowed, and Tom, Bob and Mike ready in their diving kit, the tender drove them all out to the red marker buoys.

It was a short trip, and as soon as they were there, all three descended a few metres down to the seabed to inspect the loads. The three divers only needed to clear their ears briefly. A consequence of having just flown at height more than anything. Mike inspected the D-ring on the first load and undid the shackle that connected to the lifting strop. He let the strop drop to the sea floor and it fell soundlessly before landing softly onto the sand. He reattached the D-ring to the top of the load, planning to give the flotation bags something solid to clip onto.

To look at, the loads had done pretty well. There was no wear and tear on the cargo netting, nor obvious risk of any of the buckles shearing. With all four loads eventually inspected, the three men rose to the surface. Taking their regulators out of their mouths and inflating their buoyancy jackets, they just floated on the surface. 'What do you think?' asked Tom.

Mike was the ex-SEAL and they defaulted to him. 'They look good, guys. I think we should just get on with it. Even if we have a minor problem, the sand is flat all the way to the ship.'

'Bob, why don't you and I rig up the one that's just below us, and let Mike start on the one nearest to the ship.'

'Sounds good, Tom.'

The deckhand, after a quick instruction, passed down two full air tanks to Mike, and two more to Bob. All four were dropped down to the seabed just below them, landing in a gentle cloud of sand. The flotation bags followed next. They weren't quite so easy. They were not inflated but they still had some residual air in them, and they wouldn't just sink. Bob tried for a moment to swim his bags down, but gave up very quickly having struggled in vain. Tom was laughing at him underwater, bubbles escaping from the side of his regulator, and then he pointed to Mike.

Mike of course had simply turned the mouth of the airbag up towards the surface, and then the bag naturally released the trapped air upwards. He swam gently down with it. Aware of what had gone on with Bob, Mike turned around, looked at him and exaggeratedly shook his head. Unable to talk, Bob returned a rude sign with his hand, that was pretty much the same in any language.

Mike, working quickly whilst buoyant adjacent to the load, attached the two bags to the D-ring on the top of it. Then, picking up one of the air tanks from the floor, he fed the regulator into the mouth of the bag which was now just above the load. The rest of the bag floated gently in the current looking like some monster, deflated yellow squid.

Pressing the button on the regulator Mike quickly started to fill the first bag. As the air expanded and tried to escape upwards it was captured by the bright yellow air balloon shaped bag. He only filled it halfway to start with, before he switched to the other one. After that, gently filling each of them in turn, and keeping them balanced, he soon managed to get to the point where he felt the load was reaching buoyancy. Tom and Bob had been watching him carefully and they started to duplicate what he was doing.

Mike's load started to gently lift off the floor in a slight cloud of sand. He allowed it to rise under its own buoyancy. As it rose, the air in the bag continued to expand, and it accelerated upwards until it broached the surface.

As Mike surfaced, the tender moved closer and Raj passed him a cream-coloured rope which, with a quick one-handed bowline knot, he tied around the D-ring. Raj had connected the other end to a davit on the tender and with that done they headed towards *Red Stiletto*, towing the gold underneath the bags.

As the evening was cooling, a slight breeze was picking up, and whilst it was nothing to worry about yet, a little bit of chop was forming. Once the tender reached *Red Stiletto*, Miguel was on hand and operating the small white crane that was part of the toy deck. The crane was normally used for moving jet skis in and out of the water, or the submersible, but it had enough of a lift rating for the job in hand. With the lifting cable spooled out, Mike connected the hook on the end to the D-ring of the load. With gentle, testing presses of the controls,

Miguel started to lift it out of the water. There was a bit of an issue with the canvas bag liner that they had used way back at the river. It had filled with several tons of water but Mike, quick as a flash, went under with his diving knife and slashed great rents into the fabric. He was extremely careful to avoid the cargo netting.

Finally, with water still dripping, Miguel was able to operate the crane up and sideways. Mechanically he swung it around so that it moved inboard, and he then lowered the complete package on to the deck behind him.

As the tender turned and started to head back towards the marker buoys, Mike, who was looking forward, shouted, 'Thar she blows!'

Raj, not a nautical man, didn't quite get it but looked where Mike was pointing. He was just in time to see two massively over-filled airbags broach the surface like a Polaris missile and stand there proud. It would have been funny, except for the fact that the breeze immediately caught them and started to drag the load downwind, towards the cliff edge of the sand bar and deeper water.

'Oh fuck! Get us over there, man.' Mike commanded the deckhand.

With a burst of power that nearly unseated Raj, the tender leapt forward. Bob and Tom were clinging on to the bags for dear life, trying separately to swim against the wind but making no headway. They were simply passengers clinging on. The deckhand was savvy though and went well downwind, bringing the tender to a halt in the right place and allowing the load to be pushed towards him. As it came close, Mike jumped into the water with the rope in his hand.

As he landed, he looked straight down. Gone was the nice shallow sand bar, replaced by an infinity of water that disappeared down to the point where light petered out. It was inky black down there. He performed his one-handed knot-tying trick again, surfaced and directly told Raj to get it back over the shallows and to the ship.

Slowly and carefully, they hauled the load upwind. There was plenty of power available, but the deckhand was worried about dragging such a weight and what it might do to the netting. Once over the sand they felt palpable relief. A quick conference later and it was decided that Tom would accompany the load back to the ship, and supervise the lifting, whilst Mike, helped by Bob, would prepare the next one.

Twenty minutes later, the third load was on board and the fourth was being filled with air. The radio on the tender squawked into life. 'Tender, look lively. We have company about five miles out.'

Raj looked up at the bridge, to see Chris giving the universal military signal to hurry up. He was pointing in the direction of the problem. He obviously didn't want to discuss it over the radio. Raj looked that way but couldn't see anything. He had no way of communicating with Mike underwater, so did the next best thing. Taking a deep breath, he dove off the side of the tender, swimming as deep as he could and then he tapped Mike on the shoulder.

Mike, normally such a calm man, nearly spat his regulator out in shock. Having got his attention though, Raj signalled with a thumbs down for enemy and the direction they were coming from. Mike quickly recovered and nodded. Raj made his way back up to the surface. The last load was filled with air more quickly than perhaps it wanted to be and as it broached, Raj already had the tow rope in the water.

'Hurry up, chaps, it doesn't look friendly!' came Chris's booming voice over the water.

Chapter 95

October 5th, *Red Stiletto*. The Ivory Coast.

The approaching boat definitely wasn't on a social call. It was also well outside its legal jurisdiction. The military patrol vessel that was approaching was Ghanaian. *Red Stiletto* was in Ivory Coast waters and either the patrol vessel's commander was lost, or he was under specific instructions. Chris suspected the latter. He had settled the civilian crew down, as they were beginning to panic a little about what exactly was being recovered. He had then managed a quick phone call with Max on the satphone on the bridge and filled him in. Max had told him he would come back to him as soon as possible.

Meanwhile, the tender with the last load was just pulling up alongside *Red Stiletto*. Chris could see Bob in the water and Tom now managing the lifting crane, but he couldn't see Mike, Raj or Miguel.

Chris looked at the patrol vessel, without the need for binoculars now. It was small, and it was seriously fast. Battleship grey and perhaps fifteen metres long he could see it was more of a near-shore interceptor than a deep-sea patrol vessel. That meant a crew of perhaps three or four, he thought. It was intensely sleek. A sharp pointed bow, narrow with a huge plume of white water being ejected out of the stern. With a top speed of more than fifty knots, there was no way that *Red Stiletto* was going to outrun that. It looked like a plan B was needed. Once within hailing range, the patrol vessel's loudhailer sprang into life. 'Pleasure craft, this is Ghanaian Navy patrol vessel. Turn off your engines and prepare to be boarded.'

Chris turned to the captain. 'Don't worry, Captain. It's OK. I'll speak to them, it's all going to be fine. Please do not move the ship under any circumstances.' With that, he went down the external stairwell to the rear deck.

As he went, he passed Tom and Bob ,who were lifting the final load onto the toy deck. Whilst Tom was in charge of land ops, Chris was in charge of the maritime phase. After his Royal Navy career fell off a cliff, he had moved into maritime consulting; dealing with young naval officers was certainly his domain. He might never get to command an aircraft carrier, but he could deal with some jumped up cretins, who were way out of their jurisdiction and even further out of their league.

The patrol vessel pulled up at the stern and with full volume on their hailing system assaulted the ship with noise. 'No one move! You are commanded to stop what you are doing!'

Chris winced and stuck his fingers in his ears. Tom and Bob kept going with the load, it was so nearly secure on deck. Two naval ratings looped mooring ropes over davits at the stern of *Red Stiletto* and tied them off.

'Stand still!' the Ghanaian naval officer commanded. Chris just stood there looking down at him. As he watched, the two naval ratings raised their weapons. Both were armed with American M16s, the result of some aid program or other. They did at least look like they knew which end was the pointy end.

Having decided that he had control now, the naval officer stopped using the massively loudhailing system and stepped forwards out of his console area. The patrol vessel was dwarfed by the bulk and splendour of *Red Stiletto* and the navy team had to look up at Chris to hold a conversation.

'What's in those loads and what are you doing in our national waters?'

'We are not in your national waters, old chap. What's in the loads is therefore not your jurisdiction and is none of your business.' Chris smiled blandly as he delivered the insult.

The naval officer was incensed. He was perhaps mid-twenties, a lieutenant, sufficiently connected or perhaps even competent to command one of the few sleek craft that was given the fuel to do its job. In an exuberance of youth though, he lost his composure. He started ranting, threatening, demanding. 'I am going to board you! Lower your boarding ladder!'

Chris was a picture of calm, 'No. You are outside your legal jurisdiction, and you are pointing guns at me in international waters. That would make this an act of piracy. If you want to board me, you are going to have to force your way onboard. I will however tell you that this vessel is under the flag state of France and on board are British and American citizens. If you want to force your way on board, you will find yourself in an international court before you can blink.'

The officer spoke to his two men in a language that none of the team understood. It did give Tom time to finish manoeuvring the crane though. Chris had a quick look around. Where the fuck were Mike and Raj?

The captain's voice came over the tannoy. 'This is the captain. The man you spoke to on the phone just now said you can do whatever you need to do.' Chris looked up at the top deck. He could see one of the deckhands up there with a phone, recording everything.

The young lieutenant's ears pricked up at that. 'What does that mean?'

Chris didn't reply. He looked over at Tom and received an ever so subtle nod.

'It means, old chap, that I'm in charge here, and that you are way out of line.'

The lieutenant couldn't work out why, when he was in command of all the guns, this civilian wasn't just rolling over. He had received a phone call from the Minister of the Interior himself that something wasn't right, and he should investigate any suspicious activity. A massive yacht hauling loads out of the water certainly fit the bill. Were they drug trafficking? Smuggling? And now, they were all so calm. He tried to regain the initiative. 'We are coming aboard! Nobody moves!'

'How?' asked Chris.

'What?'

'I said how? How are you coming aboard?' To Chris it was obvious that they couldn't scale the side of the vessel. They were too low in the water. This just infuriated the lieutenant even more.

'Lower your boarding ladder!'

'So let me get this straight, Captain Blackbeard. You are demanding, using force, to board this vessel in international waters, where you are out of your country's legal jurisdiction?'

Not seeing the trap, the lieutenant shouted, 'You are damn right I am!'

Chris raised his eyebrows and shook his head sadly.

There was a moment of comedy where the lieutenant tried to climb up the stern of the vessel by climbing up one of his men, however his patrol vessel started to use up the slack on the mooring ropes, while drifting away from the ship. He managed to jump back onto his own vessel instead of falling in the water and really embarrassing himself. Furious, he grabbed the rifle from one of his men, cocked it, and fired a burst up into the air.

That action was all that was needed. As the harsh sound of the M16 echoed away, Mike appeared at the stern rail, on the far side of the patrol vessel.

Chapter 96

October 5th, *Red Stiletto*. The Ivory Coast.

When the patrol vessel crew had been busy tying it up at the stern, Mike, Raj and Miguel had left the toy deck and efficiently raided the Peli cases that they had brought with them from the Chinook. Mike was still in his diving kit and between them they hatched a plan.

Working furiously, Raj had assembled a compact device using a small amount of explosives and a waterproof remote detonator. It was perhaps the size of a half-litre water bottle, plenty big enough for their purposes. Miguel had taken his weapon up onto the bridge. The captain had nearly had kittens when he saw it and didn't know whether to be relieved or horrified. Miguel crept up to the rear of the Bridge deck and hid beside the deckhand who was filming everything. He stayed low, listening to the conversation at the stern.

Mike took a harpoon from the diving stores and went forward to the bow of *Red Stiletto* where, out of sight he gently lowered himself into the water. He had to be careful not to snag the small, netted bag hooked to his weight belt, on the railing as he went in. The bag contained the explosive device. Inserting his regulator, and taking a moment to get his buoyancy right, Mike stayed as close as he could under the hull of the majestic yacht. Almost surreal in the crystal-clear waters, the bright red hull and several hundred tons of luxury looked like it was hovering about five metres above him. Staying close to the keel he finned all the way to the stern. He passed the huge bronze propeller and straight under the much smaller hull of the patrol vessel. There was only the slightest crevice of light between the two boats. Fenders preventing them from banging into each other, but there was no way the navy personnel could see his manoeuvring underneath.

The first thing he did was attach the explosive to one of the two propellers at the rear. Then carefully and slowly he came up on the far side of the patrol boat and listened to the conversation. He checked above him and made sure that he would be able to grab the side rail and then he waited.

When the burst of automatic fire happened, Mike made his decision. With immense forearms and upper body strength, cultivated by years of chin ups, he quietly hauled himself up out of the water. A quick glance told him several things. Firstly, the young lieutenant had lost his temper, secondly the two seamen were not looking in his direction and thirdly Miguel had just popped up on the Bridge and was aiming his weapon down at the patrol vessel.

A kind of Mexican standoff was happening, but still the naval personnel who had reacted with surprise at Miguel's appearance hadn't seen Mike. He raised his harpoon aiming it at the young officer and started to advance along the deck. When he was just a metre away, and the evil looking harpoon was pointed straight at the man's back, Mike went for shock and awe. 'Put your fuckin' weapons on the deck! Do it! Do it now!'

Completely surprised the officer turned, weapon swinging with him. Mike watched his eyes with absolute precision. He saw the man register shock, fear and then determination in microseconds. He had made the wrong call. Mike pressed the trigger and the harpoon launched with the shuddering force of a weapon designed to attack huge fish. Flying a metre or so only, it smacked into the officer's chest, breaking through cartilage and bone and skewering the man's heart. The head penetrated out through his back and stopped with an evil barb, shining cruelly silver against a growing red stain on his white shirt. The other two seamen began to turn, weapons rising. Miguel made sure that they wouldn't hurt Mike with a supremely fast and accurate set of double taps. From the looks on their faces they could have died from surprise.

'All clear!' Mike called sharply. From his position, looking up at *Red Stiletto*, he saw Tom and Chris appear at the stern rail. And then Raj appeared, with the detonator in his hand.

'Well that all happened quite quickly, didn't it?' said Raj. 'Shall I blow up the boat now?'

Mike ,who was standing barely a metre from the device, looked at him, rolling his eyes before calling up, 'Hey Miguel, good shooting, buddy. Thanks a million.'

Miguel stroked the scar on the side of his face, nonchalant, ice cool. 'Nah problem, man.'

'Bugger,' sighed Tom. 'This is a bit messier than I wanted it to be.'

'Yes,' agreed Chris. 'We were completely legal there though. Captain! How are you doing?' Chris called up to the Bridge.

The captain appeared and stood beside Miguel and his deckhand. 'This isn't a normal charter that's for sure. But we have all of that on video. I think we're OK. God knows what the owner will say though. He hates guns.'

'Well as long as everyone is OK,' called back Chris. 'What I suggest is that we drop that patrol vessel over the cliff so to speak. We sink her at the deepest point. It's a shame about those three young men, but it can't be helped.'

Everyone reflected for a moment. There wasn't a lot they could do. Perhaps an anonymous phone call when the task was over would notify the navy command where it was scuttled and they could do the necessary respects in due course. That was not going to happen right now though and so Mike hastily undid the patrol boat mooring lines. He started up the engines with the push of a button and then drove the vessel a couple of hundred metres away. He gathered the bodies and dragged them into the cabin area, tying them to the boat using the mooring ropes. Once he was certain it would drift over the edge of the sand bar and the cliff around it, he jumped off and swam back to *Red Stiletto*.

There was a little bit of a ceremony at the stern deck as Raj pressed the button on the transmitter. The blast wasn't particularly big, but it was enough to create a large hole in the transom at the rear. She began to settle quickly in the water, but there was a problem. She had either an air pocket or ballast tanks in her bow and so she only half sank. Her bow stood proud, desperate to be some form of floating tomb marker. The men had to pick up their weapons again. Several bursts of fire were needed to sufficiently penetrate the hull and the bow. Whilst it wasn't a military salute, ultimately it was enough. With air escaping in a bubbling white froth, she sank down into the depths taking the bodies of her crew with her.

On the bridge, the captain raised the anchor, engaged the propellers and started the long journey around the West coast of Africa, past the Mediterranean, towards the ultimate destination. The gold was finally on the way, heading towards the secure depository of the Bank of England.

Chapter 97

October 6th, Accra. Ghana.

The Minister was worried about this phone call. It was obvious to him now that he had failed. Not only had he failed but he had done so spectacularly. He tried to recall the conversations over the past couple of days. How much could really be attributed to him? How many people knew, with absolute certainty, that he had been involved in it? Without a doubt, in government everyone knew about the incident, but who could pin anything on him? And of those he had called in to his confidence just a few weeks ago? He was really only worried about the Minister of Transport. That slimy, two-faced bastard. Could he cause problems? Would he cause problems? Yes, The Minister thought grimly to himself. That toad probably would. Damnit! He had been so close! He had so nearly had the golden fortune in his hand, and then, like a jungle mist at dawn, it just… evaporated!

He pulled out his burner phone and dialled the number of The Associate. That's odd, he thought, as it went straight to a disengaged tone. He tried again. No luck. He pulled his own phone out of his pocket and dialled the number. This time it went straight through. It was picked up but there was no greeting at the other end. 'Hello? It's me.' Still silence. 'Hello, hello?' There was a click and then a heavily digitised voice at the other end.

'What do you want?'

'Oh! I am glad I got you. I was worried. I need help! I have to leave the country immediately. I think everything is falling down around me.' There was no reply. 'Are you still there?'

'I am, but I don't understand why I should help you. You failed me.'

The Minister was whining. 'But that wasn't my fault, the police, they reacted too fast, and then some foreigners got involved. Hundreds of them. They killed everyone and they stole all of the gold!'

'Are you sure they killed everyone?'

'Yes, your man, Abdi, he died in a helicopter crash! Everyone else was already dead!'

The digitised voice paused for a moment, thinking. 'Are you calling from your personal phone?'

'What's that got to do with...' The minister realised his mistake and swore internally.

'I'll have one of my team contact you.'

'But when? It must be soon. I think that they know!'

There was just a click at the other end as the phone was put down.

Once The Minister had hung up, in a room about thirty kilometres away, a young man in a pale green military uniform smiled. He was sitting at a computer console with a headset on. He started to type up the notes for the call that he had just been monitoring. When he had finished, he pushed a button on his console and was put through to the duty intelligence officer. 'Ma'am. It looks like we have a serious bite from code name Mathumba. Sending it through now for you to confirm.'

'Acknowledged. Let me listen to it and grade it for follow up.' Five minutes later, the intelligence officer was smiling grimly. Well, well, she thought. Somebody was in trouble.

Chapter 98

October 9th, *Red Stiletto*. The Atlantic.

The *Red Stiletto* had been underway for four days now and was making good progress. The crew had taken a while to come to terms with the act of piracy, and the lethal actions of Mike and Miguel. There was an intense mix of both respect and concern in their eyes. It had taken a lot of soothing from Tom to get them all to settle down a little. He had taken the whole crew aside with the captain's permission and given them as much assurance as he could, that they were in fact operating legitimately. That was a tough one to believe of course, especially with all of the bars of gold stacked up under the tarpaulins on the toy deck. There was no pretence now though and there was always someone from Tom's team, armed and overseeing the precious cargo. There was no more time for toys or a pleasure cruise and so everything was battened down. *Red Stiletto*, her bow surging through a gentle swell, was making her fastest and most fuel-inefficient way to her final destination.

Bob was on duty on the toy deck and the others were sitting at an intricately-carved glass dining room table, in a plush part of the main living area. The white suede walls were immaculately brushed, not a mark on them. Every few metres were large and stunning underwater photos, a manta ray with gaping mouth, an octopus in full tentacular colour, a submerged wreck teeming with life. Breaking up the room in its very centre was a large aquarium, two metres long, a metre wide and from floor to ceiling. It was teeming with fish, brightly coloured butterfly fish, parrot fish and angels. The pride of the collection, living in the base was a moray eel. Queen of the hand-carved coral castle.

The table was large enough to seat eight but had been set for just five. Tom, Mike, Raj, Chris, and Miguel were sitting opposite each other and between them was a seafood feast. Lobster, king prawns, scallops, calamari, and coconut rice. Food that the previously abandoned charter had ordered and paid for, and which was gratefully received by the team. The men were being good; despite the twenty-year-old malts and decadent spirits bar, they had implemented a one-beer-a-night rule. They were not worried about being hijacked but were maintaining their professionalism. Miguel, Chris, and Bob had plenty of experience of dealing with pirates, having been attacked off the coast of Somalia whilst on their way to rescue a ship that had been taken hostage. Miguel had defended their ship, taking an epic shot at distance at a moving platform. When the team had reached the captured ship, they had seen first-hand the results of being hijacked and kept in captivity. There was no way that was going to happen to them.

One of the reasons Miguel was such an effective killer was the time he had spent with the Western Cartel in Columbia. He had spent years as an enforcer. He had been retained to make sure that his boss got paid, and when that didn't happen, Miguel went visiting. Sometimes that meant killing, sometimes torture and sometimes it was just a warning. All of that was long past now though, and he had escaped that life with a small fortune to Kenya, where he had bought a new identity and a fake passport. That was what was troubling Miguel now. It had never been the intent that he would head all the way back to the UK with the team. But, with the massive number of changes in the project, he found himself sitting on this yacht with no easy way of getting off. He had had a quiet conversation with Tom just before dinner. Miguel felt that he had turned legitimate now, so he didn't really like raising the subject with one of his employers. 'Tom, I have a bit of a problem.'

'Uh huh?' Tom, who was lying down on a gorgeous white suede couch, looked up from the book he was reading.

'I'm worried that when we land in the UK, that my, ahem, Kenyan passport might set some alarm bells off.'

Tom looked at him shrewdly. 'Really? Well, we don't really want to draw any attention to ourselves, do we?'

'It's me, I'm afraid. I'm sorry to give you this problem, but we need to get me off the ship before we reach Europe.'

Tom thought for a moment. 'We don't really want to enter anyone's national waters. Who knows which powerful individuals are behind the original heist. And no matter who we are, having a vast stack of gold is going to look a touch dodgy, isn't it?'

'Yeah, sorry.'

'Not to worry old chap. I'll have a chat with Max. We'll sort something out.'

'Gracias, amigo.' Miguel left to get cleaned up. Tom thought for a moment and then realised he had time perhaps for one more chapter.

Naturally, with men around the table at supper, stories were being told, embellished, and even admitted to. Raj had just started on one that he hadn't told anyone before, not even his best buddy Mike. As he helped himself to the decadent shellfish, avoiding the carbs of course, Raj was looking a little embarrassed.

'So, it was one of my first ever close-protection tasks. Before I joined you guys, and I was pretty new to Kenya too. An old mate of mine had given me the job of looking after the CEO of the Adidas foundation. She was seriously intelligent and, as it happens, both very attractive and extremely fit. She had this thing for running which was just awe inspiring. I'd been looking after her on an East Africa tour of all the projects they were supporting. We'd been to Addis Ababa and Kampala, and now she was finishing off in Nairobi. She was staying at the Muthaiga club and, as it was one of the last nights, she offered to buy me supper. We'd been getting on pretty well, so we went to the restaurant and, well, you know me. I always had the prawn curry there. Anyway, we had a good meal, got on well and then agreed to meet at six the following morning, for a dawn run around the Muthaiga club golf course.' Raj took a breath, used a fork to scrape out a lobster tail and, a little apprehensive, carried on.

'Anyway, it was only about an hour later that night that I knew I was in trouble. I was back in my room at the club and out of nowhere, I felt really sick. Twenty minutes later, my body was in convulsions. Throwing up at the top end and the shits at the other end. I tell you, I emptied everything from my bowels!'

'Buddy, some of us are still eating!' Mike objected.

'Well, I was up for the whole night. Judging which end I had to have over the toilet. I've rarely been so ill. I got about half an hour of sleep and then, seriously dehydrated, made my way down to the first golf tee to meet the client. There she was, blonde ponytail, amazing figure. Adidas pumps obviously. As soon as I got there, she was off. Normally, I would be able to keep up, but quickly it was obvious that I couldn't! I had stomach cramps; I was retching, and I was dehydrated. She was very kind, and she slowed down a bit, but then…' Raj paused for a breath, 'I farted! And I shat myself at the same time.'

The table roared with laughter. Miguel asked, 'What did you do?'

'Well, I kept running of course, I wasn't going to leave my principal.'

'Man, that is so gross, didn't she notice?'

'Well, I was pretty sure that if I ran into wind fast enough, she wouldn't notice. I was, after all, behind her. But it got to the point where I was slowing her down too much. And there was a bit of a dog leg in the course. I told her I'd meet her at the start of the 10th hole. She kept running the perimeter and I took a short cut.'

'So, you left your principal?' asked Mike.

'Yep, I had to! I had badly digested prawn curry running down my leg! Anyway, as I was on my short cut, I came across a sand bunker. Quick as a flash, I jumped into the bunker, dropped my shorts and emptied my bowels. Man, the pain from those cramps! It took a while and when I was done, I used sand to, you know, scrub things clean. I tell you, forget waterboarding, you should try having to wipe your ass with sand, after having gotten the shits from a hot curry!'

Tom was horrified. 'Hang on, are you telling me you coiled one down in one of the bunkers at the club? *The* Club?'

'Well, it wasn't really laying one down, it was more exploding all over it. Anyway, I missed the client obviously and headed back to my room to get cleaned up. I had to stop by one of the lakes on the way to wash my hands. The worst part was, that I thought she hadn't noticed. But, when I met her about an hour later, she came down from her room and handed me a whole bloody packet of Imodium!'

Miguel was laughing, Chris was looking disgusted, Mike was staring at his best buddy, wondering how he hadn't heard that story before. Tom, though, was mortified that Raj had shat all over his favourite golf course.

Chapter 99

October 10th, Accra. Ghana.

The street was filled with blue flashing lights. They reflected off the windows of the expensive apartment blocks that towered up into the night sky. At street level, half a dozen police cars were parked up, blocking road access, lights blazing, although at least the sirens had been turned off. Despite the fact that it was two in the morning, neighbours were staring out of their windows, curtains twitching, watching the spectacle. Here in the diplomatic quarter relatively few crimes were committed. Especially not murder, and that was the rumour going around on the residential WhatsApp group. But, perhaps more sensationally, the rumour was that it was the Minister that had been killed. Such a nice man some said, a big supporter of charities. A contender for President, said others. Not any more though.

Chapter 100

October 10th, Accra. Ghana.

At nine o'clock that morning, the President was having a working breakfast. He sat at a large mahogany table at Statehouse, whilst liveried servants served him and his guest. The guest though, for some reason, didn't seem to be hungry. He was staring at the headlines on the newspapers on the table.

'So, tell me Minister, how is the transport docket for you?' The President shovelled a forkful of poached eggs and hollandaise sauce into his mouth. He dabbed at the sides with a rich red linen napkin whilst he waited for a reply.

'It's fine Mr President, some usual issues, never quite enough funds for the road development agenda.'

'Right, it was that way when I ran it too. I must say, I think you have done well enough over the past few years. I see that you are distracted by the headlines? Such a shame. Those newspapers tell me that I need a new Minister of the Interior. Do you know anything about that?' He pointed at the paper.

'Me, Mr President?' He sounded genuinely shocked. 'Oh no, sir, I haven't heard anything about that at all.'

'Well, the papers say he died of a heart attack.' The President paused, looking directly into the Minister of Transport's eyes. For a full minute, nothing was said. During that time, the President was running through the images that had been delivered to him about half an hour before the meeting.

The Minister of the Interior may well have died of a heart attack, but it certainly hadn't helped that he had had a gold bar hammered down his throat, breaking his jaw, his teeth and destroying his oesophagus. It was entirely unnecessary, therefore, to have another one forced up his arse, but the President had wanted to make a point when he had ordered it done. 'Dangerous things, heart attacks. They can happen any time, can't they, especially when you think you're at the top of your game.'

'Yes, Mr President. Most unfortunate.'

'Well, it looks like I'll need another Minister, and I am told that you're competent and above all, loyal. Is that true?'

The Minister of Transport replied, 'Absolutely, Mr President. I have always been loyal to you.' That of course was what he said, but what he was really wondering was if that arrogant idiot had talked before he died? Did the President know already that he was involved? What digital records existed? He was pretty sure that he would pass detailed inspections. He just didn't know for sure. Was he a dead man already, being toyed with by the tiger?

The President, on the other hand, knew a lot more than he was going to let on. No good politician showed all their cards until it was time to take the pot. A little innuendo, a comment here or there, sewing just enough doubt. It kept people on their toes. The funny thing was that the President did actually rate the capabilities of this man. However, that meant that with the upcoming election he would need to hold him closer. What a conundrum. The President crocodile-smiled as he drank some coffee. Kill him? Use him? Let him create his own momentum and divide the opposition vote? It was life or death decisions like those that made the game so enjoyable.

Chapter 101

October 25th, Southampton. Great Britain.

As *Red Stiletto* arrived in Southampton, one of the southernmost ports in Great Britain, she moored up in the main port facility. Despite her own size, she was dwarfed by a pair of gigantic cruise liners. They were alongside the largest wharfs, troops of camera-laden passengers coming off, and supplies being loaded on. To the embarrassment of her crew, *Red Stiletto* looked slightly less polished than usual, having spent the past two weeks transiting through the Atlantic swells. She was covered in a fine salty spray, built up layer upon layer and she needed a deep clean. Some ships were pretty as a picture, moored off Monaco, with supermodels on the top deck. Some were not designed with quite such a rough ocean life in mind.

The gold too, despite its canvas covering on the toy deck, had become covered in salt. It had lost a little of its lustre, but the important thing was that it was safe. With *Red Stiletto* tied up at her berth, six cash-in-transit vehicles had already arrived and were parked up on the jetty. Nothing was allowed on or off until customs and immigration had done their part. There was one other individual also standing on the jetty, though. A Ghanaian man by the look of it, and in his hand he was holding a manila envelope. He gathered both the customs and immigration officers together and flashed a diplomatic passport. From his envelope he took a letter and gave it to them. The officials had a quick conversation, nodded their agreement, and invited the man to join them as they walked up the boarding stair.

The Captain and Chris were waiting at the top and shook hands with all three as they came aboard. Tom and the rest of his team were sitting comfortably on sofas in the main living space watching the proceedings. The immigration officer went first. 'Captain, good afternoon. Can I have the immigration documentation and copies of the seafarers' tickets or passports for all the crew and the passengers?'

'Of course. Come on through to the main cabin so you can use a table and meet the passengers.' The Captain, despite his confidence, was a little nervous. He had everything in order except for Miguel's passport. Chris had told him that it would all be sorted out on arrival and fortunately he was correct. The Ghanaian diplomat stepped forwards again and out of his envelope he pulled a Ghanaian diplomatic passport. It had all of Miguel's details and his photograph. It looked well-worn and even had several immigration stamps in it. He passed it to the captain, who handed it straight onto the immigration officer. The immigration official spent ten minutes looking at passports, cross-referencing the faces around him and then stamping the passports. He left Miguel's until last.

'Good afternoon, sir.' he said, addressing Miguel. 'Could you confirm that you are a diplomat with the Ghanaian government?

Miguel tried to cover some of his obvious Colombian accent, adopting more Kenyan tones than anything, though he thought the official wouldn't know the difference. 'Yes Bwana, I am. Is there a problem?'

'Well, it's highly unusual, sir, but this gentleman tells me you lost your passport in transit and so has brought you your spare?'

'That's correct.' Miguel put on an imperious tone.

It was enough for the official, who just sighed, stamped the passport and went on his way.

The customs official, though, now had to play by the rules. He had been told before boarding that the ship was under diplomatic immunity, and that there was a high-ranking Ghanaian diplomat aboard. Therefore, he wasn't allowed to search the ship unless he had specific cause to assume a crime had been committed. Even then, before he did so, he would need authorisation. He addressed Miguel. 'Sir, do you have anything on board that you wish to declare?'

Tom came to his rescue. 'Hello, my friend, let me answer on my boss's behalf. As a matter of fact, we do. On the deck below, we have three hundred million dollars' worth of gold bullion. It's en route from Ghana to the Bank of England. I believe you need a cash and valuables import declaration. We have had our office fax one to us. Is a copy ok, or do you need an ink signature?'

The official's jaw was still on the floor, though he was professional enough not to show it. Sounding nonchalant he said, 'Very good sir. I think I'd better take a look, please.' He didn't really need to take a look, but it wasn't every day you got to see such a vast fortune in gold. As he was taken down below, he asked a follow-up question. 'Do you have anything else to declare sir?'

'Funnily enough, we do. In the diplomatic pouch, we have brought in several automatic weapons and a small quantity of explosives.'

'You don't need to tell me what's in the pouch sir, only what you want to declare.'

'Well in this case, we do. We no longer have need for them and we would like to hand them over to the police so that they can be properly destroyed. We won't be so worried about pirates on the way back.' Tom gave a disarming grin. By now they were all down on the Toy deck and the official saw the vast quantity of bullion laid out on the floor.

'It's a little unusual, sir. Would you mind if I made a couple of phone calls?'

Ten minutes later the man came back. 'Well, sir, that's OK. The police are on their way and will bring some paperwork. You'll be able to hand over your, ahem, items to them. I have also asked for some police and customs officer support. There really isn't a huge threat, but it's not often such a large sum comes into Southampton, sir.'

'Wonderful. I suspect we shall ask for an escort or two for the trip to London as well.'

'That's probably a good idea, sir.'

'Excellent. When the police get here, are you happy that we can start to unload to the cash-in-transit team?'

The customs officer realised that his afternoon had just been highjacked. He was going to have to stay until he had counted each and every bar off the ship. 'Yes. This is going to take a while isn't it, sir?'

Chapter 102

October 25th, The Bank of England. Great Britain.

The Bank of England was in the centre of London, close to St Paul's Cathedral and only a few hundred metres away from the iconic London Bridge. The Bank functioned as a bank, a museum and of course, a gold store. On the outside, it had fabulously-carved rich white stone walls and Roman pillars. Inside, the décor was similarly decadent, but the real wealth was stored a long way underground in nine separate vaults. Very few people ever had access to the vaults though, and it had been nearly a hundred years since the public had been allowed in to deal in real gold there. Nowadays that was the preserve of Her Majesty's government and some other friends from around the world.

Tom and his team didn't have any VIP access though and they came in through the vehicle security door at the rear. As the cash-in-transit convoy pulled into the loading bay, Tom, Mike, Raj and the Ghanaian diplomat from the port, who was keeping an eagle eye on the gold, climbed out of their Landcruiser. They stretched their legs and walked up to a high concrete platform that was obviously an unloading bay. Looking around the cavernous, concrete underground carpark, the bright white floodlighting enhanced the complete lack of character of the grey room. The six armoured vehicles reversed so that their rear doors were all lined up besides each other against the raised platform. Each of the drivers got out and proceeded to take a clip board with paperwork to a small bald fat man wearing a simple white short-sleeved shirt, and dark trousers. The co-driver of the first truck cross-checked the seal on the rear door, cracked it and opened the door wide.

The storeman swore in a thick London cockney accent. 'Bloody 'ell! 'Snot even on pallets, init! What d'ya expect me ta do wiv it? Hey?'

Tom walked up. 'Is there a problem?'

'Bloody right there is!' The man sniffed the air suspiciously. 'Ere. Sumfin smells, I dunno, fishy. Gawd! Look at tha state of it! Watz it covered in?' The man had gone into the back of the vehicle and was rubbing his finger over one of the bricks. He scraped off some of the salt that had accumulated over the journey, pulled it up to his rather large nostril, sniffing suspiciously. 'For fucks sake, mate. It ain't even clean!'

Raj stepped in trying to calm the man down a little. 'We only arrived this morning I am afraid. And we haven't had time to go through a car wash.' He was trying to add a little humour, but it failed miserably.

'You're not funny, mate. How am I goin' ta weigh it all, make sure it's all kosher. It's all gotta be unloaded from yer bloody trucks by 'and. Then we 'ave ta wash it, stack it, dry it, weigh it. It ain't easy!'

'Well, it looks like you have a little work to do then doesn't it, *mate*' Raj put his best English accent on the word mate, and it earned him a scowl from the receiver.

Tom, ever the diplomat asked, 'How can we help?'

'Well you can't, Guv, can ya. Once it's in 'ere, it's all in my domain. I'm goin' ta 'ave ta get the boys off their tea break, ain't I?

'That's very kind of you.' Tom turned to the Ghanaian. 'As we have never weighed this, shall we start with a basic brick count and then let this fine gentleman get on with it?'

'Yes, I think you can sign for the count by brick and then we let them do their jobs. It looks like it may take some time, but I am happy to monitor from here on in.'

The receiver butted into the conversation. 'Well, that's bloody luvely. Glad we are in agreement.' He pulled out his own clipboard, pulled a cheap biro from behind his hairy ear and asked. 'What's the origin of this lot then?'

The diplomat replied. 'It belongs to the people of Ghana.'

'Well, ain't they lucky, but that ain't the question I asked. I need to know where it came from.'

The diplomat was becoming less than amused with the man but kept his composure. 'It comes from Ghana.'

'Lovely, and 'ave ya got any provenance documentation?'

'Just my credentials as the deputy Ambassador to London.' He held out his diplomatic passport.

The short fat receiver realised he may have been a little too brash and rude. He changed his tone immediately and ticked a box on his form. 'Right, sir. Umm. Let me go and get my lads. Back in a jiffy.'

When he had gone, Tom turned to Mike and Raj. 'It's lovely fellows like that which make me really miss Blighty.'

Chapter 103

October 26th, Accra. Ghana

Statehouse hadn't changed at all in the month since Max had last been there. He had received the same treatment at the airport, collected off the plane and bundled into a government Landcruiser. As he left the airport boundary though, several police outriders appeared on motorbikes and with sirens blaring he was driven quickly to his meeting with the President. He had only waited in the anteroom for about twenty minutes before he was joined on the sofa by the man himself. He spoke again in his deep melodious voice. 'I have received word from the Embassy in London overnight. A total of just over three hundred million dollars in gold bullion was received by The Bank of England yesterday evening.'

Max took a sip of his coffee, 'Yes, my team deposited it yesterday and are already airborne and heading back to Nairobi.'

'Tell me, was this a difficult… task, or project, or whatever you call them?'

'Well, it wasn't easy, Mr President. It was extremely fluid, and anything that's last minute carries a lot of planning risks. If we don't mitigate them effectively then the operational risks kick in and people die.'

'We're any of your team injured?'

'Sadly yes. One of our aircraft was shot down by the thieves and we lost the pilot. Your aviation authority are currently investigating it. But of course, there isn't much we can directly say.'

'Right, and what about your team on the ground. I am told there was some fighting?'

'Yes, but we were fortunate. We had two short contact battles. One planned, and one unavoidable.'

'You are referring to my missing naval patrol vessel?' The President raised his eyebrow.

'Yes. The patrol boats commander tried to pirate the gold in international waters. My team had to defend themselves.'

'It was lucky that your team were so well armed then, wasn't it?'

The way that he said it brought a revelation to Max's mind. The team had all assumed that someone else had tried to capture the gold. Had it in fact been the President all along? Had the man rolled the dice and tried to steal it for himself? After everything that Max had done for him? It would have saved him the success fee, that was for sure, but on top of that, a vast sum of gold would still have disappeared from the Ghanaian economy and ended up in the President's hands. Max answered carefully, 'Yes. But the whole situation was unfortunate. I will send you the approximate location of the wreck. Your navy may wish to recover it or mark it as a war grave. But I have to ask, Mr President, have your security services found anything useful about the organisation that tried to capture the gold in the first place?'

'Only a little. We had a few insiders, well-established senior people in my government who went rogue. They were being manipulated by a foreign power or organisation. With a little persuasion, we did get a name. Someone called The Associate. We also think there was another person called Abdi.'

'Now that's remarkable. I hadn't heard of The Associate, but we know Abdi from another project. Did you hear about the oil tanker that was captured off the coast of Somalia last year?'

'The Hibernian something, wasn't it?'

'That's right, the *Hibernia III*. Well, that project was one of our response files. The lead pirate negotiator was called Abdi. My team thought they recognised him during the ambush. What's interesting, though, is we never knew who the kingpin behind that piracy problem was. I think now we can take an educated guess.'

'I'll pass that on to my intelligence chief. I want to know who The Associate is and then we shall see what he's up to. Now do we have anything else?'

'Just the small matter of our final invoice Mr President.'

'That's fine. If you want to send it to me, I'll make sure it gets approved quickly.'

'Thank you, we'd appreciate that.'

'No, no, Max. I think you and your team did a great job. I just hope I don't need to use your services again.'

'Thank you, Mr President, that's very kind.'

Chapter 104

October 27th, The Bank of England. Great Britain.

The gold was sitting there, doing what it did best, representing wealth, value, tangible things and of course power. It was stacked up on pallets, sitting on wide two-tiered steel shelving that stretched the length of the vault. In this room, such a vast sum was just a small proportion of the overall quantity. Billions of dollars' worth of gold were kept in the quiet, still vaults below the bank. It was a sterile environment, bright halogen lights shining from almost every angle. Security cameras, monitored from some far distant room, moved silently, persistently scanning. The vault was deep underground, far from the bustling city on the surface, but if you listened carefully, every now and then a dull throb reached your ears. One of the multitudes of underground trains, its vibration passing through many metres of rock and reinforced concrete. To get down there, the gold had taken an elevator. And now, finally, it was safe, guarded, monitored.

It was lustrous and clean. Well, clean in the way that something can be washed. But this gold was dirty. Scrape past the veneer of what it symbolised, and it was in fact covered in blood. The blood of the guards and the mine workers. The blood of the soldiers that tried to recover it in the jungle. The blood of the thieves themselves, and finally the blood of those dead naval personnel. Was that gold really a symbol of wealth and power, or was it a dirty emblem of blood and death? In actual fact, it was of course both.

Chapter 105

October 27th, The Jungle. Ghana.

Abdi was in pain. A deep throbbing pain that he felt throughout his body. He was lying on a crude bed made from branches, sticks and leaves. He was in a simple house made from wattle and daub. Sticks intricately sewn together to make the walls, the gaps filled with thick mud that was allowed to dry. The roof was built of wide palm leaves and had been surprisingly effective over the past few weeks at keeping the rain out. Yesterday, for the first time since he could remember, Abdi had been able to get out of the rickety bed and he had walked around the village. Perhaps settlement was a better word. A collection of shacks on the bank of the river. Close enough to get water and light, but far enough away that humanity could sail on past and not interfere with the inhabitants' way of life.

Abdi had been found, walking delirious through the jungle by one of the settlement's hunters. His head wound had finally gone septic enough for the antibiotics he was using to be overcome. The hunter had carried him back, and the village had done their best to treat him, feed him and even at times wash him. A poultice made from a combination of roots and leaves had miraculously soothed the wound and he was getting better now. Abdi was even able to eat what little food was spared for him. It was sheer self-determination that had forced his hand, holding the spoon of crushed jungle insects, bush honey and bitter leaves into his mouth. Hot or cold, it looked like a filthy mix, and tasted even worse, but it was what the toothless old village healer said he must eat.

Abdi was definitely getting better though. He was still weak, but his determination was building, and most importantly, though he was in the middle of nowhere, he was alive!

Chapter 106

October 28th, Hyde Park. London.

Max walked out of the Lancaster Gate tube station, crossed the busy road and walked into Hyde Park near the Italian gardens. The water gardens were spectacular in the summer, but now, in the autumn, the four rectangular ponds were cold and grey. The pale paving stone paths around the circumference were mossed and slippery. Interspersed amongst the statues around the perimeter, were well worn concrete bench seats spaced about ten metres apart. Even in the grey weather, well-wrapped-up office workers were out in the fresh air eating their lunches. On one bench sat an elegant woman in her middle fifties. A black trench coat, woolly hat and scarf meant that she blended in with every other Londoner there. Max strolled casually around the path until he saw her. Without catching her eye or acknowledging her, he sat down on the other end of the bench. In his past career Max had been a spook and he knew the lady very well.

Nancy pulled out a small thermos flask, unscrewed the top and poured some coffee into the lid. 'Max, dharling! How are you?' Nancy was unwrapping a plain-looking sandwich. 'Do excuse me whilst I eat, busy day.'

'Fine, thank you. Is Her Majesty's Government talking to me again?'

'Well, you know how fickle we are. That ransom drop wasn't popular with the Prime Minister, but you've made up for it with that daring adventure in the jungle.'

'Really?'

'Truly. We have a real ally on the West coast of Africa in Ghana. We've spent years developing that relationship. The last thing we wanted was a regime change. We're still working on who was behind it, of course.'

'Yes, well that's why I asked to meet.'

'Oh goody, you do know something!'

'Only a couple of names. The first one, you already know. The chap who was orchestrating the heist was Abdi, the negotiator from that Somali piracy ring. You remember the *Hibernia III*?

'Now that *is* interesting. And the other?'

'It was a new name to me. The Associate?'

Even being the seasoned spook that Nancy was couldn't stop her from a sharp intake of breath. 'Bugger. Are you sure?'

'That came from the President himself, who was intimately involved in the 'questioning', shall we say, of one of the ring leaders.'

'The Minister of the Interior?'

'I assume so. It's never so subtle when a fit, middle-aged man has a heart attack just before campaign season.'

'Quite. Of course, the information is less reliable when it's tortured out of someone. But I think it must be genuine. There's no reason why they would know that name.'

Max looked at her. 'What can you tell me?'

'Officially? Nothing, dharling!' She took a bite of her sandwich.

'Of course.'

'But if I were to think out loud and someone who happened to be sitting on a bench next to me accidently heard, then I would say that The Associate is a very dangerous person. The Marble Arch of arch-criminals if you like. We don't yet know what his or even her agenda is, we don't even know their real identity. Just the name. The Associate has mixed fortunes. Some successes, some failures. It looks like your little ransom drop did even more damage than we thought, if the money ended up there.' Nancy pouted.

Max reflected, 'It's very odd that two of our largest, most recent projects have had The Associate backing them. If I were a betting man, I would say that The Associate has suddenly switched focus to Africa.'

Nancy looked at Max, wiping some crumbs off her lip with a gloved hand. Then she stood up and began to walk away. 'Be careful Max. You don't want The Associate to learn that you interfered with whatever their grand plan was. Do let me know if you find out anything more about him or her.'

'Actually, Nancy, I was about to say the same thing.'

'Dharling, how funny! But I thought you had left the service?'

Chapter 107

October 30th, Nairobi. Kenya.

The Muthaiga Club, an idyllic space for the Kenyan elite, situated in the wealthiest suburb of Nairobi; established in 1913 and originally the preserve of the white Kenyan aristocracy, it had fortunately matured into 21st century equality. The club had expansive gardens, a pro-tour level golf course and a strong air of nostalgia throughout the tastefully-decorated rooms. The Club suited all sorts of members, from those who chose to sit in a corner on a brown leather-studded chair, snooze or do the crossword, to those who would dine in the al fresco dining room, whilst sipping cocktails from the extensively-stocked bar. As a member-only club, it was steeped in traditions, wearing a jacket and tie to dinner being one.

And as with traditions, Max had invited the Project Inca team to dine at The Club. He always hosted dinner after successful projects. It was a chance to feed back informally, decompress and develop the camaraderie that his teams were legendary for. Tonight was the first night that many of the team members had been in the same country together, since the end of the project. At a large round table at the edge of the outside dining space, in jackets and ties, sat Max, Tom, Mike, Raj, Miguel and Chris. Bob was already away on another project.

By agreement, Max had ordered a huge beef fillet and the chef had prepared it just for the team. A selection of vegetables, salads and sauces had all been laid on the table and the team had eaten well. As was ever the case at the end of a project, the banter increased when Raj assumed the role of fines master. He had signalled the waiter, and as planned, a tray of Jägermeister shots had been delivered.

Never a shy one, Raj stood up and began proceedings. 'Team, once again it has fallen to me to feed back on a project well done. For once, we don't have everyone's Apple watch heart rate data. And that means I can't tell you who was flapping the most at key points during the project. So, the first fine will go to Max, for giving us bugger all planning time.' A shot was passed around the table and Max took his medicine.

'Next up, for making us trek through the jungle for no purpose whatsoever, and then lifting us out by helicopter again, the next one goes to Tom.' There was a resounding 'hear, hear!' from Mike on that one.

'Mike, you're getting fined for getting laid on the airplane on the way to a project.'

'I'll happily take that one, buddy.'

Max looked at Tom with a questioning eyebrow, but Tom just gave him a "don't ask" kind of look in reply.

Raj continued. 'Chris, for spending the entire bloody time on a floating gin palace, whilst we were sweating our butts off in the jungle, you have both the fine *and* you're paying the bloody bill for dinner!'

'Ha!' said Chris. 'That's why I joined the navy and not the infantry, old chap.'

'And the last fine," he continued, "goes to Miguel, for being a lucky bugger.'

Miguel just looked at him.

'Miguel not only managed to get a new, legitimate identity, but the lucky bugger got a working diplomatic passport.'

'Yep, and it's got five years of validity left.'

'Well, that's it, gentlemen, except for who gets to wear this!' Raj held up the garish yellow Hawaiian shirt. It was a team tradition that whoever had cocked up the most, won the wooden spoon, or in this case they had to wear the dodgy shirt at dinner. With it being the Muthaiga club, the individual would either get thrown out, or at the very minimum get stern-faced looks from all the members.

'And the winner is… Mike!'

'What, no way buddy, what did I do?'

'You were screaming like a little boy when you found that rubber snake in your rucksack!'

Mike was deadpan. 'I would like to suggest another recipient.'

The table was listening carefully and Raj tried to cut him off, but Mike succeeded in overruling him. 'I think the biggest fuckup on this project was you, Raj.'

'No way! I didn't do anything wrong.'

'Yeah, you did. That story you told about taking a runny dump on the 10th hole of this very golf course!'

A couple of club members at nearby tables who had overheard, looked over with horror on their faces.

'Mike, shush!'

'Nah way buddy, not until you agree to wear the shirt. It's only right. I mean who the hell takes a dump…'

'OK! OK! Shut up, buddy. I'll do it!'

There was a roar of laughter as Raj took the shirt and buttoned it up over the top of his single-breasted lightweight beige jacket. The positive hum of conversation resumed in The Club. The waiters floated discreetly around the tables filling glasses and clearing plates. The cool Nairobi evening breeze wafted the sounds of laughter across the manicured lawns.

Afterword

I have managed security risks for more than twenty years, but without doubt, one of the fastest-evolving technologies, that in my opinion is most understated as a security threat, is drones.

Don't get me wrong. There are vast benefits from drone technologies in activities such as logistics, surveying, security applications, remote area pharmaceutical deliveries and fire fighting in high rise buildings, to name just a few.

However, in terms of providing capability for delivery of a package to the lowest common denominator, drones are in a league of their own. It takes virtually no technical knowledge for the computer-game generation to fly anything from a camera to narcotics, and even homemade explosives or incendiaries into the location of their choice.

Perhaps my tale here of an attack against a facility is a little far-fetched. Perhaps. But let's bring it closer to home. What about drones dropping acid from height above Times Square on New Year's Eve? What about half a dozen half-kilo lead weights dropped from two hundred feet above a packed sports stadium? In some countries, explosives can be bought with just a driving licence or simply-acquired permit. A single drone with the right payload, hitting a car or going off in a school playground. The imagination can be terrifying.

This easy offensive capability, bought for a few hundred dollars, cannot be defended against until you start spending many thousands, hundreds of thousands and even millions in defence. Given the vast number of potential targets and the huge number of individuals with a far-right, far-left, or other extremist agenda, the threat is real.

Rob Phayre on his writing journey.
'They' say that everyone has at least one book in them. I'm delighted to find that I have many. As has been commented on publicly, my first fictional novel, The Ransom Drop, was heavily based on my actual experiences delivering ransoms to Somali pirates, so I was always a little apprehensive starting a project which was proportionally more fiction than not. I was delighted to receive an award for the audio book,

but perhaps more so was giving my friends and family a little glimpse into some of the 'fun' things I used to do.

When deciding what adventure I would pen next, it was actually an easy decision. During my military career, as a young officer and pilot, I was lucky to deploy to the jungles of a West African country for three months with my team and a couple of helicopters. We lived in the jungle for about half of that time and the rest was spent on an almost abandoned airfield.

We had an absolute blast and I learned vast amounts about living in the jungle and leadership.

I can safely say I had nothing to do with any thefts of gold bullion, though we did see the bullion planes flying overhead on several occasions. With a twinkle in my eye, I can admit to wondering (as a planning exercise of course), how we could steal it!

 I do hope you enjoy the story. If you do, then please take a moment to share your thoughts at robphayre.com or on Amazon.
I would love to hear from you.

Acknowledgements and Thanks

Firstly, to my wife and children, thank you. I know that you know that writing is my new happy place, and I appreciate the hour every evening that you give me to do it, even after my working day is done.

Victoria, for being a fab 'older' sister. I love you more than I can ever express in words. You were always there for me when we were younger, and I am here for you, anytime.

I want to thank both Terry and Siri, for agreeing yet again to edit for me, despite having done it the first time around as well and for not learning their lesson! Thank you for your love and support, and for the sacrifices you made for me, to be able to do what I have done.

My thanks to Andy too, for not only adding considerable extra polish to this work, but for being such a fabulous uncle. One who has always stepped up to the plate when needed!

Gordon, what can I say? Thank you for your 'charming' stories about snakes!

Stu, one of the best Chinook pilots I know, and a mate from the old days, thanks for your technical expertise.

And, as always, to those courageous people, too often taken for granted, who risk their all to keep others safe. Thank you for all that you do, every day.

Other Books by Rob Phayre

The Ransom Drop

The Response Files Book 1

When an oil tanker is hijacked by a novice band of Somali pirates, It's a near impossible problem to solve in one of the most remote and dangerous places on earth.

A team of negotiators, security and maritime experts are called in with one job to do, save the lives of the crew.

Can this 'A-team' of experts do so? Can they prevent a massive environmental disaster, rescue the ship and its hundred-million-dollar cargo? There are reputations to be made, or lost...

The Ransom Drop is a true to real life, military suspense thriller that reveals the secrets behind the resolution of Somali piracy. It's factually correct, fictionally fantastic and written by a guy who delivered some of the largest ransoms ever paid at sea.

Available in hardback, paperback, e-book, and as an award-winning audiobook. www.theransomdrop.com

The Insurgency

The Response Files Book 3

Coming in 2022 - Book 3 of The Response Files.

The vast infrastructure of the natural gas plant was completely alien to that remote part of Africa. An insurgency had been brewing for years stoked by the hand of The Associate and all the usual problems. Corruption, politics and brewing fundamentalism.

When the insurgents attack the site, they don't just intend to behead the foreigners. They want to grab the government by the balls and get what they feel is their right.

Of course, they need to discover that they are wrong. And it needs Max and his team to show them why.

To find out more visit: www.theresponsefiles.com

For more books by Rob Phayre or to learn more about the author visit: www.robphayre.com

To ask Rob Phayre a question, or leave feedback, visit: Goodreads.com

Printed in Great Britain
by Amazon

87489842R00163